DATE DUE	
JY 28 '04		
AG 12 '04		
DE 2 '04		
2/26/19		
4/3/19		

THE FLYING U'S LAST STAND

**Center Point
Large Print**

**This Large Print Book carries the
Seal of Approval of N.A.V.H.**

THE FLYING U'S
LAST STAND

———◦∞◦———

B. M. BOWER

CENTER POINT PUBLISHING

THORNDIKE, MAINE

This Center Point Large Print edition
is published in the year 2004 by arrangement with
Golden West Literary Agency.

The text of this Large Print edition is unabridged. In other
aspects, this book may vary from the original edition. Printed in
Thailand. Set in 16-point Times New Roman type.

ISBN 1-58547-420-7

Library of Congress Cataloging-in-Publication Data

Bower, B. M., 1874-1940.
    The flying U's last stand / B. M. Bower.--Center Point large print ed.
      p. cm.
    ISBN 1-58547-420-7 (lib. bdg. : alk. paper)
      1. Ranch life--Fiction. 2. Cowboys--Fiction. 3. Montana--Fiction. 4. Large type books.
I. Title.

PS3503.O8193F585 2004
813'.52--dc22

                                                                    2003027834

CHAPTER I

OLD WAYS AND NEW

Progress is like the insidious change from youth to old age, except that progress does not mean decay. The change that is almost imperceptible and yet inexorable is much the same, however. You will see a community apparently changeless as the years pass by; and yet, when the years have gone and you look back, there has been a change. It is not the same. It never will be the same. It can pass through further change, but it cannot go back. Men look back, sick sometimes with longing for the things that were and that can be no more; they live the old days in memory—but try as they will they may not go back. With intelligent, persistent effort they may retard further change considerably, but that is the most that they can hope to do. Civilization and Time will continue the march in spite of all that man may do.

That is the way it was with the Flying U. Old J. G. Whitmore fought doggedly against the changing conditions—and he fought intelligently and well. When he saw the range dwindling and the way to the watering places barred against his cattle with long stretches of barbed wire, he sent the herds deeper into the Badlands to seek what grazing was in the hidden, little valleys and the deep, sequestered canyons. He cut more hay for winter feeding, and he sowed his meadows to alfalfa that he might increase the crops. He shipped old cows and dry cows with his fat steers in the fall, and he bettered the blood of his herds and raised bigger cattle. Therefore, if his cattle grew fewer in number, they improved in quality and prices went higher, so that the result was much the same.

It began to look, then, as though J. G. Whitmore was cunningly besting the situation, and was going to hold out indefinitely against the encroachments of civilization upon the old order of things on the range. And it had begun to look as though he was going to best Time at his own game, and refuse also to grow old; as though he would go on being the same pudgy, grizzled, humorously querulous Old Man beloved of his men, the Happy Family of the Flying U.

Sometimes, however, Time will fill a four-flush with the joker, and then laugh while he rakes in the chips. J. G. Whitmore had been going his way and refusing to grow old for a long time—and then an accident, which is Time's joker, turned the game against him. He stood for just a second too long on a crowded crossing in Chicago, hesitating between going forward or back. And that second gave Time a chance to play an accident. A big seven-passenger touring car mowed him down and left him in a heap for the ambulance from the nearest hospital to gather on its stretcher.

The Old Man did not die; he had lived long on the open range and he was pretty tough and hard to kill. He went back to his beloved Flying U, with a crutch to help him shuffle from bed to easy chair.

The Little Doctor, who was his youngest sister, nursed him tirelessly; but it was long before there came a day when the Old Man gave his crutch to the Kid to use for a stick-horse, and walked through the living room and out upon the porch with the help of a cane and the arm of the Little Doctor, and with the Kid galloping before him on the crutch.

Later he discarded the help of somebody's arm, and hobbled down to the corral with the cane, and with the Kid still galloping before him on "Uncle Gee-Gee's" crutch. He stood for some time leaning against the corral watching some of the boys halter-breaking a horse that was later to be sold—when he was "broke gentle"—and then he hobbled back again, thankful for the soft comfort of his big chair.

That was well enough, as far as it went. The Flying U took it for granted that the Old Man was slowly returning to the old order of life, when rheumatism was his only foe and he could run things with his old energy and easy good management. But there never came a day when the Old Man gave his cane to the Kid to play with. There never came a day when he was not thankful for the soft comfort of his chair. There never came a day when he was the same Old Man who joshed the boys and scolded them and threatened them. The day was always coming when his back would quit aching if he walked to the stable and back without a long rest between, but it never actually arrived.

So, imperceptibly but surely, the Old Man began to grow old. The thin spot on top of his head grew shiny, so that the Kid noticed it and made blunt comments upon the subject. His rheumatism was not his worst foe, now. He had to pet his digestive apparatus and cut out strong coffee with three heaping teaspoons of sugar in each cup, because the Little Doctor told him his liver was torpid. He had to stop giving the Kid jolty rides on his knees—but that was because the Kid was getting too big for baby play. The Kid was big enough to ride real horses now, and he ought to be ashamed to ride knee-horses any more.

To two things the Old Man clung almost fiercely; the old regime of ranging his cattle at large and starting out the wagons in the spring just the same as if twenty-five men instead of twelve went with them; and the retention of the Happy Family on his payroll, just as if they were actually needed. If one of the boys left to try other things and other fields, the Old Man considered him gone on a vacation and expected him back when spring roundup approached.

True, he was seldom disappointed in that. For the Happy Family looked upon the Flying U as home, and six months was about the limit for straying afar. Cowpunchers to the bone though they were, they bent backs over irrigating ditches and sweated in the hayfields just for the sake of staying together on the ranch. I cannot say that they did it uncomplainingly—for the bunk-house was saturated to the ridge-pole with their maledictions while they compared blistered hands and pitchfork callouses, and mourned the days that were gone; the days when they rode far and free and scorned any work that could not be done from the saddle. But they stayed, and they did the ranch work as well the range work, which is the main point.

They became engaged to certain girls who filled their dreams and all their waking thoughts—but they never quite came to the point of marrying and going their way. Except Pink, who did marry impulsively and unwisely, and who suffered himself to be bullied and called Percy for seven months or so, and who balked at leaving the Flying U for the city and a vicarious existence in theaterdom, and so found himself free quite as suddenly as he had been tied.

They intended to marry and settle down—sometime. But there was always something in the way of carrying those intentions to fulfilment, so that eventually the majority of the Happy Family found themselves not even engaged, but drifting along toward permanent bachelorhood. Being of the optimistic type, however, they did not worry; Pink having set before them a fine example of the failure of marriage and having returned with manifest relief to the freedom of the bunk-house.

CHAPTER II

ANDY GREEN'S NEW ACQUAINTANCE

Andy Green, chief prevaricator of the Happy Family of the Flying U—and not ashamed of either title or connection—pushed his new Stetson back off his untanned forehead, attempted to negotiate the narrow passage into a Pullman sleeper with his suitcase swinging from his right hand, and butted into a woman who was just emerging from the dressing-room. He butted into her so emphatically that he was compelled to swing his left arm out very quickly, or see her go headlong into the window opposite; for a full-sized suitcase propelled forward by a muscular young man may prove a very efficient instrument of disaster, especially if it catches one just in the hollow back of the knee. The woman tottered and grasped Andy convulsively to save herself a fall, and so they stood blocking the passage until the porter arrived and took the suitcase from Andy with a tip-inviting deference.

Andy apologized profusely, with a quaint, cow-punchery phrasing that caused the woman to take a second look at him. And, since Andy Green would look good to any woman capable of recognizing—and appreciating—a real man when she saw him, she smiled and said it didn't matter in the least.

That was the beginning of the acquaintance. Andy took her by her plump, chiffon-veiled arm and piloted her to her seat, and he afterward tipped the porter generously and had his own belongings deposited in the section across the aisle. Then, with the guile of a foreign diplomat, he betook himself to the smoking-room and stayed there for three quarters of an hour. He was not taking any particular risk of losing the opportunity of an unusually pleasant journey, for the dollar he had invested in the goodwill of the porter had yielded the information that the lady was going through to Great Falls. Since Andy had boarded the train at Harlem there was plenty of time to kill between there and Dry Lake, which was his destination.

The lady smiled at him rememberingly when finally he seated himself across the aisle from her, and without any serious motive Andy smiled back. So presently they were exchanging remarks about the journey. Later on,

Andy went over and sat beside her and conversation began in earnest. Her name, it transpired, was Florence Grace Hallman. Andy read it engraved upon a card which added the information that she was engaged in the real estate business—or so the three or four words implied. "Homeseekers' Syndicate, Minneapolis and St. Paul," said the card. Andy was visibly impressed thereby. He looked at her with swift appraisement and decided that she was "all to the good."

Florence Grace Hallman was tall and daintily muscular as to figure. Her hair was a light yellow—and not quite the shade which peroxide gives, and therefore probably natural. Her eyes were brown, a shade too close together but cool and calm and calculating in their gaze, and her eyebrows slanted upward a bit at the outer ends and were as heavy as beauty permitted. Her lips were very red, and her chin was very firm. She looked the successful business woman to her fingertips, and she was eminently attractive for a woman of that self-assured type.

Andy was attractive also, in a purely Western way. His gray eyes were candid and his voice was pleasant with a humorous drawl that matched well the quirk of his lips when he talked. He was headed for home—which was the Flying U—sober and sunny and with enough money to see him through. He told Florence Hallman his name, and said that he lived "up the road a ways" without being too definite. Florence Hallman lived in Minneapolis, she said; though she traveled most of the time, in the interests of her firm.

Yes, she liked the real estate business. One had a

chance to see the world, and keep in touch with people and things. She liked the West especially well. Since her firm had taken up the homeseekers' line she spent most of her time in the West.

They had supper—she called it dinner, Andy observed—together, and Andy Green paid the check, which was not so small. It was after that, when they became more confidential, that Florence Hallman, with the egotism of the successful person who believes herself or himself to be of keen interest to the listener, spoke in greater detail of her present mission.

Her firm's policy was, she said, to locate a large tract of government land somewhere, and then organize a homeseekers' colony, and settle the land-hungry upon the tract—at so much per hunger. She thought it a great scheme for both sides of the transaction. The men who wanted claims got them. The firm got the fee for showing them the land—and certain other perquisites at which she merely hinted.

She thought that Andy himself would be a success at the business. She was quick to form her opinions of people whom she met, and she knew that Andy was just the man for such work. Andy, listening with his gray eyes straying often to her face and dwelling there, modestly failed to agree with her. He did not know the first thing about the real estate business, he confessed, nor very much about ranching. Oh, yes—he lived in this country, and he knew *that* pretty well, but—

"The point is right here," said Florence Grace Hallman, laying her pink fingertips upon his arm and glancing behind her to make sure that they were practically alone—their immediate neighbors being still in the diner. "I'm speaking merely upon impulse—which isn't a wise thing to do, ordinarily. But—well, your eyes vouch for you, Mr. Green, and we women are bound to act impulsively sometimes—or we wouldn't be women, would we?" She laughed—rather, she gave a little, infectious giggle, and took away her fingers, to the regret of Andy who liked the feel of them on his forearm.

"The point is here. I've recognized the fact, all along, that we need a man stationed right here, living in the country, who will meet prospective homesteaders and talk farming; keep up their enthusiasm; whip the doubters into line; talk climate and soil and the future of the country; *look* the part, you understand."

"So I look like a rube, do I?" Andy's lips quirked a half smile at her.

"No, of course you don't!" She laid her fingers on his sleeve again, which was what Andy wanted—what he had intended to bait her into doing; thereby proving that, in some respects at least, he amply justified Miss Hallman in her snap judgment of him.

"Of course you don't look like a rube! I don't want you to. But you do look Western—because you *are* Western to the bone. Besides, you look perfectly dependable. Nobody could look into your eyes and even think of doubting the truth of any statement you made to them." Andy snickered mentally at that though his eyes never lost their clear candor. "And," she concluded, "being a bona fide resident of the country, your word would carry more weight than mine if I were to talk myself black in the face!"

"That's where you're dead wrong," Andy hastened to correct her.

"Well, you must let me have my own opinion, Mr. Green. You would be convincing enough, at any rate. You see, there is a certain per cent. of—let us call it waste effort—in this colonization business. We have to reckon on a certain number of nibblers who won't bite—" Andy's honest, gray eyes widened a hair's breadth at the frankness of her language. "—when they get out here. They swallow the folders we send out, but when they get out here and see the country, they can't see it as a rich farming district, and they won't invest. They go back home and knock, if they do anything.

"My idea is to stop that waste; to land every home-seeker that boards our excursion trains. And I believe the way to do that is to have the right kind of a man out here, steer the doubtfuls against him—and let his personality and his experience do the rest. They're hungry enough to come, you see; the thing is to keep them here. A man that lives right here, that has all the earmarks of the West, and is not known to be affiliated with our Syndicate (you could have rigs to hire, and drive the doubtfuls to the tract)—don't you see what an enormous advantage he'd have? The class I speak of are the suspicious ones—those who are from Missouri. They're inclined to want salt with what *we* say about the resources of the country. Even our chemical analysis of the soil, and weather bureau dope, don't go very far with those hicks. They want to talk with someone who has *tried* it, you see."

"I—see," said Andy thoughtfully, and his eyes narrowed a trifle. "On the square, Miss Hallman, what *are* the natural advantages out here—for farming? What line of talk do you give those come-ons?"

Miss Hallman laughed and made a very pretty gesture with her two ringed hands. "Whatever sounds the best to them," she said. "If they write and ask about spuds, we come back with illustrated folders of potato crops and statistics of average yields and prices and all that. If it's dairy, we have dairy folders. And so on. It isn't any fraud—there *are* sections of the country that produce almost anything, from alfalfa to strawberries. You know that," she challenged.

"Sure. But I didn't know there was much tillable land left lying around loose," he ventured to say.

Again Miss Hallman made the pretty gesture, which might mean much or nothing. "There's plenty of land 'lying around loose,' as you call it. How do you know it won't produce, till it has been tried?"

"That's right," Andy assented uneasily. "If there's water to put on it—"

"And since there is the land, our business lies in getting people located on it. The towns and the railroads are back of us. That is, they look with favor upon bringing settlers into the country. It increases the business of the country—the traffic, the freights, the merchants' business, everything."

Andy puckered his eyebrows and looked out of the window upon a great stretch of open, rolling prairie, clothed sparely in grass that was showing faint green in the hollows, and with no water for miles—as he knew well—except for the rivers that hurried through narrow bottom lands guarded by high bluffs that were for the most part barren. The land was there, all right. But—

"What I can't see," he observed after a minute during which Miss Florence Hallman studied his averted face, "what I can't see is, where do the settlers get off at?"

"At Easy Street, if they're lucky enough," she told him lightly. "My business is to locate them on the land. Getting a living off it is *their* business. And," she added defensively, "people do make a living on ranches out here."

"That's right," he agreed again—he was finding it very pleasant to agree with Florence Grace Hallman. "Mostly off stock, though."

"Yes, and we encourage our clients to bring out all the young stock they possibly can; young cows and horses and—all that sort of thing. There's quantities of open country around here, that even the most optimistic of homeseekers would never think of filing on. They can make out, all right, I guess. We certainly urge them strongly to bring stock with them. It's always been famous as a cattle country—that's one of our highest cards. We tell them—"

"How do you do that? Do you write to them and *talk* to them?"

"Yes, if they show a strong enough interest—and bank account. I follow up the best prospects and visit them in person. I've talked to fifty horny-handed hoemen in the past month."

"Then I don't see what you need of anyone to bring up the drag," Andy told her admiringly. "If *you* talk to 'em, there oughtn't be any drag!"

"Thank you for the implied compliment. But there *is* a

'drag,' as you call it. There's going to be a big one, too, I'm afraid—when they get out and see this tract we're going to work off this spring." She stopped and studied him as a chess player studies the board.

"I'm very much tempted to tell you something I shouldn't tell," she said at length, lowering her voice a little. Remember, Andy Green was a very good looking man, and his eyes were remarkable for their clear, candid gaze. Even as keen a business woman as Florence Grace Hallman must be forgiven for being deceived by them. "I'm tempted to tell you where this tract is. You may know it."

"You better not, unless you're willing to take a chance," he told her soberly. "If it looks too good, I'm liable to jump it myself."

Miss Hallman laughed and twisted her red lips at him in what might be construed as a flirtatious manner. She was really quite taken with Andy Green. "I'll take a chance. I don't think you'll jump it. Do you know any-thing about Dry Lake, up above Havre, toward Great Falls—and the country out east of there, towards the mountains?"

The fingers of Andy Green closed into his palms. His eyes, however, continued to look into hers with his most guileless expression.

"Y-es—that is, I've ridden over it," he acknowledged simply.

"Well—now this is a secret; at least we don't want those mossback ranchers in there to get hold of it too soon, though they couldn't really *do* anything, since it's all government land and the lease has only just run out.

There's a tract lying between the Bear Paws and—do you know where the Flying U ranch is?"

"About where it is—yes."

"Well, it's right up there on that plateau—bench, you call it out here. There are several thousand acres along in there that we're locating settlers on this spring. We're just waiting for the grass to get nice and green, and the prairie to get all covered with those blue, blue wind flowers, and the meadow larks to get busy with their nests, and then we're going to bring them out and—" She spread her hands again. It seemed a favorite gesture grown into a habit, and it surely was more eloquent than words. "Those prairies will be a dream of beauty, in a little while," she said. "I'm to watch for the psychological time to bring out the seekers. And if I could just interest you, Mr. Green, to the extent of being somewhere around Dry Lake, with a good team that you will drive for hire and some samples of oats and dry-land spuds and stuff that you raised on your claim—" She eyed him sharply for one so endearingly feminine. "Would you do it? There'd be a salary and besides that a commission on each doubter you landed. And I'd just love to have you for one of my assistants."

"It sure sounds good," Andy flirted with the proposition, and let his eyes soften appreciably to meet her last sentence and the tone in which she spoke it. "Do you think I could get by with the right line of talk with the doubters?"

"I think you could," she said, and in her voice there was a cooing note. "Study up a little on the right dope, and I think you could convince—even me."

"Could I?" Andy Green knew that cooing note, himself, and one a shade more provocative. "I wonder!"

A man came down the aisle at that moment, gave Andy a keen glance and went on with a cigar between his fingers. Andy scowled frankly, sighed and straightened his shoulders.

"That's what I call hard luck," he grumbled. "I've got to see that man before he gets off the train—and the h— worst of it is, I don't know just what station he'll get off at." He sighed again. "I've got a deal on," he told her confidentially, "that's sure going to keep me humping if I pull loose so as to go in with you: How long did you say?"

"Probably two weeks, the way spring is opening up, out here. I'd want you to get perfectly familiar with our policy and the details of our scheme before they land. I'd want you to be familiar with that tract, and be able to show up its best points when you take seekers out there. You'd be so much better than one of our own men, who have the word 'agent' written all over them. You'll come back and—talk it over, won't you?" For Andy was showing unmistakable symptoms of leaving her to follow the man.

"You *know* it," he declared in a tone of intimacy. "I won't sleep nights till this thing is settled—and settled right." He gave her a smile that dazzled the lady, got up with much reluctance and with a glance that had in it a certain element of longing went down the aisle after the man who had preceded him.

Andy's business with the man consisted solely in mixing cigarette smoke with cigar smoke and of helping to stare moodily out of the window. Words there were none, save when Andy was proffered a match and muttered his thanks. The silent session lasted for half an hour. Then the man got up and went out, and the breath of Andy Green paused behind his nostrils until he saw that the man went only to the first section in the car and settled there behind a spread newspaper, invisible to Florence Grace Hallman unless she searched the car and peered over the top of the paper to see who was behind.

After that Andy Green continued to stare out of the window, seeing nothing of the scenery but the flicker of telegraph posts before his eyes that were visioning the future.

The Flying U ranch hemmed in by homesteaders from the East, he saw; homesteaders who were being urged to bring all the stock they could, and turn it loose upon the shrinking range. Homesteaders who would fence the country into squares, and tear up the grass and sow grain that might never bear a harvest. Homesteaders who would inevitably grow poorer upon the land that would suck their strength and all their little savings and turn them loose finally to forage a living where they might. Homesteaders who would ruin the land that ruined them. . . . It was not a pleasing picture, but it was more pleasing than the picture he saw of the Flying U after these human grasshoppers had settled there.

The range that fed the Flying U stock would feed no more and hide their ribs at shipping time. That he knew too well. Old J. G. Whitmore and Chip would have to sell out. And that was like death; indeed, it *is* death of a sort, when one of the old outfits is wiped out. It had happened before—happened too often to make pleasant memories for Andy Green, who could name outfit after outfit that had been forced out of business by the settling of the range land; who could name dozens of cattle brands once seen upon the range, and never glimpsed now from spring roundup until fall.

Must the Flying U brand disappear also? The good old Flying U, for whose existence the Old Man had fought and schemed since first was raised the cry that the old range was passing? The Flying U that had become a part of his life? Andy let his cigarette grow cold; he roused only to swear at the porter who entered with dust cloth and a deprecating grin.

After that, Andy thought of Florence Grace Hallman—and his eyes were not particularly senti-mental. There was a hard line about his mouth also; though Florence Grace Hallman was but a pawn in the game, after all, and not personally guilty of half the crimes Andy laid upon her shoulders. With her it was pure, cold-blooded business, this luring of the land-hungry to a land whose fertility was at best problemat-ical; would, for a price, turn loose the victims of her greed to devastate what little grazing ground was left.

The train neared Havre. Andy roused himself, rang for the porter and sent him after his suitcase and coat. Then he sauntered down the aisle, stopped beside Florence Grace Hallman and smiled down at her with a gleam behind the clear candor of his eyes.

"Hard luck, lady," he murmured, leaning toward her. "I'm just simply loaded to the guards with responsibili-ties, and here's where I get off. But I'm sure glad I met yuh, and I'll certainly think day and night about you and—all you told me about. I'd like to get in on this land deal. Fact is, I'm going to make it my business to get in on it. Maybe my way of working won't suit you—but I'll sure work hard for any boss and do the best I know how."

"I think that will suit me," Miss Hallman assured him, and smiled unsuspectingly up into his eyes, which she thought she could read so easily. "When shall I see you again? Could you come to Great Falls in the next ten days? I shall be stopping at the Park. Or if you will leave me your address—"

"No use. I'll be on the move and a letter wouldn't get me. I'll see yuh later, anyway. I'm bound to. And when I do, we'll get down to cases. Good bye."

He was turning away when Miss Hallman put out a soft, jewelled hand. She thought it was diffidence that made Andy Green hesitate perceptibly before he took it. She thought it was simply a masculine shyness and confusion that made him clasp her fingers loosely and let them go on the instant. She did not see him rub his palm down the leg of his dark gray trousers as he walked down the aisle, and if she had she would not have seen any significance in the movement.

Andy Green did that again before he stepped off the train. For he felt he had shaken hands with a traitor to himself and his outfit, and it went against the grain. That the traitor was a woman, and a charming woman at that, only intensified his resentment against her. A man can fight a man and keep his self respect; but a man does mortally dread being forced into a position where he must fight a woman.

CHAPTER III

The Kid—Chip's Kid and the Little Doctor's—was six years old and big for his age. Also he was a member in good standing of the Happy Family and he insisted upon being called Buck outside the house; within it the Little Doctor insisted even more strongly that he answer to the many endearing names she had invented for him, and to the more formal one of Claude, which really belonged to Daddy Chip.

Being six years old and big for his age, and being called Buck by his friends, the Happy Family, the Kid decided that he should have a man's-sized horse of his own, to feed and water and ride and proudly call his "string." Having settled that important point, he began to cast about him for a horse worthy his love and owner-ship, and speedily he decided that matter also.

Therefore, he ran bareheaded up to the blacksmith shop where Daddy Chip was hammering upon the anvil, and delivered his ultimatum from the doorway.

"Silver's going to be my string, Daddy Chip, and I'm going to feed him myself and ride him myself and nobody else can touch him 'thout I say they can."

"Yes?" Chip squinted along a dully-glowing iron bar, laid it back upon the anvil and gave it another whack upon the side that still bulged a little.

"Yes, and I'm going to saddle him myself and every-thing. And I want you to get me some jingling silver

23

spurs like Mig has got, with chains that hang away down and rattle when you walk." The Kid lifted one small foot and laid a grimy finger in front of his heel by way of illustration.

"Yes?" Chip's eyes twinkled briefly and immediately became intent upon his work.

"Yes, and Doctor Dell has got to let me sleep in the bunk-house with the rest of the fellers. And I ain't going to wear a nightie once more! I don't have to, do I, Daddy Chip? Not with lace on it. Happy Jack says I'm a girl long as I wear lace nighties, and I ain't a girl. Am I, Daddy Chip?"

"I should say not!" Chip testified emphatically, and carried the iron bar to the forge for further heating.

"I'm going on roundup too, tomorrow afternoon." The Kid's conception of time was extremely sketchy and had no connection whatever with the calendar. "I'm going to keep Silver in the little corral and let him sleep in the box stall where his leg got well that time he broke it. I 'member when he had a rag tied on it and teased for sugar. And the Countess has got to quit a kickin' every time I need sugar for my string. Ain't she, Daddy Chip? She's got to let us men alone or there'll be something doing!"

"I'd tell a man," said Chip inattentively, only half hearing the war-like declaration of his offspring—as is the way with busy fathers.

"I'm going to take a ride now on Silver. I guess I'll ride in to Dry Lake and get the mail—and I'm 'pletely outa the makings, too."

"Uh-hunh—a—what's that? You keep off Silver. He'll

24

kick the daylights out of you, Kid. Where's your hat? Didn't your mother tell you she'd tie a sunbonnet on you if you didn't keep your hat on? You better hike back and get it before she sees you."

The Kid stared mutinously from the doorway. "You said I could have Silver. What's the use of having a string if a feller can't ride it? And I *can* ride him, and he don't kick at all. I rode him just now, in the little pasture to see if I liked his gait better than the others. I rode Banjo first and I wouldn't own a thing like him, on a bet. Silver'll do me till I can get around to break a real one."

Chip's hand dropped from the bellows while he stared hard at the Kid. "Did you go down in the pasture and—" Words failed him just then.

"I'd *tell* a man I did!" the Kid retorted with a perfect imitation of Chip's manner and tone when crossed. "I've been trying out all the darned benches you've got—and there ain't a one I'd give a punched nickel for but Silver. I'd a' rode Shootin' Star, only he wouldn't stand still so I could get onto him. Whoever broke him did a bum job. The horse *I* break will stand, or I'll know the reason why. Silver'll stand, all right. And I can guide him pretty well by slapping his neck. You did a pretty fair job when you broke Silver," the Kid informed his father patronizingly.

Chip said something which the Kid was not supposed to hear, and sat suddenly down upon the stone rim of the forge. It had never before occurred to Chip that his Kid was no longer a baby but a most adventurous man-child who had lived all his life among men and whose mental development had more than kept pace with his growing body. He had laughed with the others at the Kid's quaint precociousness of speech and at his frank worship of range men and range life. He had gone to some trouble to find a tractable Shetland pony the size of a burro, and had taught the Kid to ride, decorously and fully protected from accident. He and the Little Doctor had been proud of the Kid's masculine traits as they manifested themselves in the management of that small specimen of horse flesh. That the Kid should have outgrown so quickly his content with Stubby seemed much more amazing than it really was. He eyed the Kid doubtfully for a minute, and then grinned.

"All that don't let you out on the hat question," he said, evading the real issue and laying stress upon the small matter of obedience, as is the exasperating habit of parents. "You don't see any of the bunch going around bareheaded. Only women and babies do that."

"The bunch goes bareheaded when they get their hats blowed off in the creek," the Kid pointed out unmoved. "I've seen you lose your hat mor'n once, old-timer. That's nothing." He sent Chip a sudden, adorable smile which proclaimed him the child of his mother and which never failed to thrill Chip secretly—it was so like the Little Doctor. "You lend me your hat for a while, dad," he said. "She never said what hat I had to wear, just so it's a hat. Honest to gran'ma, my hat's in the creek and I couldn't poke it out with a stick or anything. It sailed into the swimmin' hole. I was goin' to go after it," he explained further, "but—a snake was swimmin'—and I hated to 'sturb him."

Chip drew a sharp breath and for one panicky moment considered imperative the hiring of a bodyguard for his Kid.

"You keep out of the pasture, young man!" His tone was stern to match his perturbation. "And you leave Silver alone—"

The Kid did not wait for more. He lifted up his voice and wept in bitterness of spirit. Wept so that one could hear him a mile. Wept so that J. G. Whitmore, reading the Great Falls *Tribune* on the porch, laid down his paper and asked the world at large what ailed that doggoned kid now.

"Dell, you better go see what's wrong," he called afterwards through the open door to the Little Doctor, who was examining a jar of germ cultures in her "office." "Chances is he's fallen off the stable or something— though he sounds more mad than hurt. If it wasn't for my doggoned back—"

The Little Doctor passed him hurriedly. When her man-child wept, it needed no suggestion from J. G. or anyone else to send her flying to the rescue. So presently she arrived breathless at the blacksmith shop and found Chip within, looking in urgent need of reinforcements, and the Kid yelling ragefully beside the door and kicking the log wall with vicious boot-toes.

"Shut up, now, or I'll spank you!" Chip was saying desperately when his wife appeared. "I wish you'd take that Kid and tie him up, Dell," he added snappishly. "Here he's been riding all the horses in the little pasture—and taking a chance of breaking his neck! And he ain't satisfied with Stubby—he thinks he's entitled to Silver!"

"Well, why not? There, there, honey—men don't cry

27

when things go wrong—"

"No—because they can take it out in cussing!" wailed the Kid. "I wouldn't cry either, if you'd let me swear all I want to!"

Chip turned his back precipitately and his shoulders were seen to shake. The Little Doctor looked shocked.

"I want Silver for my string!" cried the Kid, artfully transferring his appeal to the higher court. "I can ride him—'cause I have rode him, in the pasture; and he never bucked once or kicked or anything. Doggone it, he likes to have me ride him! He comes a-runnin' up to me when I go down there, and I give him sugar. And then he waits till I climb on his back, and then we chase the other horses and play ride circle. He wants to be my string!" Something in the feel of his mother's arm around his shoulder whispered hope to the Kid. He looked up at her with his most endearing smile. "You come down there and I'll show you," he wheedled. "We're pals. And I guess you wouldn't like to have the boys call you Tom Thumb, a-ridin' Stubby. He's nothing but a five-cent sample of a horse. Mig Medicine says so. I—I'd rather walk than ride Stubby. And I'm going on roundup. The boys said I could go when I get a real horse under me— and I want Silver. Daddy Chip said I could have him. And now he's Injun-giver. Can't I have him, Doctor Dell?"

The gray-blue eyes clashed with the brown. "It wouldn't hurt anything to let the poor little tad show us what he can do," said the gray-blue eyes.

"Oh—all right," yielded the brown, and their owner threw the iron bar upon the cooling forge and began to turn down his sleeves. "Why don't you make him wear a hat?" he asked. "A little more and he won't pay any attention to anything you tell him. I'd carry out that sunbonnet bluff, anyway, if I were you."

"Now, Daddy Chip! I 'splained to you how I lost my hat," reproached the Kid, clinging fast to the Little Doctor's hand.

"Yes—and you 'splained that you'd have gone into that deep hole and drowned—with nobody there to pull you out—if you hadn't been scared of a water snake," Chip pointed out relentlessly.

"I wasn't 'zactly scared," amended the Kid gravely. "He was havin' such a good time, and he was swimmin' around so—comf'table—and it wasn't polite to 'sturb him. Can't I have Silver?"

"We'll go down and ask Silver what he thinks about it," said the Little Doctor, anxious to make peace between her two idols. "And we'll see if Daddy Chip can get the hat. You must wear a hat, honey; you know what mother told you—and you know mother keeps her word."

"I wish dad did," the Kid commented, passing over the hat question. "He said I could have Silver, and keep him in a box stall and feed him my own self and water him my own self and nobody's to touch him but me."

"Well, if daddy said all that—we'll have to think it over, and consult Silver and see what he has to say about it."

Silver, when consulted, professed at least a willingness to own the Kid for his master. He did indeed come trotting up for sugar; and when he had eaten two grimy lumps from the Kid's grimier hand, he permitted the Kid to entice him to a high rock, and stood there while the Kid clambered upon the rock and from there to his sleek back. He even waited until the Kid gathered a handful of silky mane and kicked him on the ribs; then he started off at a lope, while the Kid risked his balance to cast a triumphant grin—that had a gap in the middle—back at his astonished parents.

"Look how the little devil guides him!" exclaimed Chip surrenderingly. "I guess he's safe enough—old Silver seems to sabe he's got a kid to take care of. He sure would strike a different gait with me! Lord! how the time slides by; I can't seem to get it through me that the Kid's growing up."

The Little Doctor sighed a bit. And the Kid, circling grandly on the far side of the little pasture, came galloping back to hear the verdict. It pleased him—though he was inclined to mistake a great privilege for a right that must not be denied. He commanded his Daddy Chip to open the gate for him so he could ride Silver to the stable and put him in the box stall; which was a superfluous kindness, as Chip tried to point out and failed to make convincing.

The Kid wanted Silver in the box stall, where he could feed him and water him his own self. So into the box stall Silver reluctantly went, and spent a greater part of the day with his head stuck out through the window, staring enviously at his mates in the pasture.

For several days Chip watched the Kid covertly whenever his small feet strayed stableward; watched and was full of secret pride at the manner in which the Kid rose to his new responsibility. Never did a "string" receive the care which Silver got, and never did rider sit more proudly upon his steed than did the Kid sit upon Silver. There seemed to be practically no risk—Chip was amazed at the Kid's ability to ride. Besides, Silver was growing old—fourteen years being considered old age in a horse. He was more given to taking life with a placid optimism that did not startle easily. He carried the Kid's weight easily, and he had not lost all his springiness of muscle. The Little Doctor rode him sometimes, and loved his smooth gallop and his even temper; now she loved him more when she saw how careful he was of the Kid. She besought the Kid to be careful of Silver also, and was most manfully snubbed for her solicitude.

The Kid had owned Silver for a week, and considered that he was qualified to give advice to the Happy Family, including his Daddy Chip, concerning the proper care of horses. He stood with his hands upon his hips and his feet far apart, and spat into the corral dust and told Big Medicine that nobody but a pilgrim ever handled a horse the way Big Medicine was handling Dence. Whereat Big Medicine gave a bellowing haw-haw-haw and choked it suddenly when he saw that the Kid desired him to take the criticism seriously.

"All right, Buck," he acceded humbly, winking openly at the Native Son. "I'll try m'best, old-timer. Trouble with me is, I never had nobody to learn me how to handle a hoss."

"Well, you've got me, now," Buck returned calmly. "I don't ride *my* string without brushing the hay out of his tail. There's a big long hay stuck in your horse's tail." He pointed an accusing finger, and Big Medicine silently edged close to Dence's rump and very carefully removed the big, long hay. He took a fine chance of getting himself kicked, but he did not tell the Kid that.

"That all right now, Buck?" Big Medicine wanted to know, when he had accomplished the thing without accident.

"Oh, it'll do," was the frugal praise he got. "I've got to go and feed my string, now. And after a while I'll water him. You want to feed your horse always before you water him, 'cause eatin' makes him firsty. You 'member that, now."

"I'll sure try to, Buck," Big Medicine promised soberly, and watched the Kid go striding away with his hat tilted at the approved Happy-Family angle and his small hands in his pockets. Big Medicine was thinking of his own kid, and wondering what he was like, and if he remembered his dad. He waved his hand in cordial farewell when the Kid looked back and wrinkled his nose in the adorable, Little-Doctor smile he had, and turned his attention to Dence.

The Kid made straight for the box stall and told Silver hello over the half-door. Silver turned from gazing out of the window, and came forward expectantly, and the Kid told him to wait a minute and not be so impatient. Then he climbed upon a box, got down a canvas nose bag with leather bottom, and from a secret receptacle behind the oats box he brought a bag of sugar and poured about a tea-cupful into the bag. Daddy Chip had impressed upon him what would be the tragic consequences if he fed oats to Silver five times a day. Silver would die, and it would be the Kid that killed him. Daddy Chip had not said any-thing about sugar being fatal, however, and the Countess could not always stand guard over the sugar sack. So Silver had a sweet taste in his mouth twelve hours of the twenty-four, and was getting a habit of licking his lips reminiscently during the other twelve.

The Kid had watched the boys adjust nose bags ever since he could toddle. He lugged it into the stall, set it artfully upon the floor and let Silver thrust in his head to the eyes: then he pulled the strap over Silver's neck and managed to buckle it very securely. He slapped the sleek neck afterward as his Daddy Chip did, hugged it the way Doctor Dell did, and stood back to watch Silver revel in the bag.

" 'S good lickums?" he asked gravely, because he had once heard his mother ask Silver that very question, in almost that very tone.

At that moment an uproar outside caught his youthful attention. He listened a minute, heard Pink's voice and a shout of laughter, and ran to see what was going on; for where was excitement, there the Kid was also, as nearly in the middle of it as he could manage. His going would not have mattered to Silver, had he remembered to close the half-door of the stall behind him; even that would not have mattered, had he not left the outer door of the stable open also.

The cause of the uproar does not greatly matter, except that the Kid became so rapturously engaged in watching the foolery of the Happy Family that he forgot all about Silver. And since sugar produces thirst, and Silver had not smelled water since morning, he licked the last sweet grain from the inside of the nose bag and then walked out of the stall and the stable and made for the creek— and a horse cannot drink with a nose bag fastened over his face. All he can do, if he succeeds in getting his nose into the water, is to drown himself most expeditiously and completely.

Silver reached the creek unseen, sought the deepest hole and tried to drink. Since his nose was covered with the bag he could not do so, but he fussed and splashed and thrust his head deeper, until the water ran into the bag from the top. He backed and snorted and strangled, and in a minute he fell. Fortunately he struggled a little, and in doing so he slid backward down the bank so that his head was up the slope and the water ran out of the bag, which was all that saved him.

He was a dead horse, to all appearances at least, when Slim spied him and gave a yell to bring every human being on the ranch at a run. The Kid came with the rest, gave one scream and hid his face in the Little Doctor's skirts, and trembled so that his mother was more frightened for him than for the horse, and had Chip carry him to the house where he could not watch the first-aid efforts of the Happy Family.

They did not say anything much. By their united strength they pulled Silver up the bank so that his limp head hung downward. Then they began to work over him exactly as if he had been a drowned man, except that they did not, of course, roll him over a barrel. They moved his legs backward and forward, they kneaded his paunch, they blew into his nostrils, they felt anxiously for heart-beats. They sweated and gave up the fight, saying that it was no use. They saw a quiver of the muscles over the chest and redoubled their efforts, telling one another hopefully that he was alive, all right. They saw finally a quiver of the nostrils as well, and one after another they laid palms upon his heart, felt there a steady beating and proclaimed the fact profanely.

They pulled him then into a more comfortable position where the sun shone warmly and stood around him in a crude circle and watched for more pronounced symptoms of recovery, and sent word to the Kid that his string was going to be all right in a little while.

The information was lost upon the Kid, who wept in his Daddy Chip's arms and would not listen to anything they told him. He had seen Silver stretched out dead, with his back in the edge of the creek and his feet sprawled at horrible angles, and the sight obsessed him and forbade comfort. He had killed his string; nothing was clear in his mind save that, and he screamed with his face hidden from his little world.

The Little Doctor, with anxious eyes and puckered eyebrows, poured something into a teaspoon and helped Chip fight to get it down the Kid's throat. And the Kid shrieked and struggled and strangled, as is the way of kids the world over, and tried to spit out the stuff and couldn't, so he screamed the louder and held his breath until he was purple, and his parents were scared stiff. The Old Man hobbled to the door in the midst of the uproar and asked them acrimoniously why they didn't make that doggoned Kid stop his howling; and when Chip, his nerves already strained to the snapping point, told him bluntly to get out and mind his own business, he hobbled away again muttering anathemas against the whole outfit.

The Countess rushed in from out of doors and wanted to know what under the shin' sun was the matter with that kid, and advised his frantic parents to throw water in his face. Chip told her exactly what he had told the Old Man, in exactly the same tone; so the Countess retreated, declaring that he wouldn't be let to act that way if he was *her* kid, and that he was plumb overlastingly spoiled.

The Happy Family heard the disturbance and thought the Kid was being spanked for the accident, which put every man of them in a fighting humor toward Chip, the Little Doctor, the Old Man and the whole world. Pink even meditated going up to the White House to lick Chip—or at least tell him what he thought of him—and he had plenty of sympathizers; though they advised him half-heartedly not to buy in to any family mixup.

It was into this storm-centre that Andy Green rode headlong with his own burden of threatened disaster.

CHAPTER IV

ANDY TAKES A HAND IN THE GAME

Andy Green was a day late in arriving at the Flying U. First he lost time by leaving the train thirty miles short of the destination marked on his ticket, and when he did resume his journey, on the next train, he traveled eighty-four miles beyond Dry Lake, which landed him in Great Falls in the early morning. There, with the caution of a criminal carefully avoiding a meeting with Miss

Hallman, he spent an hour in poring over a plat of a certain section of Chouteau County, and in copying certain descriptions of unoccupied land.

He had not slept very well the night before and he looked it. He had cogitated upon the subject of land speculations and the welfare of his outfit until his head was one great, dull ache. But on general principles it seemed wise to learn all he could concerning the particular tract of land about which Florence Grace Hallman had talked.

The day was past when range rights might be defended honorably with rifles and six-shooters and iron-nerved men to use them—and I fear that Andy Green sighed because it was so. But such measures were not to be thought of; if they fought at all they must fight with the law behind them—and even Andy's optimism did not see much hope from the law; none, in fact, since both the law and the moneyed powers were eager for the coming of homebuilders into that wide land. All up along the Marias they had built their board shacks, and back over the benches as far as one could see. There was nothing to stop them, everything to make their coming easy.

Andy scowled at the plat he was studying, and admitted to himself that it looked as though the Homeseekers' Syndicate were going to have things their own way; unless— There he stuck. There must be some way out. In this case it was the clerk in the office who pointed the way with an idle remark.

"Going to take up a claim, are you?"

Andy looked up at him with the blank stare of preoccupation, and changed expression as the question filtered into his brain and fitted somehow into the puzzle. He grinned, said maybe he would, folded the sheet of paper filled with what looked like a meaningless jumble of letters and figures, bought a plat of that township and begged some government pamphlets, and went out humming a little tune just above a whisper. At the door he tilted his hat at an angle and took long, eager steps toward an obscure hotel.

There was no train going east until midnight, and he caught that train. This time he actually got off at Dry Lake, got his horse out of the livery stable and dug up the dust of the lane with rapid hoof-beats.

When he rode down the Hog's Back he saw the Happy Family benched around some object on the creek-bank, and he heard the hysterical screaming of the Kid up in the house, and saw the Old Man limping excitedly up and down the porch. A man less astute than Andy Green would have known that something had happened. He hurried down the last slope, galloped along the creek-bottom, crossed the ford in a couple of leaps and pulled up beside the group that surrounded Silver.

"What's been taking place here?" he demanded curiously, skipping the usual greetings.

"Hell," said the Native Son succintly, glancing up at him.

"Old Silver looked over the fence into Kingdom Come," Weary enlarged the statement a little. "Tried to take a drink with a nose bag on. I guess he'll come through all right."

"What ails the Kid?" Andy demanded, glancing toward

the house whence issued a fresh outburst of shrieks.

The Happy Family looked at one another and then at the White House.

"Aw, some folks hain't got a lick of sense when it comes to kids," Big Medicine accused gruffly.

"The Kid," Weary explained, "put the nose bag on Silver and then left the stable door open."

"They ain't—spanking him for it, are they?" Andy demanded belligerently. "By gracious, how'd a kid know any better? Little bit of a tad like that—"

"Aw, they don't never spank the Kid!" Slim defended the parents loyally. "By golly, they's been times *I* would-a spanked him, if it'd been me. Countess says it's plumb ridiculous the way that Kid runs over 'em—rough shod. If he's gittin' spanked now, it's the first time."

"Well," said Andy, looking from one to another and reverting to his own worry as he swung down from his sweating horse, "there's something worse than a spanked kid going to happen to this outfit if you fellows don't get busy and do something. There's a swarm of dry-farmers coming in on us, with their stock to eat up the grass and their darned fences shutting off the water—"

"Oh, for the Lord's sake, cut it out!" snapped Pink. "We ain't in the mood for any of your joshes. We've had about enough excitement for once."

"Ah, don't be a damn' fool," Andy snapped. "There's no josh about it. I've got the scheme, just as they framed it up in Minneapolis. I got to talking with a she-agent on the train, and she gave the whole snap away. I laid low, and made a sneak to the land office and got a plat of the land, and all the dope—"

"Get any mail?" Pink interrupted him, in the tone that took no notice whatever of Andy's ill news. "Time I was hearing from them spurs I sent for."

Andy silently went through his pockets and produced what mail he had gleaned from the post-office, and led his horse into the shade of the stable and pulled off the saddle. Every movement betrayed the fact that he was in the grip of unpleasant emotions, but to the Happy Family he said not another word.

The Happy Family did not notice his silence at the time. But afterwards, when the Kid had stopped crying and Silver had gotten to his feet and wobbled back to the stable, led by Chip, who explained briefly and satisfactorily the cause of the uproar at the house, and the boys had started up to their belated dinner, they began to realize that for a returned traveler Andy Green was not having much to say.

They asked him about his trip, and received brief answers. Had he been anyone else they would have wanted to know immediately what was eatin' on him; but since it was Andy Green the boldest of them were cautious. For Andy Green had fooled them too often with his lies. They waited, and they watched him covertly and a bit puzzled.

Silence and gloom were not boon companions of Andy Green, at any time. So Weary, having the most charitable nature of any among them, sighed and yielded the point of silent contention.

"What was all that you started to tell us about the dry-farmers, Andy?" he asked indulgently.

"All straight goods. But there's no use talking to you

boneheads. You'll set around chewing the rag and looking wise till it's too late to do anything but holler your heads off." He got up from where he had been lounging on a bench just outside the mess house and walked away, with his hands thrust deep into his pockets and his shoulders drooped forward.

The Happy Family looked after him doubtfully.

"Aw, it's just some darned josh uh his," Happy Jack declared. "I know *him*."

"Look at the way he slouches along—like he was loaded to the ears with trouble!" Pink pointed out amusedly. "He'd fool anybody that didn't know him, all right."

"And he fools the fellows that do know him, often than anybody else," added the Native Son negligently. "You're fooled right now if you think that's all acting. That *hombre* has got something on his mind."

"Well, by golly, it ain't dry-farmers," Slim asserted boldly.

"If you fellows wouldn't say it was a frame-up between us two, I'd go after him and find out. But . . ."

"But as it stands, you'd believe Andy Green a whole lot quicker'n what we would you," supplemented Big Medicine loudly. "You're dead right there."

"What was it he said about it?" Weary wanted to know. "I wasn't paying much attention, with the Kid yelling his head off and old Silver gaping like a sick turkey, and all. What was it about them dry-farmers?"

"He said," piped Pink, "that he'd got next to a scheme to bring a big bunch of dry-farmers in on this bench up here, with stock that they'd turn loose on the range.

That's what he *said.* He claims the agent wanted him to go in on it."

"Mamma!" Weary held a match poised midway between his thigh and his cigarette while he stared at Pink. "That would be some mixup—if it was to happen. Where's the josh?" he questioned the group.

"The josh is, that he'd like to see us all het up over it, and makin' war-talks and laying for the pilgrims some dark night with our six-guns, most likely," retorted Pink, who happened to be in a bad humor because in ten minutes he was due at a line of post-holes that divided the big pasture into two unequal parts. "He can't agitate me over anybody's troubles but my own. Happy, I'll help Bud stretch wire this afternoon if you'll tamp the rest uh them posts."

"Aw, you stick to your own job! How was it when I wanted you to help pull the old wire off the hill fence and git it ready to string down here? You wasn't crazy about workin' with bob wire then, I noticed. You said—"

"What I said wasn't a commencement to what I'll say again," Pink began truculently, and so the subject turned effectually from Andy Green.

Weary smoked while they wrangled, and when the group broke up for the afternoon's work he went in search of Andy. He was not quite easy in his mind concerning the alleged joke. He found Andy replacing some broken strands in his cinch, and he went straight at the mooted question.

Andy looked up from his work and scowled. "This ain't any joke with me," he stated grimly. "It's something that's going to put the Flying U out of business if it ain't stopped before it gets started. I've been worrying my head off, ever since day before yesterday; I ain't in the humor to take anything off those joshers up there— I'll tell yuh that much."

"Well, but how do you figure it can be stopped?" Weary sat soberly down on the oats box and absently watched Andy's expert fingers while they knotted the heavy, cotton cord through the cinch-rings. "We can't stand 'em off with guns."

Andy dropped the cinch and stood up, pushing back his hat and then pulling it forward into place with the gesture he used when he was very much in earnest. "No, we can't. But if the bunch is game for it there's a way to block their play—and the law does all our fighting for us. It's like this, Weary: Counting Chip and the Little Doctor and the Countess there's 'leven of us that can use our rights up here on the bench. If we can get Irish and Jack Bates to come back and help us out, there's thirteen of us. And we can take homesteads along the creeks and deserts back on the bench, and—say, do you know how much land we can corral, the bunch of us? Four thousand acres! We'll have the creeks, and also we'll have the breaks corralled for our own stock.

"I've gone over the plat—I brought a copy to show you fellows what we can do. And by taking up our claims right, we keep a deadline from the Bear Paws to the Flying U. Now the Old Man owns Denson's ranch, all south uh here is fairly safe—unless they come in between his south line and the breaks; and there ain't room for more than two or three claims there. Maybe we can get some of the boys to grab what there is, and string ourselves out north uh here too.

"That's the only way on earth we can save what feed there is left. This way, we get the land ourselves and hold it, so there don't any outside stock come in on us. If Florence Grace Hallman and her bunch lands any settlers here, they'll be between us and Dry Lake; and they're welcome to squat on them dry pinnacles—so long as we keep their stock from crossing our claims to get into the breaks. Savvy the burro?"

"Yes-s—but how'd yuh *know* they're going to do all this? Mamma? I don't want to turn dry-farmer if I don't have to!"

Andy's face clouded. "That's just what'll block the game, I'm afraid. I don't want to, either. None of the boys'll want to. It'll mean going up there and baching, six or seven months of the year, by our high lonesomes. We'll have to fulfill the requirements, if we start in— because them pilgrims'll be standing around like dogs at a picnic, waiting for something to drop so they can grab it and run. It ain't going to be any snap.

"And there's another thing bothers me, Weary. It's going to be one peach of a job to make the boys believe it hard enough to make their entries in time." Andy grinned wrily. "By gracious, this is where I could see a gilt-edged reputation for telling the truth!"

"You could, all right," Weary agreed sympathetically. "It's going to strain our swallowers to get all that down, and that's a fact. You ought to have some proof, if you want the boys to grab it, Andy." His face sobered. "Who is this Florence person? If you could get some kinda proof—a letter, say . . ."

"Easiest thing in the world! She's stopping at the Park, in Great Falls, and she wanted me to come up or write. I'll send that foxy dame a letter that'll produce proof enough. You've helped me a lot, Weary."

Weary scrutinized him sharply and puckered his lips into a doubtful expression. "I wish I knew for a fact whether all this is straight goods, Andy," he said pensively. "Honest, Andy, is this some josh, or do you mean it?"

"By gracious, I wish it was a josh! But it ain't, darn it. In about two weeks or so you'll all see the point of this joke—but whether the joke's on us or on the Homeseekers' Syndicate depends on you fellows. Lord! I wish I'd never told a lie!"

Weary sat knocking his heels rhythmically against the side of the box while he thought the matter over. Meanwhile Andy Green went on with his work and scowled over his well-earned reputation that hampered him now just when he needed the confidence of his fellows. Perhaps his mental suffering could not rightly be called remorse, but a poignant regret it most certainly was, and a sense of complete bafflement which came out in his next sentence.

"Even if she wrote me a letter, the boys'd call it a frame-up just the same. They'd say I had it fixed before I left town. Doctor Cecil's up at the Falls. They'd lay it to her."

"I was thinking of that, myself. What's the matter with getting Chip to go up with you? Couldn't you ring him in on the agent somehow, so he can get the straight of it?"

Andy stood up and looked at Weary a minute. "How'd I make Chip believe me enough to *go?*" he countered. His eyes were too full of trouble to encourage levity in his listener. "You remember that time the boys rode off and left me laying out here on the prairie with my leg broke?" he went on dismally. "I'd rather have that happen to me a dozen times than see 'em set back and give me the laugh now, just when— Oh, hell!" He dropped the finished cinch and walked moodily to the door. "Weary, if them dry-farmers come flockin' in on me while this bunch stands around callin' me a liar, I—" He did not attempt to finish the sentence; but Weary, staring curiously at Andy's profile, saw a quivering of the muscles around his lips.

Spite of past experience he believed, at that moment, every word which Andy Green had uttered upon the subject of the proposed immigration. He was about to tell Andy so, when Chip walked unexpectedly out of Silver's stall and glanced from Weary to Andy standing still in the doorway. Weary looked at him inquiringly; for Chip must have heard every word they said, and if Chip believed it—

"Have you got that plat with you, Andy?" Chip asked tersely and with never a doubt in his tone.

Andy swung toward him like a prisoner who has just heard a jury return a verdict of not guilty to the judge. "I've got it, yes," he answered simply, with only his voice betraying the emotions he felt—and his eyes. "Want it?"

"I'll take a look at it, if it's handy," said Chip.

Andy felt in his inside coat pocket, drew out a thin,

folded map of that particular part of the county. He singled out a couple of pamphlets and gave them to Chip also.

"That's a copy of the homestead and desert laws," he said. "I guess you heard me telling Weary what kinda deal we're up against, here. Better not say anything to the Old Man till you have to; no use worrying him—he can't do nothing." It was amazing, the change that had come over Andy's face and manner since Chip first spoke. Now he grinned a little.

"If you want to go in on this deal," he said quizzically, "maybe it'll be just as well if you talk to the bunch yourself about it, Chip. You ain't any tin angel, but I'm willing to admit the boys'll believe you a whole lot quicker than they would me."

"Yes—and they'll probably hand me a bunch of pity for getting stung by you," Chip retorted. "I'll take a chance, anyway—but the Lord help you, Andy. If you can't produce proof when the time comes."

CHAPTER V

THE HAPPY FAMILY TURN NESTERS

"Say, Andy, where's them dry-farmers?" Big Medicine inquired at the top of his voice when the Happy Family had reached the biscuit-and-syrup stage of supper that evening.

"Oh, they're trying to make up their minds whether to bring the old fannin'-mill along or sell it and buy new when they get here," Andy informed him imperturbably.

"The women-folks are busy going through their rag bags, cutting the buttons off all the pants that ain't worth patching no more."

The Happy Family snickered appreciatively; this was more like the Andy Green with whom they were accustomed to deal.

"What's daughter doin', about now?" asked Cal Emmett, fixing his round, baby-blue stare upon Andy.

"Daughter? Why, daughter's leaning over the gate telling him she wouldn't never *look* at one of them wild cowboys—the idea! She's heard all about 'em, and they're too rough and rude for *her*. Pass the cane juice, somebody."

"Yeah—all right for daughter. If she's a good looker we'll see if she don't change her verdict about cowboys."

"Who will? You don't call yourself one, do yuh?" Pink flung at him quickly.

"Well, that depends; I know I ain't any *lady* broncho—hey, cut it out!" This last because of half a biscuit aimed accurately at the middle of his face. If you want to know why, search out the history of a certain War Bonnet Roundup, wherein Pink rashly impersonated a lady broncho-fighter.

"Where they going to live when they git here?" asked Happy Jack, reverting to the dry-farmers.

"Close enough so you can holler from here to their back door, my boy," Andy assured him. Andy felt that he could afford to be facetious now that he had Chip and Weary on his side.

"Aw, gwan! I betche there ain't a word of truth in all

that scarey talk," Happy Jack fleered heavily.

"Name your bet. I'll take it." Andy stirred up the sugar in his coffee like a man who is occupied chiefly with the joys of the table.

"Aw, you ain't going to git me that way again," Happy Jack declared. "They's some ketch to it."

"There sure is, Happy. The biggest ketch you ever seen. It's ketch the Flying U outfit and squeeze the life out of it." Andy's tone had in it considerable earnestness. For, though Chip would no doubt convince the boys that the danger was very real, there was a small matter of pride to urge Andy into trying to convince them himself.

"Well, I'd like to see anybody try that scheme," blurted Slim.

"Oh, you'll see it, all right. Just set around on your haunches a couple of weeks or so."

Pink eyed him with a wide glance. "You'd like to make us fall for that, wouldn't you?" he challenged.

Andy gave him a level look. "No, I wouldn't. I'd like to put one over on you smart gazabos that think you know it all; but I don't want to bad enough to see the Flying U go outa business just so I could holler didn't-I-tell-you. There's a limit to what I'll pay for a josh."

"Well," put in the Native Son with his easy drawl, "I'm coming to the centre with my auto, just for the sake of seeing the cards turned. Deal 'em out, *amigo;* state your case once more, so we can take a good, square look at these dry-farmers."

"What's the use?" Andy argued. "You'd all just holler your heads off. You wouldn't *do* anything about it—not if you knew it was the truth!" This, of course, was pure guile upon his part.

"Oh, wouldn't we? I guess, by golly, we'd do as much for the outfit as what you would." Slim swallowed the bait.

"Maybe you would, if you could take it out in talking," snorted Andy. "My chips are in. I've got three-hundred-and-twenty acres picked out, up here, and I'm going to file on 'em before these damned nesters get off the train. Uh course, that won't be more'n a flea bite—but I can make it interesting for my next-door neighbors, anyway; and every flea bite helps to keep a dog moving, yuh know."

"I'll go along and use my rights," Weary offered seriously. "That'll make one section they won't get, anyway."

Pink gave him a startled look across the table. "You ain't going to grab it, are yuh?" he demanded.

"I sure am—if it's three-hundred-and-twenty acres of land you mean. If I don't, somebody else will." He sighed humorously. "Next summer you'll see me hoeing spuds, most likely—if the law says I got to."

"Haw-haw-haw-w!" laughed Big Medicine suddenly. "It'd sure be worth the price, jest to ride up and watch you two marks down on all fours weedin' onions."

"We don't have to do anything like that if we don't want to," put in Andy Green calmly. "I've been reading up on the law. There's one little joker in it. It says that homestead land can be used for grazing purposes if it's more valuable for pasture than for crops, and that actual grazing will be accepted instead of cultivation—if it *is* grazing land. So—"

"I betche you can't prove that," Happy Jack interrupted him. "I never heard of that before—"

"The world's plumb full of things you never heard of Happy," Andy told him witheringly. "I gave Chip my copy of the homestead laws, and a plat of the land up here; soon as he hands 'em back I can show you in cold print where it says that very identical thing.

"That's what makes it look good to me, just on general principles," he went on. "If the bunch of us could pool our interests and use what rights we got, we can corral about four thousand acres—and we can head off outsiders from grazing in the Badlands, if we take our land right. We've been fooling around, just putting in our time and drawing wages, when we could be owning our own grazing land by now and shipping our own cattle, if we had enough sense to last us overnight.

"A-course, I ain't crazy about turning nester, myself—but we've let things slide till we've got to come through or get outa the game. That Minneapolis bunch that the blonde lady works for is sending out a colony of farmers to take up this land between here and the Bear Paws. The lady tipped her hand, not knowing where I ranged. She's a real nice lady, too, and goodlooking—but a grafter to her last eyewinker. And she hit too close to home to suit me, when she named the place where they're going to dump their colony."

"Where does the graft come in?" inquired Pink cautiously. "The farmers get the land, don't they?"

"Sure, they get the land. And they pungle up a good-sized fee to Florence Grace Hallman and her outfit, for locating 'em. Also there's side money in it, near as I can

51

find out. They skin the farmers somehow on the fare out here. They prowl around through the government plats till they spot a few thousand acres of land in a chunk; they take a look at it, maybe, and then they boom it like hell, and get them eastern marks hooked—them with money, the lady said. Then they ship a bunch out here, locate 'em on the land and leave it up to *them,* whether they scratch a living or not. She said they urge the rubes to bring all the stock they can, because there's plenty of range left. You can see for yourself how that'll work out, around here!"

Pink eyed him attentively, and suddenly his dimples stood deep. "All right, I'm It," he surrendered.

"It'd be a sin not to fall for a yarn like that, Andy. I expect you made it all up outa your own head, but that's all right. It's a pleasure to be fooled by a genius like you. I'll go raising turnips and cabbages myself."

"By golly, you couldn't raise nothing but hell up on that dry bench," Slim observed. "There ain't any water. What's the use uh talking foolish?"

"They're going to tackle it, just the same," Andy pointed out patiently.

"Well, if you ain't just lyin' to hear yourself, that there graftin' bunch had oughta be strung up!"

"Sure, they had. Nobody's going to argue about that. If they came out here with their herd of pilgrims and found the land all took up—" Andy smiled hypnotically upon the goggling group.

"Haw-haw-haw-w!" bawled Big Medicine. "It'd be wuth it, by cripes!"

"Yeah—it would, all right. If that talk Andy's been

giving us is straight, about grazing the land instead uh working it—"

"You can mighty quick find out," Andy retorted. "Go up and ask Chip for them land laws, and that plat. And ask him what he thinks about the deal. You don't have to take *my* word for it." Andy grinned virtuously and pushed back his chair. From their faces, and the remarks they had made, he felt very confident of the ultimate decision. "What about you, Patsy?" he asked, turning to the bald German cook who was thumping bread dough in a far corner. "You got any homestead rights you ain't used?"

"Py cosh, I got all der rights dere iss," Patsy returned querulously. "I got more rights as you shmartys. I got soldier's rights mit fightin'. Und py cosh, I use him too if dem fellers coom by us mit der dry farms alreatty!"

"Well, you son-of-a-gun!" Andy smote him elatedly upon a fat shoulder. "By gracious, that makes another three hundred and twenty to the good. Gee, it's lucky this bunch has gone along turning up their noses at nesters and thinkin' they couldn't be real punchers and hold down claims too. If any of us had had sense enough to grab a piece of land we'd be right up against it now. We'd have to set back and watch a bunch of down-east rubes light down on us like flies on spilt molasses, and we couldn't do a thing."

"As it is, we'll all turn nesters for the good of the cause!" finished Pink somewhat cynically, getting up and following Cal and Slim to the door.

"Aw, I betche they's some ketch to it!" gloomed Happy Jack. "I betche Andy jest wants to see us takin' up claims on that dry bench, and then set back and laugh at us fer bitin' on his josh."

"Well, you'll have the claims, won't you? And if you hang onto them there'll be money in the deal someday. Can't you get it into your system that all this country's bound to settle up?" Andy's eyes snapped angrily. "Can't you see the difference between us owning the land between here and the mountains, and a bunch of out-siders that'll cut it all up into little fields and try to farm it? If you can't see that, you better go hack a hole in your head so an idea can squeeze in now and then when you ain't looking!"

"Well, I betche there ain't no colony comin' to settle that there bench," Happy Jack persisted stubbornly.

"Yes there is, by cripes!" trumpeted Big Medicine behind him. "And that colony is goin' to be *us*. It's time I was doin' somethin' fer that there boy uh mine. And soon as we git that fence strung I'm goin' to hit the trail for the nearest land office. Honest to grandma, if Andy's lyin' it's goin' to be the prof''t'blest lie *he* ever told. I don't care a cuss about whether them dry-farmers is fixin' to light here or not. That there land-pool looks good to *me,* and I'm comin' in on it with all four feet!"

Big Medicine was nothing less than a human landslide when once he threw himself into anything, be it a fight or a frolic. Now he blocked the way to the door with his broad shoulders and his frog-like eyes fixed their pro-truding stare accusingly upon the reluctant ones.

"Cal, you git up there and git that plat and bring it here," he ordered. "And for criminy sake git that table cleared off, Patsy. Ain't you got head enough to see what a cinch we got? Down in Conconino County the boys wouldn't stand back and wait to be purty-pleased into a thing like this. You'd pass up a Chris'mas turkey if yuh seen Andy washin' his face and lookin' hungry! You'd—"

What further reproach he would have heaped upon them was interrupted by Chip, who opened the door just then and bumped Big Medicine in the back. In his hand Chip carried the land plat and the pamphlets, and in his keen, brown eyes he carried the light of battle for his outfit. The eyes of Andy Green sent bright glances from him to Big Medicine, and on to the others. He was too wise then to twit those others with their unbelief. His wisdom went farther than that; for he remained very much in the background of the conversation and contented himself with answering, briefly and truthfully, the questions they put to him about Florence Grace Hallman and the things she had so foolishly divulged concerning her plans.

Chip spread the plat upon an end of the table hastily and the Happy Family crowded close. They did not doubt, now—nor did they hang back reluctantly. Instead they followed eagerly the trail Chip's finger took across the map, and they listened intently to what he said about that trail.

The clause about grazing the land, he said, simplified matters a whole lot. It was a cinch you couldn't turn loose and dry-farm that land and have even a fair chance of reaping a harvest. But as grazing land they could hold all the land along One Man Creek. The land lying back of that, and higher up toward the foothills, they could stretch a line of claims that would protect the Badland grazing.

"I wouldn't ask you fellows to go into this," said Chip, looking from one sober face to another, "just to help the outfit. But it'll be a good thing for you boys. It'll give you a foothold—something better than wages, if you stay with your claims and prove up. Of course, I can't say anything about us buying out your claims—that's fraud, according to Hoyle; but you ain't simple-minded—you know your land won't be begging for a buyer, in case you should ever want to sell.

"There's another thing. This will not only head off the dry-farmers from overstocking what little range is left—it'll make a dead-line for sheep, too. With all our claims under fence, do you realize what that'll mean for the grass?"

"Josephine! There's feed for considerable stock, right over there on our claims, to say nothing of what we'll cover," exclaimed Pink.

"I'd tell a man! And if we get water on the desert claims—" Chip grinned down at him. "See what we've been passing up, all this time? We've had some of it leased, of course—but that can't be done again. There's been some wire-pulling, and because we ain't politicians we got turned down when the Old Man wanted to renew the lease. I can see now why it was, maybe. This dry-farm business had something to do with it, if you ask me."

"Gee whiz! And here we've been calling Andy a liar," sighed Cal Emmett.

"Aw, jest because he happened to tell the truth once,

don't cut no ice," Happy Jack maintained with sufficient ambiguity to avert the natural consequences.

"Of course, it won't be any gold-mine," Chip added dispassionately. "But it's worth picking up, all right; and if it'll keep out a bunch of tight-fisted settlers that don't give a darn for anything but what's inside their own fence, that's worth a lot, too."

"Say, my dad's a farmer," Pink declared. "And while I think of it, them eastern farmers ain't so worse—not the brand I've seen, anyway. Damn it, you fellows have got to quit talking about 'em as if they were blackleg stock."

"We ain't saying nothing against farmers *as* farmers, Little One," Big Medicine explained. "As men, and as women, and as kids, they're mighty nice folks. My folks have got an eighty-acre farm in Wisconsin," he confessed unexpectedly, "and I think a pile of 'em. But if they was to come out here, trying to horn in on our range, I'd lead 'em gently to the railroad and tell 'em goodbye so's't they'd know I meant it! Can't yuh see the difference?" he bawled, goggling at Pink with misleading savageness in his ugly face.

"Oh, I see," Pink admitted mildly. "I only just wanted to remind you fellows that I don't mean anything personal and I don't want you to. Say, what about One Man Coulee?" he asked suddenly. "That's marked vacant on the map. I always thought—"

"Sure, you did!" Chip grinned at him wisely, "because we used it for a line camp, you thought we owned a deed to it. We had that land leased, is all."

"Say, by golly, I'll file on that, then," Slim declared selfishly. "If Happy's ghost don't git to playin' music too much," he added with his heavy-handed wit.

"No, sir! You ain't going to have One Man Coulee unless Andy says he don't want it!" shouted Big Medicine. "I leave it to Chip if Andy hadn't oughta have first pick. He's the feller that's put us onto this and he's the feller that's going to pick his claim first."

Chip did not need to sanction that assertion. The whole Happy Family agreed unanimously that it should be so—except Slim, who yielded a bit unwillingly.

Till midnight and after, they made plans for the future and took no thought whatever of the difficulties that might lie before them. For the coming colony they had no pity, and for the balked schemes of the Homeseekers' Syndicate no compunctions whatever.

So Andy Green, having seen his stratagem well on the way to success, slept soundly that night in his own bed, serenely sure of the future.

CHAPTER VI

THE FIRST BLOW IN THE FIGHT

Letters went speeding to Irish and Jack Bates, absent members of the Happy Family of the Flying U; letters that explained the situation, set forth briefly the plan of the proposed pool, and which importuned them to come home or make haste to the nearest land-office and file upon certain quarter-sections therein described. Those men who would be easiest believed wrote and signed the letters, and certain others added characteristic postscripts best calculated to bring results.

After that, the Happy Family debated upon the bold-ness of going in a body to Great Falls to file upon their claims, or the caution of proceeding instead to Glasgow where the next nearest land-office might be found. Slim and Happy Jack favored caution and Glasgow. The others sneered at their timidity, as they were wont to do.

"Yuh think Florence Grace Hallman is going to stand guard with a six-gun?" Andy challenged at last. "She's tied up till her colony gets there. She can't file on all that land herself, can she?" He smiled reminiscently. "The lady asked me to come up to the Falls and see her," he said softly. "I'm going. The rest of you can take the same train, I reckon—she won't stop you from it, and I won't. And who's to stop you from filing? The land's there, open for settlement. At least it was open, day before yes-terday."

"Well, the sooner we go the better," Slim declared. "That fencin' kin wait. We gotta git back before Chip wants to start out the wagons, too."

"Listen here, *hombres,*" called the Native Son from the window, where he had been studying the pamphlet con-taining the homestead law. "If we want to play safe on this, we all better quit the outfit before we go. I don't like the way some of this stuff reads."

"I don't like the way none of it reads," grumbled Happy Jack. "I betche we can't make it go. We'll never git a patent."

"Well, pull out of the game, then!" snapped Andy Green, whose nerves were beginning to feel the strain put upon them.

"I ain't in it yet," said Happy Jack sourly, and banged

59

the door shut upon his departure.

Andy returned to studying the map. Finally he reached for his hat in the manner of one who had definitely made up his mind to something.

"Well, the rest of you can do as you darned please," he delivered his ultimatum from the doorway. "I'm going to draw a month's wages and hit the trail. I can catch the evening train to the Falls and be ready to file on my chunk in the morning."

"Ain't in any rush, are yuh?" Pink inquired facetiously. "If I had my dinner settled and this cigarette smoked, I might go along—provided you don't take the trail with yuh."

"Hold on, boys," the Native Son called out. "I think we better get a move on, too; but we want to get a fair running start, and not fall over this hump. Listen here! We've got to swear that it is 'not for the benefit of any other person, persons or corporation' and so on; and farther along it says we must not act in collusion with any person, persons or corporation, to give them the benefit of the land."

"Well, who's acting in collusion? What's collusion mean anyhow?" Slim demanded aggressively.

"It means what we're aiming to do—if anybody could prove it on us," explained the Native Son. "My oldest brother's a lawyer, and I caught some of it from him. And my advice is this: to get into a row with the Old Man, maybe—anyway, quit him cold, so we get our time. We must let that fact percolate the alleged brains of Dry Lake and vicinity—and if we give any reason for taking claims right under the nose of the Flying U, why, we're doing it to spite the Old Man. Otherwise we're going to have trouble—unless that colony scheme is just a pipe dream of Andy's."

The Happy Family had learned to respect the opinions of the Native Son. Once, as you may have heard, the Native Son even scored in a battle of wits with Andy Green. And he had helped Andy pull the Flying U out of an extremely ticklish situation, by his keen wit saving the outfit much trouble and money. Wherefore they heeded now his warning to the extent of discussing the obstacle he had pointed out. One after another they read the paragraph and sensed the possibilities of its construction. Afterward they went into consultation as to ways and means, calling Happy Jack back so that he might understand what must be done. For the Happy Family was nothing if not thorough, and their partisanship that had been growing stronger through the years was roused as it had not been since Dunk Whittaker drove sheep in upon the Flying U.

The Old Man, having eaten a slice of roast pork in defiance of his sister's professional prohibition of the indulgence, was sitting on the sunny side of the porch trying to ignore the first uneasy symptoms of indigestion. The Little Doctor had taken his pipe away from him that morning, and had badgered him into taking a certain decoction whose taste lingered bitterly. Ranch work was growing heavier each year in proportion to the lightening of range work. He had not been able to renew his lease of government land—which also went against the grain. And the Kid, like the last affliction which the Lord sent unto Job—I've forgotten whether that was boils or the butchery of his offspring—came loping down the length of the porch and kicked the Old Man's bunion with a stubby boot-toe.

Thus was born the psychological moment when the treachery of the Happy Family would cut deepest.

They came, bunched and talking low-voiced together with hatbrims hiding shamed eyes, a type-true group of workers bearing a grievance. Not a man was absent. Even Patsy, big and sloppy and bearing with him stale kitchen odors, limped stolidly in the rear beside Slim, who looked guilty as though he had been strangling somebody's favorite cat.

The Old Man, bent head-foremost over his growing paunch that he might caress his outraged bunion, glared at them with belligerent curiosity. The group came on and stopped short at the steps. The Old Man straightened with a grunt of pain because of his lame back, and waited. Which made it all the harder for the Happy Family, especially for Andy Green who had been chosen spokesman.

"We'd like our time," blurted Andy and fixed his eyes upon the lowest rung of the Old Man's chair.

"Oh, you would, hunh? The whole bunch of yuh?" The Old Man eyed them incredulously.

"Yes, the whole bunch of us. We're going to quit."

The Old Man's jaw dropped a little, but eyes did not waver from their faces. "Well, I never coaxed a man to stay yet," he stated grimly, "and I'm gittin' too old in the business to start coaxin' now. Dell!" He turned in his chair so that he faced the open door. "Bring me my time and check books outa the desk!"

A gray hardness came slowly to the Old Man's face while he waited, his seamed hands gripping the padded arms of his chair. It never occurred to him now that the Happy Family might be perpetrating one of their jokes. He had looked at their faces, you see. They meant to quit him—quit him cold just as spring work was beginning. They were ashamed of themselves, of course; they had a right to be ashamed, he thought bitterly. It hurt—hurt so that he would have died before he would ask for excuse, reason, grievance or explanation. So he waited, and he gripped the arms of his chair, and did not speak a word.

The Happy Family had expected him to swear at them stormily; to call them such names as his memory could seize upon. They had been careful to prepare a list of plausible reasons for having them. They had first invented a gold rumor that they hoped would sound convincing, but Andy had insisted upon telling him straightforwardly that they did not favor fence-building and ditch-digging and such back-breaking toil; that they were range men and they demanded range work or none; that if they must dig ditches and build fences they preferred doing it for themselves. "That," said Andy, "makes us out such low-down sons-of-guns we'd have to look a snake in the eye, but it's got the grain of truth that'll make it go down. We *don't* love this farming graft, and the Old Man knows it. He's heard us kicking often enough. He'll believe this last stretch of fence is what made us throw him down, and he'll be so mad he'll cuss us out till the neighbors'll think the smoke's a prairie fire. We'll get our time, and the things he'll say will likely make us so hot we can all talk convincing when we hit town. Keep a stiff upper lip, boys. We got to do it, and he'll make us mad, so it won't be as hard as you imagine."

The theory was good, and revealed a knowledge of human nature that made one cease to wonder why Andy was a prince of convincing liars. The theory was good—nothing was the matter with it, except that in this instance it did not work. The Old Man did not ask for their reasons or explanations. Neither did he say anything to make them mad. He just sat there, with his face gray and hard, and said nothing at all.

The Little Doctor appeared with the books and a fountain pen; saw the Happy Family standing there like condemned men at the steps; saw the Old Man's face, and trembled wide-eyed upon the verge of speech. Then she decided that this was no time for questioning and hurried away. The Happy Family did not look at one another—they looked chiefly at the wall of the house.

The Old Man reckoned the wages due each one, and wrote a check for the exact amount. And he spoke no word that did not concern the matter in hand. He still had that gray, hard look in his face that froze whatever explanation they would otherwise have volunteered. And when he handed the last man—who was Patsy—his check, he got up stiffly and turned his back upon them, and went inside and closed the door while yet they lingered, waiting to explain.

At the bunk-house, whence they walked silently, Slim turned upon their leader. His face had gone white, and his eyes were veined with red.

"If that there land business falls down anywhere

because you lied to us, Andy Green, I'll kill you for this," he stated flatly.

"If it does, Slim, I'll stand and let yuh shoot me as full of lead as you like," Andy promised. Then he strove to shake off the spell of the Old Man's stricken silence. "Buck up, boys. He'll thank us for what we aim to do— when he knows all about it."

"Well, it seems to me," sighed Weary lugubriously, "we mighta managed it without hitting the Old Man a wallop in the back, like that."

"How'n hell did *I* know he'd take it the way he did?" Andy questioned sharply, and began throwing his personal belongings into his "war-bag."

"Aw, looks to me like he was glad to git shet of us!" grumbled Happy Jack. "I betche he's more tickled than sorry, right now."

In spite of Chip's assurance that he would tell the Old Man all about it as soon as he could, it was an ill-humored Family that rode into Dry Lake and cashed their several checks at the desk of the General Store which also did an informal banking business, and afterwards took the train for Great Falls.

The news spread through the town that old J. G. Whitmore had fired the Happy Family in a bunch for some unforgivable crime against the peace of the outfit, and that the boys were hatching up some scheme to get even. From the gossip that was rolled upon the tongues of the Dry Lake scandal lovers, the Happy Family must have been more than sufficiently convincing.

CHAPTER VII

THE COMING OF THE COLONY

If you would see northern Montana at its most beau-
tiful best, you should see it in mid-May when the
ground-swallows are nesting and the meadow larks are
singing of their sweet ecstasy with life; when curlews go
sailing low over the green, grassy billows, peering and
perking with long bills thrust rapier-wise through the
sunny stillness, and calling shrilly, "Cor-r-*eck,* cor-r-
eck!" You should see the high prairies then, when all the
world is a-shimmer with green velvet brocaded brightly
in blue and pink and yellow flower-patterns; when the
heat waves go quivering up to meet the sun, so that the
far horizons wave like painted drop-scenes stirred by a
breeze; when a hypnotic spell of peace and bright
promises is woven over the rangeland—you should see
it then, if you would love it with a sweet unreason that
will last you through all the years to come.

The Homeseekers' Syndicate, as represented by Florence Grace Hallman—she of the wheat-yellow hair and
the tempting red lips and the narrow, calculating eyes—
did well to wait for the spell of the prairies when the
wind flowers and the lupines blue the hillsides and the
new grass paints green the hollows.

There is in us all a deep-rooted instinct to create, and
never is that instinct so nearly dominant as in the spring
when the grass and the flowers and the birds all sing the
song of Creation together. Then is when city-dwellers

study the bright army of seed-packets in the stores, and meditate rashly upon the possibilities of back-yard gardening. Then is when the seasoned country-dwellers walk over their farms in the sunset and plan largely for harvest time. Then is when the salaried-folk read avidly the real-estate advertisements, and dream of chicken ranches and fruit ranches. Surely, then, the Homeseekers' Syndicate planned well the date of their excursion into the land of large promise which lay east of Dry Lake.

Rumors of the excursion seeped through the channels of gossip and set the town talking and speculating—after the manner of very small towns. Rumors grew to definite though erroneous statements. Definite statements became certified facts that bore fruit in detailed arrangements.

Came Florence Grace Hallman from Great Falls, to canvass the town for "accommodations." Florence Grace Hallman was a capable woman though perhaps a shade too much inclined to take certain things for granted—such as Andy's anchored interest in her and her project, and the probability of the tract remaining just as it had been when last she went over the plat in the land office. Florence Grace Hallman had been busy arranging the details of the coming of the colony, and she had neglected to visit the land office lately. Since she cannily represented the excursion as being merely a sight-seeing trip she failed also to receive any inkling of recent settlements.

On a certain sunny morning in mid-May, the Happy Family stood upon the depot platform and waited for the special car of the Homeseekers' Syndicate. The Happy Family had been very busy. They had taken all the land they could, and had sighed because they could still look from their claims upon pinnacles as yet unclaimed save by the government. From the south line of Meeker's land in the foothills of the Bear Paws, to the north line of the Flying U, the chain of newly-filed claims remained unbroken. It had taken some careful work upon the part of the Happy Family to do this and still choose land not absolutely worthless except from a scenic viewpoint. But they had managed it. Also they had hauled loads of lumber from Dry Lake, wherewith to build their modest ten-by-twelve shacks with one door and one window apiece and a round hole in the roof big enough for a length of stove-pipe. And now, having heard of the mysterious excursion due that day, they had come to see just what would take place.

"She's fifteen minutes late," the agent volunteered, thrusting his head through the open window. "Looking for friends, boys?"

"Andy is," Pink informed him cheerfully. "The rest of us are just hanging around through sympathy. It's his girl coming."

"Well, I guess he thinks he needs a housekeeper now," the agent grinned. "Why don't you fellows get busy now and rustle some cooks?"

"Girls don't like to cook over a camp-fire," Cal Emmett told him soberly. "We kinda thought we ought to build our shacks first."

"You can pick you out some when the train gets in," said the agent. "There's a carload of—" He pulled in his head hurriedly and laid supple fingers on the telegraph key to answer a call, and the Happy Family moved down to the other end of the platform where there was more shade.

The agent presently appeared pushing the truck of out-going express, a cheap trunk and a basket "telescope" belonging to one of the hotel girls—who had quit her job and was sitting now inside waiting for the train. He placed the truck where the baggage car would come to a halt, stood for a minute looking down the track, glanced at the lazy group in the patch of shade and went back into the office.

"There's her smoke," Cal Emmett announced in the midst of an apathetic silence.

Weary looked up from whittling a notch in the end of a platform plank and closed his jack-knife languidly. Andy pushed his hat backward and then tilted it forward over one eyebrow and threw away his cigarette.

"Wonder if Florence Grace will be riding point on the bunch?" he speculated aloud. "If she is, I'm liable to have my hands full. Florence Grace will sure be sore when she finds out how I got into the game."

"Aw, I betche there ain't no such a person," said Happy Jack, doubter to the last.

"I wish there wasn't," sighed Andy. "If I done what I feel like doing, I'd crawl under the platform and size up the layout through a crack. Honest to gracious, boys, I hate to meet that lady."

They grinned at him and stared at the black smudge that was rolling toward them. "She's sure hittin' her up," Pink vouchsafed with a certain tenseness of tone. That train was not as ordinary trains; they felt that it was relentlessly bringing them trouble, perhaps; certainly a problem—unless the homeseekers hovered only so long as it took them to see that wisdom lay in looking elsewhere for a home.

"If this was August instead of May, I wouldn't worry about them pilgrims staying long," Jack Bates voiced the thought that was uppermost in their minds.

"There comes two livery rigs to haul 'em to the hotel," Pink pointed out as he glanced toward town. "And there's another one. Johnny told me every room they've got is spoke for, and two in every bed."

"That wouldn't take no crowd," Happy Jack grumbled, remembering the limitations of Dry Lake's hotel. "Here come Chip and the missus."

The Little Doctor left Chip to get their tickets and walked quickly toward them.

"Hello, boys! Waiting for someone, or just going somewhere?"

"Waiting. Same to you, Mrs. Chip," Weary replied.

"To me? Well, we're going up to make our filings. Claude won't take a homestead, because we'll have to stay on at the Flying U, of course, and we couldn't hold one. But we'll both file desert claims. J. G. hasn't been a bit well, and I didn't dare leave him before—and of course Claude wouldn't go till I did. That the passenger coming, or a freight?"

"It's the train—with the dry-farmers," Andy informed her with a glance at the nearing smoke-smudge.

"Is it? We aren't any too soon then, are we? I left Son at home—and he threatened to run away and live with

70

you boys. I almost wish I'd brought him along. He's been perfectly awful. So have the men Claude hired to take your places. I believe that is what made J. G. sick—having those strange men on the place. He's been like a bear."

"Didn't Chip tell him—"

"He did, yes. He told him right away, that evening. But—J. G. has such stubborn ideas. We couldn't make him believe that anyone would be crazy enough to take up that land and try to make a living farming it. He—" She looked sidewise at Andy and pursed her lips to keep from smiling.

"He thinks I lied about it, I suppose," said that young man shrewdly.

"That's what he says. He pretends that you boys meant to quit, and just thought that up for an excuse."

"Here she comes!"

A black nose thrust through a deep cut that had a curve to it. At their feet the rails began to hum. The Little Doctor turned hastily to see if Chip were coming. The agent came out with a handful of papers. Stragglers moved quickly, and the discharged waitress appeared and made eyes at Pink, whom she considered the handsomest one of the lot.

The train slid up, slowed and stopped. Two coaches beyond the platform a porter descended and placed the box-step for landing passengers. From that particular coach began presently to emerge a fluttering steam of humanity—at first mostly feminine. They hovered there upon the cindery path and lifted their faces to watch for others yet to come, and the babble of their voices could be heard above the engine sounds.

"Aw, I knowed there was some ketch to it!" blurted Happy Jack. "That there ain't no colony— It's nothin' but a bunch of school-ma'ams!"

"That lady ridin' point is the lady herself," Andy murmured, edging behind Weary and Pink as the flutter came closer. "That's Florence Grace Hallman."

"Well, by golly, git out and speak your little piece, then!" muttered Slim, and gave Andy an unexpected push that sent him staggering out into the open.

"Why, how de do, Mr. Green!" cried the blonde leader of the flock. "This is an unexpected pleasure."

"Yes ma'am, it is," Andy assented mildly, with an eye cocked sidewise in search of the guilty man.

The blonde leader paused, her flock coming to a fluttering stand behind her. The nostrils of the astonished Happy Family caught a mingled odor of travel and perfume.

"Well, Mr. Green, why didn't you come and see me?" demanded Florence Grace Hallman in the tone of one who has a right to ask leading questions. Her cool, brown eyes went appraisingly over the Happy Family while she spoke.

"I've been right around here, all the time," Andy gave meek account of himself. "I've been busy."

"Oh. Did you go over the tract, Mr. Green?"

"Yes-s—I went over it."

"And what do you think of it—privately?"

"Privately—it's pretty big." Andy sighed. The bigness of that tract had worried the Happy Family a good deal.

"Well, the bigger the better. You see I've got 'em

72

started." She flicked a glance backward at her waiting colony. "You men are perfectly exasperating! Why didn't you tell me where you were and what you were doing?" She looked up at him with charming disapproval. "I feel like shaking you! I could have made good use of you, Mr. Green."

"I was making pretty good use of myself," Andy explained, and wished he knew who gave him that surreptitious kick on the ankle. Did the chump want an introduction? Well! In that case—

"Miss Hallman, if you don't mind I'd like to introduce some men I rounded up," he began before the Happy Family could move out of the danger zone of his imagination. "Representative citizens, you see. You can sic your bunch onto 'em and get a lot of information. This is Mr. Weary Davidson, Miss Hallman: He's a hayseed that lives out that way and he talks spuds better than anything else. And here's Slim. He raises hogs to a fare-you-well. And this is Percy Perkins"—meaning Pink— "and he's another successful dry-farmer. Goats is his trade. And Mr. Jack Bates, he raises peanuts—or he's trying 'em this year—and has contracts to supply the local market. Mr. Happy Jack is our local undertaker. He wants to sell out if he can because nobody ever dies in this country. He's thinking some of starting a duck-ranch. This man—" indicating Big Medicine—"has got the finest-looking crop of volunteer wild oats in the country. He knows all about 'em. Mr. Emmett, here, can put you wise to cabbage-heads; that's his specialty. And Mr. Miguel Rapponi is up here from Old Mexico looking for a favorable location for a rubber plantation.

The natural advantages here are great for rubber.

"I've gone to some trouble gathering this bunch together for you, Miss Hallman. I don't reckon you knew there was that many dry-farmers in the country. Your bunch won't have to listen to one man, only— here's half a dozen ready and waiting to talk."

Miss Hallman was impressed. A few of the closest homeseekers she beckoned and introduced to the perspiring Happy Family—mostly feminine homeseekers, of whom there were a dozen or so. The men whom the hotel had sent down with rigs waited impatiently and the unintroduced male colonists stared at the low rim of Lonesome Prairie and wondered if over there lay their future prosperity.

When the Happy Family finally made their escape, Andy Green had disappeared. He was not in Rusty Brown's place when the Happy Family went to that haven and washed down their wrongs in beer. Pink made a hurried trip to the livery stable and reported that Andy's horse was gone.

They were wondering whether he would have the nerve to go home and await their coming—home at this stage of the game meaning One Man Coulee, which Andy had taken as a homestead and desert claim and where the Happy Family camped together until such time as their claim shacks were habitable. Some thought that he was hiding in town, and advised a thorough search before they took to their horses. The Native Son told them with languid certainty that Andy was headed straight for the camp because he would figure that in camp was where they would least expect to find him.

The opinions of the Native Son were usually worth adopting. In this case, however, it brought them into the street at the moment when Florence Grace Hallman and two homeseekers had ventured from the hotel in search of them. Slim and Jack Bates and Cal Emmett saw them in time and shied across the street and into the barber shop where they sat down and demanded unnecessary hair-cuts and spied upon their unfortunate fellows through the window while they waited; but the others met the women fairly since it was too late to turn back without making themselves ridiculous.

"I was wondering," began Miss Hallman, "if some of you gentlemen could not help us out in the matter of conveyances. I have made arrangements for most of my guests, but we simply can't squeeze another one into the rigs I have engaged."

"How many are left out?" asked Weary, since no one else showed any symptoms of speech.

"Just us three, here. You've met Miss Allen, Mr. Davidson—and Miss Price. And so have you other gentlemen, because I introduced you at the depot. I told everybody just which rig they were to ride in, and put three in a seat, at that, and in counting noses I forgot to count our own—"

"I really don't see how she managed to overlook mine," sighed Miss Allen, laying a dainty, gloved finger upon a nose that had the tiniest possible tilt to it. "Nobody ever overlooked my nose before."

Irish, standing close beside Weary and looking enough like him to be a twin instead of a mere cousin, smiled down at her. Miss Allen's nose was a nice nose, and above it twinkled a pair of warm brown eyes, and still above them fluffed a kinky-curly mass of brown hair.

"—So if any of you gentlemen could possibly take us out to the tract, we'd be eternally grateful, besides keeping our independence intact with the usual payment. Could you help us out?"

"We all came in on horseback," Weary stated with a gentle firmness that was intended to kill their hopes as painlessly as possible.

"Wouldn't there be room on behind?" asked Miss Allen with hope still alive and flourishing.

"Lots of room," Weary assured her. "More room than you could possibly use."

"But isn't there any kind of a rig that you could buy, beg, borrow or steal?" Miss Hallman insisted. "These girls came from Wisconsin to take up claims, and I've promised to see that they get the best there is to be had. I have a couple of claims in mind, that I want them to see—and that's why we three hung back till the rest were all arranged for. There's no use talking; we just must get out to the tract as soon as the others do—a little sooner wouldn't hurt. Couldn't you think of some way?"

"We'll try," Irish promised rashly, his eyes trying to meet Miss Allen's and succeeding admirably.

"What has become of Mr. Green?" Miss Hallman demanded after she had thanked Irish with a smile.

"We don't know," Weary answered mildly. "We were trying to locate him ourselves."

"He seems a rather uncertain young man. I rather counted on his assistance; he promised—"

"Mr. Irish has thought of a rig he can use, Miss

Hallman," said the Allen girl suddenly. "He's going to drive us out himself. Let's hurry and get ready. How many minutes will it take you, Mr. Irish, to have that team here for us?"

Irish turned red. He *had* thought of a rig, and he had thought of driving them himself, but he could not imagine how Miss Allen could possibly have known his thoughts. Then and there he knew who would occupy the other half of the front seat, in case he did really drive the team he had in mind.

"I told you she's a hustler," laughed Miss Hallman. "She'll be raising bigger crops than you men—give her a year to get started. Well, girls, come on, then."

They turned away, and walked toward the livery stable—where was manifested an unwonted activity— waiting for Irish to clear himself; which he did not do.

"You going to drive them women out there?" Pink demanded after an impatient silence.

"Why not? Somebody'll have to."

"What team are you going to use?" asked Jack Bates.

"Chip's." Irish did not glance around, but kept striding down the middle of the road.

"Don't you think you need help, *amigo?*" the Native Son insinuated craftily. "You can't talk to three girls at once; I could be hired to go along and take one off your hands. That should help some."

"Like hell you will!" Irish retorted. Then he added cautiously, "Which one?"

"That old girl with the blue eyes should not be permitted to annoy the driver," drawled the Native Son. "Also, Florence Grace might want some intelligent person to talk to."

"Well, I got my opinion of any man that'll throw in with that bunch," Pink declared hotly. "They can do just as much harm. You make me sick."

"Let 'em go," Weary advised calmly. "Come on, boys—let's pull out, away from all these lunatics. I hate to see them get stung, but I don't see what we can do about it—only, if they come around asking me what I think of that land, I'm going to tell 'em."

"And then they'll ask you why you took claims up there, and you'll tell 'em that, too—will you?"

That was it. They could not tell the truth without harming their own cause. They thought that Irish and the Native Son were foolish to take Chip's team and drive those women fifteen miles or so that they might seize upon land much better left alone; but that was the business of Irish and the Native Son, who did not ask for the approval of the Happy Family before doing anything they wanted to do.

The Happy Family saddled and rode back to their claims, gravely discussing the potentialities of the future. Since they rode slowly while they talked, they were presently overtaken by a swirl of dust, behind which came the matched browns which were the Flying U's crack driving team, bearing Irish and Miss Allen upon the front seat of a two-seated spring-wagon that had seen far better days than this. Native Son helped to crowd the back seat and waved a hand with reprehensible cheerfulness as they went past.

The Happy Family stared after them with frowning disapproval, and Weary turned in the saddle and looked ruefully at his fellows.

"Things won't ever be the same around here," he predicted. "There goes the beginning of the end of the Flying U and we ain't big enough to stop it."

CHAPTER VIII

FLORENCE GRACE HALLMAN SPEAKS PLAINLY

Andy Green rode thoughtfully up the trail from his cabin in One Man Coulee, his eyes fixed absently upon the yellow soil of the hillside. Andy was facing a problem that concerned the whole Happy Family—and the Flying U as well. He wanted Weary's opinion, and Miguel Rapponi's, and Pink's—when it came to that, he wanted the opinion of them all.

Thus far the boys had been wholly occupied with getting their shacks built and getting themselves settled upon their claims with an air of convincing permanency. Also they had watched with keen interest developments where the homeseekers were concerned, and had not given very much thought to their next step, except in a general way.

They all recognized the fact that, with all these new hunting claims where there was some promise of making things grow, they would have to sit very tight upon their own land if they would avoid trouble with "jumpers." Not all the homeseekers were women. There were men, plenty of them; a few of them were wholly lacking in experience it is true, but perhaps the more greedy for land because of their ignorance. The old farmers had wanted to know about sub-soil, and average rainfall, and late frosts, and markets. The illustrated folders that used blue print for emphasis here and there, seemed no longer to satisfy them.

The Happy Family did not worry much about the old farmers who knew the game, but there were town men who had come to see the fulfilment of their dreams. These the Happy Family knew for incipient enemies. And there were the women—daring rivals of the men in their fight for independence—who had raised up ideals for which they would fight tenaciously. School-teachers who hated the routine of the schools, and who wanted freedom; who would cheerfully endure loneliness and spoiled complexions and roughened hands and see the prairie winds and sun wipe the sheen from their hair; who would wear heavy-soled shoes and keep all their pretty finery packed carefully away in their trunks, and take all their pleasure in dreaming of the future; these would fight also to have and to hold—and they would fight more dangerously than the men, because they would fight differently.

The Happy Family, then, having measured the fighting-element, knew that they were up against a grim, relentless war if they would save the Flying U. They knew that it was going to be a stiff proposition, and that they would have to obey the letter and the spirit of the land laws, or there would be trouble without end.

So they hammered and sawed and fitted boards and swore and jangled and joshed one another and badgered the life out of Patsy. Py cosh, he wouldn't cook for the whole country just because they were too lazy to cook for themselves, and py cosh if they wanted him to cook for them they could pay him sixty dollars a month, as the Old Man did.

The Happy Family were no millionaires, and they made the fact plain to Patsy to the full extent of their vocabularies. But still they begged bread from him, and couldn't see why he objected to making pie, if they furnished the stuff. Why had they planted him in the middle of their string of claims, then? With a dandy spring too, that never went dry except in the driest years, and not more than seventy-five yards, at the outside, to carry water. Up hill? Well, what of that? Hadn't they clubbed together and put up his darned shack first thing, just so he *could* get busy and cook?

Well—you see that the Happy Family had been fully occupied since the arrival of the homeseekers' excursion. As fast as the shacks were up, the Happy Family had taken possession, so that now Andy was alone, stuck down there in the coulee out of sight of everybody. Pink had once named One Man Coulee as the lonesomest hole in all that country. But at any rate the lonesomeness had served one good purpose, for it had started Andy to thinking out the details of their so-called land-pool. Now the thinking had borne fruit to the extent that he felt an urgent need of the Happy Family in council upon the subject.

As he topped the final rise which put him on a level with the undulating benchland, he lifted his head and gazed about him half regretfully, half proudly. He hated to see that wide upland dotted here and there with new, raw buildings, which proclaimed themselves claim-shacks as far as one could see them. Andy hated the sight of claim-shacks with a hatred born of long range experience. A claim-shack stuck out on the prairie meant a barbed wire fence somewhere in the immediate vicinity; and that meant a hindrance to the easy handling of herds. A claim-shack meant a nester with his plowed fields and his few head of cattle that must be painstakingly weeded out of a herd to prevent a howl going up to high heaven. Therefore, Andy Green instinctively hated the sight of a shack on the prairie. On the other hand, those shacks belonged to the Happy Family—and that pleased him. From where he sat on his horse he could count five in sight, and there were more tucked away in hollows.

But there were others going up—shacks whose owners he did not know. To be sure, they had as much right to take government land as had he or any of his friends—but Andy, being a normally selfish person, did not think so.

From one partially built shack three quarters of a mile away on a bald ridge which the Happy Family had passed up because of its barrenness and because no one was willing to waste even a desert right on that particular eighty acres, a team and light buggy came swiftly toward him. Andy, trained to quick thinking, was puzzled at the direction the driver was taking. That eighty acres joined his own west line, and unless the driver was lost or on the way to One Man Coulee, there was no reason whatever for coming this way.

He watched and saw that the team was coming straight toward him, and at a pace that threatened damage to the buggy-springs. He turned his spurred heels against his horse and went loping over the grassland to meet the person who drove in such haste; and the probability that he was meeting trouble halfway only sent him the more eagerly forward.

Trouble met him with hard, brown eyes and corn-yellow hair blown in loose strands across cheeks roughened by the spring winds. Trouble pulled up and twisted sidewise in the seat and flicked the heads off some wild larkspurs with her whip while her tongue flayed the soul of Andy Green with sarcasm.

"Well, I have found out just how you helped me colonize this tract, Mr. Green," she began with a hard inflection. "You have made a remarkable showing—in—in treachery and deceit."

"Remember, I told you I might buy in if it looked good to me," Andy reminded her in the mildest tone of which he was capable.

Florence Grace Hallman looked at him with a lift of her full upper lip at the left side. "It does look good, then? You told Mr. Graham and that Mr. Wirt a different story, Mr. Green. Both Mr. Wirt and Mr. Graham had some capital to invest here, and now they are leaving, and they persuaded several others to leave with them. Does it really look good to you—this land proposition?"

"Not your proposition—no, it don't." Andy faced her with a level glance as hard as her own. "You're trying to cold-deck this bunch. The land won't raise white beans or anything else without water, and you know it. You can plant folks on the land and collect your money and tell 'em goodbye and that settles your part of it. But how about the poor devils that put in their time and money?"

Florence Grace Hallman smiled unpleasantly. "And yet, you nearly broke your neck filing on the land yourself and getting a lot of your friends to file," she retorted. "What was your object, Mr. Green—since the land is worthless?"

"My object don't matter to anyone but myself."

"Oh, but it does! It matters to me, Mr. Green, and to my company, and to our clients."

"I'll have to buy me a new dictionary," Andy observed casually, reaching behind him to scratch a match on the skirt of his saddle. "The one I've got don't say anything about 'client' and 'victim' meaning the same thing. It's getting outa date."

"I brought enough clients—" she emphasized the word—"to settle every eighty acres of land in that whole tract. The policy of the company was eminently fair. We guaranteed to furnish a claim of eighty acres to every person who joined our Homeseekers' Club, and free pasturage to all the stock they wanted to bring. Failing to do that, we pledged ourselves to refund the fee and pay all return expenses. We could have located every member of this lot, only for *you*."

"Say, it'd be just as easy to swear as to say 'you' in that tone uh voice," Andy pointed out placidly.

"You managed to gobble up just exactly four thousand acres of this tract—and you were careful to get all the water and all the best land. That means you have knocked us out of fifty settlements—"

"Fifty wads of coin to hand back to fifty come-ons, and fifty return tickets for fifty fellows glad to get back—tough luck, ain't it?" Andy smiled sympathetically. "You oughta be glad I saved your conscience that much of a load, anyway."

Florence Grace Hallman bit her lip to control her rage. "Smart talk isn't going to help you, Mr. Green. I've investigated you thoroughly, and it's easy to guess what your object is. Mr. Green, let me advise you to abandon your claims now, before we begin action in the matter. We have the law all on our side. These are bona fide settlers we are bringing in. The land laws are pretty strict, Mr. Green. If we set the wheels in motion they will break the Flying U."

Andy grinned while he inspected his cigarette. "Funny—I heard a man brag once about how he'd break the Flying U, with sheep," he drawled. "He didn't connect, though; the Flying U broke him." He smoked until he saw an angry retort parting the red lips of the lady and then continued calmly:

"The Flying U has nothing to do with this case. As a matter of fact, old man Whitmore is pretty sore at us fellows right now. Miss Hallman, you'll have one sweet time proving that we ain't bona fide settlers. We're real sorry we didn't find it necessary to pay your folks for the fun of pointing out the land to us, but we can't help that. We needed the money to buy plows." He looked at her full with honest, gray eyes. "And that reminds me, I've got to go and borrow a garden rake. I'm planting a patch of onions," he explained engagingly. "Well, good day, Miss Hallman. Glad I happened to meet you."

"You won't be when I get through with you!" predicted the lady. "You think you've got everything your own way, don't you? Well, you've just put yourself in a position where we can get at you. You deceived me from the very start—and now you shall pay the penalty. I've got our clients to protect—and besides that I shall dearly love to get even." She touched up the horses with her whip and went bumping away over the tough sod.

"Wow!" ejaculated Andy, looking after her with laughter in his eyes. "She's sure one mad lady, all right. But shucks!" He turned and galloped off toward the farthest claim, which was Happy Jack's and the last one to be furnished with a lawful habitation.

He was lucky. The Happy Family were foregathered there, wrangling with Happy Jack over some trifling thing. He joined zealously in the argument and helped them thrash Happy Jack in the word-war, before he came at his errand.

"Say, boys, we'll have to get busy now," he told them at last. "Florence Grace is onto us bigger'n a wolf—and if I'm any judge, that lady's going to be some fighter. We've either got to plow up a bunch of ground and plant some darn thing, or else get stock on and pasture it. I met her back here on the bench. She was so mad she talked too much and I got next to their scheme;—seems like we've knocked the Syndicate outa quite a bunch of money. They want this land, and they think they're going to get it.

"Now my idea is this: We've got to have stock, or we can't graze the land. And if we take Flying U cattle and throw 'em on here, they'll contest us for taking fake claims, for the outfit. So what's the matter with us buying a bunch from the Old Man?"

"I'm broke," began Pink, but Andy stopped him.

"Listen here. We buy a bunch of stock and give him mortgages for the money, with the cattle for security. We graze 'em till the mortgage runs out—till we prove up, that means—and then we don't spot up, and the Old Man takes the stock back. See? We're grazing our own stock, according to law—but the outfit—"

"Where do we git off at?" demanded Happy Jack suspiciously. "We got to live—and it takes money to buy grub, these days."

"Well, we'll make out all right. By the time we all prove up we'll have a little bunch of stock of our own, d'yuh see? And we'll have the range—what there is left. And it'll be a long, cold day when another bunch of greenhorns bites on any colony scheme."

"How do you know the Old Man'll do that, though?" Weary wanted to know. "He's pretty mad. I rode over to the ranch last week to see Chip, and the Old Man wouldn't have anything to say to me."

"Well, what's the matter with all of us going? We can put it up to him and he'll see where it's going to be to his interest to let us have the cattle. Why, darn it, he can't help seeing now why we quit!" Pink looked ready to start then, while his enthusiasm was fresh.

"Neither can Florence Grace help seeing why we did it," Andy supplemented drily. "She can think what she darn pleases—all we got to do is deliver the goods right to the handle, on the claims, and not let her prove anything on us."

"It'll take a lot uh fencing," Happy Jack croaked pessimistically. "We ain't got the money to buy wire and posts, nor the time to build the fence."

"What's the matter with range-herding 'em?" Andy seemed to have an answer for every objection. "We can take turns at that—and we must all be careful and don't let 'em graze on our neighbors!"

Whereat the Happy Family grinned understandingly.

"Maybe the Old Man'll let us have three or four hundred head uh cows on shares," Cal hazarded.

"Can't take 'em that way," said the Native Son languidly. "It wouldn't be safe. I think we better split the bunch, and let every fellow buy a few head. We can graze 'em together—and the law can't stop us from doing that."

"Sounds good—if the Old Man will come to the centre," said Weary dubiously. The chill atmosphere of Flying U Coulee, with strangers in the bunk-house and the Old Man scowling at his paper on the porch, had left its effect upon Weary, sunny-souled as he was.

"Oh, he'll come through," cried Cal, moving toward his horse. "Come on—let's go and get it done with. First thing we know, our neighbors will be saying we ain't improving our claims!"

"You improve yours every time you git off it!" stated Happy Jack because of past wrongs. "You could improve mine a whole lot that way, too," he added when he heard the laugh of approval from the others.

They mounted and rode away, every man of them secretly glad of some excuse for making overtures to the Old Man. They had felt keenly their exile from the Flying U ranch. They had stayed away, for two reasons: one was a latent stubbornness; the other was a matter of policy, as preached by Andy Green and the Native Son.

It would not do, said these two cautious ones, to be running to the Flying U outfit all the time.

So the Happy Family had steered clear since that afternoon when they had simulated treachery to the outfit. And fate played them a scurvy trick in spite of their caution for just as they rode down the Hog's Back and across the ford, Florence Grace Hallman rode away from the White House and met them at the stable.

Florence Grace smiled a peculiar smile as she went past them. A smile that told them how sure she felt of having caught them fairly. With the smile went a supercilious bow that was worse than a direct cut, and which the Happy Family returned doubtfully, not at all sure of the rules governing warfare with a woman.

Warfare it would be; of that they had no doubt.

CHAPTER IX

THE HAPPY FAMILY BUYS A BUNCH OF CATTLE

With the Kid riding gleefully upon Weary's shoulder they trooped up the path their own feet had helped wear deep to the bunk-house. They looked in at the open door and snorted at the cheerlessness of the place.

"Why don't you come back here and stay?" the Kid demanded. "I was going to sleep down here with you—and now Doctor Dell won't let me. These hoboes are no good. They're boneheads. I wish you'd come back, so I can sleep with you. One man's named Ole and he's got a funny eye that looks at the other one all the time. I wish you'd come back."

The Happy Family wished the same thing, but they did not say so. Instead they told the Kid to ask his mother if he couldn't visit them in their shacks, and promised indulgencies that would have shocked the Little Doctor had she heard them. So they went on to the house, where the Old Man sat on the porch looking madder than when they had left him three weeks before.

"Why don't yuh run them nesters outa the country?" he demanded when they were close enough for speech. "Here they come and accuse me to my face of trying to defraud the gov'ment. Doggone you boys, what you think you're up to? What's four thousand acres when they're swarming in here like flies to a butcherin'? They can't make a living—serve 'em right. What you doggone rowdies want now?"

Not a cordial welcome, that—if they went no deeper than his words. But there was the old twinkle back of the querulousness in the Old Man's eyes. "You've got that doggone Kid broke to foller yuh so we can't keep him on the ranch no more," he added fretfully. "Tried to run away twice, on Silver. Chip had to go round him up. Found him last time pretty near over to Antelope Coulee. Might as well take yuh back, I guess, and save time running after the Kid."

"We've got to hold down our claims," Weary reminded him regretfully. In three weeks, he could see a difference in the Old Man, and the change hurt him. Lines were deeper drawn, and the kind old eyes were a shade more sunken.

"What's that amount to?" grumbled the Old Man. "You can't stop them dry-farmers from taking the country. They'll flood the country with stock—"

"No they won't," put in Big Medicine, impatient for the real meat of their errand. "By cripes, we got a scheme to beat that—you tell 'im, Weary."

"We want to buy a bunch of cattle from you," Weary said obediently. "We want to graze our claims, instead of trying to crop the land. And seeing our land runs straight through from Meeker's line fence to yours, we kinda think we've got the nesters pretty well corralled. Soon as we can afford it," he added tranquilly, "we'll stretch a fence along our west line that'll hold all the darn milk-cows they've a mind to ship out here."

"Huh!" The Old Man studied them quizzically.

"How many yuh want?" he asked abruptly.

"All you'll sell us. We want to give mortgages, with the stock for security."

"Oh, yuh do, ay? What if I have to foreclose on you? Where do you get off at, then?"

"Well, we kinda thought we could fix it up to save part of the increase outa the wreck anyway."

"Oh. That's it, ay?" He studied them another minute. "You'll want all my best cows, too, I reckon—all that grade stock I shipped in last spring. Ay?"

"We wouldn't mind," grinned Weary.

"Think you could handle five hundred head—the pick uh the bunch?"

"Sure, we could! We'd rather split 'em up amongst us, though—let every fellow buy so many."

"Think you can keep the milk-cows between you and Dry Lake, ay?" The Old Man chuckled—the first little chuckle since the Happy Family left him three weeks

91

before. "How about that, Pink?"

"Why, I think we can," chirped Pink cheerfully.

"Huh! Well, you're the toughest bunch I ever seen keep outa jail—I guess maybe you can do it. But lemme tell you boys something. You don't want to get the idea in your heads you're going to have any snap. If I know B from a bull's foot you've got your work cut out for yuh. I've been keeping cases pretty close on this dry-farm craze. Folks are land crazy. They've got the idea that a few acres of land is going to make 'em free and independent—and it don't matter much what the land is, or where it is. Yuh don't want to take it for granted they're going to take a look at your deadline and back up. If they ship in stock, they're going to see to it that stock don't starve. You'll have to hold off men and women that's making their last stand, some of 'em, for a home of their own. You get a man with his back agin the wall, and he'll fight till he drops. I don't need to tell yuh that."

The Happy Family listened to him soberly, their eyes staring broodily at the picture he conjured.

"Well, by golly, we're makin' our last stand, too," Slim blurted with his customary unexpectedness. "Our back's agin the wall right now. If we can't hold 'em back from takin' what little range is left, this outfit's going under. We got to hold 'em, by golly, or there won't be no more Flyin' U."

"Well," said Andy Green quietly, "that's all right. We're going to hold 'em."

The Old Man lifted his bent head and looked from one to another. Pride shone in his eyes. "Yuh know, don't yuh, the biggest club they can use?" He leaned forward, his lips working under his beard.

"Sure, we know. We'll look out for that." Weary smiled hearteningly.

"We want a good lawyer to draw up those mortgages," put in the Native Son lazily. "And we'll pay eight percent interest."

"Doggonedest crazy bunch ever I struck," grumbled the Old Man with grateful insincerity. "What you fellers don't think of, there ain't any use in mentioning. Oh, Dell! Bring out that jug Blake sent me! Doggoned thirsty bunch out here—won't stir a foot till they sample that wine! Got to get rid of 'em somehow—they claim to be full uh business as a jack rabbit is of fleas! When yuh want to git out and round up them cows? Wagon's over on Dry Creek som'ers. Yuh might take your soogans and ride over there tomorrow or next day and ketch 'em. I'll write a note to Chip and tell 'im what's to be done. And while you're pickin' your bunch, yuh can draw wages the same as ever, and help them milk-fed pilgrims with the calf-crop."

"We'll sure do that," promised Weary for the bunch.

"Take a taste uh this wine. This comes straight from Fresno. Senator Blake sent it the other day. Fill up that glass, Dell! What yuh want to be so doggone stingy for? They can't git the taste outa less'n a pint. This ain't any doggone liver-tonic like you dope out."

The Little Doctor smiled and filled their glasses with wine. She did not know what had happened, but she did know that the Old Man had seized another hand-hold on life in the last hour, and she was grateful. She even permitted the Kid to take a sip, because the Happy Family hated to see him refused anything he wanted.

So Flying U Coulee was for the time being filled with the same atmosphere of care-free contentment with life. The Countess stewed in the kitchen, cooking dinner for the boys. The Old Man grumbled hypocritically at them from his big chair, and named their faults in the tone that transmuted them into virtues. The Little Doctor heard about Miss Allen and her three partners, who were building a four-room shack on the four corners of tour claims, and how Irish had been caught more than once in the act of staring fixedly in the direction of that shack.

By mid afternoon the Old Man was fifty per cent. brighter than he had been in the morning, and he bullied them as of old. When they left he told them to clear out, and that if he caught them hanging around his ranch, and making it look as if he was backing them and trying to defraud the government, he'd sic the dog onto them. Which tickled the Kid immensely, because there wasn't any dog to sic.

CHAPTER X

WHEREIN ANDY GREEN LIES TO A LADY

In the soft-creeping dusk came Andy Green, slouched in the saddle with the weariness of riding since dawn; slouched to one side and singing, with his hat far back on his head and the last of a red sunset tinting darkly the hills above him. Tip-toe on a pinnacle a great, yellow star poised and winked at him knowingly. Andy's eyes twinkled answer as he glanced up that way. "We've got her going, old-timer," he announced lazily to the star.

Six miles back toward the edge of the "breaks" which are really the beginning of the Badlands that border the Missouri River an even five hundred head of the Flying U's best grade cows and their calves were settling down for the night upon a knoll that had been the bed-ground of many a herd. At the Flying U ranch were the mortgages that would make the Happy Family nominal owners of those five hundred cows and their calves. In the morning Andy would ride back and help bring the herd upon its spring grazing ground, which was the claims; in the meantime he was leisurely obeying an impulse to ride into One Man Coulee and spend the night under his own roof. And, say what you will, there is a satisfaction not to be denied in sleeping sometimes under one's own roof; and it doesn't matter in the least that the roof is made of prairie dirt thrown upon cottonwood poles. So he sang while he rode, and his voice boomed loud in the coulee:

"We're here because we're here, because we're here,
    because we're here,
We're here because we're here, because we're here,
    because we're here!"

That, if you please, is a song; there are a lot more verses exactly like this one, which may be sung to the tune of Auld Lang Syne with much effectiveness when one is in a certain mood. So Andy sang, while his tired horse picked its way among the scattered rocks of the

95

trail up the coulee.

"It's time you're here, it's time you're here,
It's time that you were here—"

mocked an echo not of the hills.

Andy swore in his astonishment and gave his horse a kick as a mild hint for haste. He thought he knew every woman-voice in the neighborhood, but this voice, high and sweet and with a compelling note that stirred him, was absolutely strange. While he loped forward he was conscious of a keen thankfulness that Pink had decided to stay in camp that night instead of accompanying Andy to One Man. He was in that mood when a sentimental encounter appealed to him strongly; and a woman's voice, singing to him from One Man cabin, promised undetermined adventure.

He did not sing again. There had been something in the voice that held him quiet, listening, expectant. But she also was silent after that last, high note—like a meadow lark startled in the middle of his song.

He came within sight of the cabin, squatting in the shadow of the grove at its back. He expected to see a light, but the window was dark, the door closed. He felt a faint unreasoning disappointment that it was so. But he had heard her. That high note that lingered upon the word "here" still tingled his senses. His eyes sent seeking glances here and there as he rode up.

Then a horse nickered, and someone rode out from the shadow at the corner of the cabin, hesitated as though tempted to flight, and came on uncertainly. They met before the cabin, and the woman peered through the dusk at Andy.

"Is this—Mr. Mallory—Irish?" she asked nervously. "Oh dear! Have I gone and made a fool of myself again?"

"Not at all! Good evening, Miss Allen." Andy folded his hands upon the saddle horn and regarded her with a little smile, keen for what might come next.

"But you're not Irish Mallory. I thought I recognized the voice, or I wouldn't have—" She urged her horse a step closer, and Andy observed from her manner that she was not accustomed to horses. She reined as if she were driving, so that the horse, bewildered, came sidling up to him. "Who are you?" she asked him sharply.

"Me? Why, I'm a nice young man—a lot better singer than Irish. I guess you never heard him, did you?" He kept his hands folded on the horn, his whole attitude passive—a reassuring passivity that lulled her uneasiness more than words could have done.

"Oh, are you Mr. Green? I seem to connect that name with your voice—and what little I can see of you."

"That's something, anyway." Andy's tone was one of gratitude. "It's two per cent. better than having to tell you right out who I am. I met you three different times, Miss Allen," he reproached.

"But always in a crowd," she defended, "and I never talked with you, particularly."

"Oh, well, that's easily fixed," he said. "It's a nice night," he added, looking up appreciatively at the brightening star-sprinkle. "Are you living on your claim now? We can talk particularly on the way over."

Miss Allen laughed and groped for a few loose hairs, found them and tucked them carefully under her hat-crown. Andy remembered that gesture; it helped him to visualize her clearly in spite of the deepening night.

"How far have you ridden today, Mr. Green?" she asked irrelevantly.

"Since daylight? Not so very far counting miles— We were trailing a herd, you see. But I've been in the saddle since sunrise, except when I was eating."

"Then you want a cup of coffee, before you ride any further. If I get down, will you let me make it for you? I'd love to. I'm crazy to see inside your cabin, but I only rode up and tried to peek in the window before you came."

"Are you living on your claim?" he asked again.

"Why, yes. We moved in last week."

"Well, we'll ride over, then, and you can make coffee there. I'm not hungry right now."

"Oh." She leaned again and peered at him, trying to read his face. "You don't *want* me to go in!"

"Yes, I do—but I don't. If you stayed and made coffee, tomorrow you'd be kicking yourself for it, and you'd be blaming me." Which, considering the life he lived, almost wholly among men, was rather astute of Andy Green.

"Oh." Then she laughed. "You must have some sisters, Mr. Green." She was silent for a minute, looking at him. "You're right," she said quietly then. "I'm always making a fool of myself. The girls will be worried about me, as it is. But I don't want you to ride any farther, Mr. Green. What I came to say need not take very long, and

I think I can find my way home alone."

"I'll take you home when you're ready to go," said Andy quietly. All at once he had wanted to protect her from even so slight an unconventionality as making his coffee for him. He had felt averse to putting her at odds with her conventional self, of inviting unfavorable criticism of himself; dimly, because instinct rather than analysis impelled him. What he had told her was the total of his formulated ideas.

"Well, I'm ready to go now, since you insist on my being conventional. I did not come West with the expectation of being tied to a book of etiquette, Mr. Green. But I find one can't get away from it after all. Still, living on one's own claim twelve miles from a town is something!"

"That's a whole lot, I should say," Andy assured her politely, and refrained from asking her what she expected to do with that eighty acres of arid land. He turned his tired horse and rode alongside her, prudently waiting for her to give the key.

"I'm not supposed to be away over here, you know," she began when they were near the foot of the bluff up which the trail wound. "I'm supposed to be just out riding, and the girls expected me back by sundown. But I've been trying to find some of you 'Flying U boys'— as they call you men who have taken so much land—on your claims. I don't know that what I could tell you would do you a particle of good. But I wanted to tell you, anyway, just to clear my own mind."

"It does lots of good just to meet you," said Andy with straightforward gallantry. "Pleasures are few and far between, out here."

"You said that very nicely, I'm sure," she snubbed. "Well, I'm going to tell you, anyway—just on the chance of doing some good." Then she stopped.

Andy rode a rod or two, waiting for her to go on. She was guiding her horse awkwardly where it needed only to be let alone, and he wanted to give her a lesson in riding. But it seemed too early in their acquaintance for that, so he waited another minute.

"Miss Hallman is going to make you a lot of trouble," she began abruptly. "I thought it might be better for you—all of you—if you knew it in advance, so there would be no sudden anger. All the settlers are antagonistic, Mr. Green—all but me, and one or two of the girls. They are going to do everything they can to prevent your land-scheme from going through. You are going to be watched and your land contested—"

"Well, we'll be right there, I guess, when the dust settles," he filled in her thought unmoved.

"I—almost hope so," she ventured. "For my part, I can see where it is very hard for the cattle men to give up their range. They resent it deeply; deeply enough to shed blood—and that is one thing I dread here. I hope, Mr. Green, that you will not resort to violence."

"I understand," said Andy softly. "We're liable to ride up on dark nights and shoot our enemies through the window—I can't deny it, Miss Allen. But now that ladies have come into the country we'll try and hold our tempers down all we can. We take pride in being polite to women. You've read that about us, haven't you, Miss Allen? And you've seen us on the stage—well, it's a fact, all right. Bad as we are, a lady can just do anything with us, if she goes at it the right way."

"Thank you. I felt sure that you would not harm any of us. Will you promise not to be violent—not to—to—"

Andy sat sidewise in the saddle, so that he faced her. Miss Allen could just make out his form distinctly; his face was quite hidden, except that she could see the shine of his eyes.

"Now, Miss Allen," he protested with soft apology. "You musta known what to expect when you moved out amongst us rough characters. I know I can't answer for myself, what I'm liable to do; and I'm about the mildest in the bunch. What the rest of the boys would do—Irish Mallory for instance—I hate to think, Miss Allen."

Afterward, when he thought it all over dispassionately, Andy wondered why he had talked to Miss Allen like that. He had not done it deliberately, just to frighten her—yet he had frightened her to a certain extent. He wished, on the way home, that he knew just what Florence Grace Hallman intended to do.

Not that it mattered greatly. Whatever she did, Andy felt that it would be futile. The Happy Family were obeying the land laws implicitly. And was not the taking of land for the preservation of a fine, fair dealing outfit that had made itself a power for prosperity and happiness in that country, a perfectly laudable enterprise? Andy believed so.

Even though they did, down in their deepest thoughts, think of the Flying U's interest, Andy did not believe that Florence Grace Hallman or anyone else could produce any evidence that would justify a contest for their land.

They were not conspiring against the prosperity of the country in the hope of great personal gain. When you came to that, they were saving fifty men from bitter disappointment—counting one settler to every eighty acres, as the Syndicate apparently did.

Still, Andy wondered why he had represented himself and his friends to be such bloodthirsty devils. If she repeated half to Florence Grace Hallman, that lady would maybe think twice before she tackled the contract of boosting the Happy Family off their claims. So at the last he managed to justify his lying to her.

He went to sleep worrying not over the trouble which Florence Grace Hallman might be plotting to bring upon him but about Miss Allen's given name and her previous condition of servitude. He hoped that she was not a stenographer, and he hoped her first name was not Mary; and if you know the history of Andy Green you will remember that he had a reason for disliking both the name and the vocation.

CHAPTER XI

A MOVING CHAPTER IN EVENTS

Having nothing more than a general warning of trouble ahead to disturb him, Andy rode blithely back down the coulee and met the herd just after sunrise. Having represented himself to be an exceedingly dangerous man, and having permitted himself to be persuaded into promising reform he felt tolerably sure of her interest in him. He had heard that a woman loves best the taming of a dangerous man, and he whistled and sang until the dust of the coming herd met him full. He hoped that Florence Grace Hallman would start something, just so that he might show Miss Allen how potent was her influence over a bad man who still has virtues worth nurturing.

Weary, riding point on the loitering herd, grinned a wordless greeting. Soon he heard Andy singing, and his own thoughts fell into accord with the words of the ditty. He began to sing also. Farther back, Pink took it up, and then the others joined in, until all unconsciously they had turned the drive into a triumphal march.

"They're a little bit rough I must confess, the most of them at least," prompted Andy, starting on the second verse alone because the others didn't know the song as well as he. He waited a second for them to join him, and went on extolling the valor of all true cowboys:

"But long's you do not cross their trail you can live with them in peace.
"But if you do they're sure to rule, the day you come to their land,
"For they'll follow you up and shoot it out, and do it man to man."

"Say, Weary! They tell me Florence Grace is sure hittin' the warpost! Ain't yuh scared?"

Weary shook his head and rode forward to ease the leaders into a narrow gulch that would cut off a mile or so of the journey.

"Taking 'em up One Man?" called Pink, and got a nod

for answer. There was a lull in the singing while they shouted at those stubborn cows who would have tried to break back on the way to a clover patch, until the gulch broadened into an arm of One Man Coulee itself. It was all peaceful and easy and just as they had planned. They were nearing their claims, and all that would remain for them to do was the holding of their herd upon the appointed grazing ground. So would the requirements of the law be fulfilled and the machinations of the Syndicate thwarted.

And then the leaders, climbing the hill at a point half a mile below Andy's cabin, snorted and swung back. Weary spurred up to push them forward, and so did Andy and Pink. They rode up over the ridge urging the reluctant cattle ahead, and came plump into the very dooryard of a brand new shack. A man was standing in the doorway watching the disturbance his presence had created; when he saw the three riders come over the crest of the bluff, his eyes widened.

The three came to a stop before him, too astonished to do more than stare. Once past the fancied menace of the new building and the man, the cattle went trotting awkwardly across the level.

"Hello," said Weary at last, "what do you think you're doing here?"

"Me? I'm holding down a claim. What are you doing?" The man did not seem antagonistic or friendly or even neutral toward them. He seemed to be waiting. He eyed the cattle that kept coming, urged on by those who shouted at them in the coulee below.

"Say, when did yuh take this claim?" Andy leaned

negligently forward and looked at him curiously.

"Oh, a week or so ago. Why?"

"I just wondered. I took it up myself, four weeks ago. Four forties I've got, strung out in a line that runs from here to yonder. You've got on my land—by mistake, of course. I just thought I'd tell yuh," he added casually, straightening up, "because I didn't think you knew it before."

"Thanks." The man smiled one-sidedly and began filling a pipe while he watched them.

"A-course it won't be much trouble to move your shack," Andy continued with neighborly interest. "A wheelbarrow will take it, easy. Back here on the bench yuh may find a patch of ground that nobody claims."

"Thanks." The man picked a match from his pocket and striking it on the door-casing lighted his pipe.

Andy moved uneasily. He did not like that man, for all he appeared so thankful for information. The fellow had a narrow forehead and broad, high cheek bones and a predatory nose. Andy studied him curiously. Did the man know what he was up against, or did he not? Was he sincere in his ready thanks, or was he sarcastic? The man looked up at him then. His eyes were clean of any hidden meaning, but they were the wrong shade of blue—the shade that is opaque and that you feel hides much that should be revealed to you.

"Seems like there's been quite a crop of shacks grown up since I rode over this way," Weary announced suddenly, returning from a brief scurry after the leaders, that inclined too much toward the south in their travel.

"Yes, the country's settling up pretty fast," conceded

the man in the doorway.

"Well, by golly!" bellowed Slim, popping up from below on a heaving horse. His round eyes glared resentfully at the man and the shack and at the three who were sitting there so quietly on their horses—just as if they had ridden up for a friendly call. "Ain't this shack on your land?" he spluttered to Andy.

"Why, yes. It is, just right at present," Andy admitted, following the man's example in the matter of a smoke, except that Andy rolled and lighted a cigarette. "He's going to move it, though."

"Oh. Thanks." With the one-sided smile.

"Say, you needn't thank *me*," Andy protested in his polite tone. "*You're* going to move it, you know."

"You may know, but I don't," corrected the other.

"Oh, that's all right. You may not know right now, but don't let that worry yuh. This is sure a great country for pilgrims to wise up in."

Big Medicine came up over the hill a hundred feet or so from them; goggled a minute at the bold trespass and came loping across the intervening space. "Say, what's this mean?" he bawled. "Claim-jumper, hey? Say, young feller, do you realize what you're doing—squattin' down on another man's land? Don't yuh know claim-jumpers git shot, out here?"

"Oh, cut out all that rough stuff!" advised the man wearily. "I know you can't hold a foot of land if anybody is a mind to contest your claims. I've filed a contest on this eighty, here, and I'm going to hold it. I don't want any trouble—I'm even willing to take a good deal in the way of bluster, rather than have trouble. But I'm going to stay. See?" He waved his pipe in a gesture of finality and continued to watch them impersonally, leaning against the door in that lounging negligence which is so irritating to a disputant.

"Oh, all right—if that's the way you feel about it," Andy replied, and turned away. "Come on, boys—no use trying to bluff that gazabo. He's wise."

He rode away with his face turned over his shoulder to see if the others were going to follow. When he was past the corner and therefore out of the man's sight, he raised his arm and beckoned to them. The four of them looked after him uncertainly. Weary kicked his horse and started, then Pink did the same. Andy beckoned again, more emphatically than before, and Big Medicine, who loved a fight as he loved to win a jackpot, turned and glared at the man in the doorway as he passed.

"Pink, you go on back and put the boys next, so when they come up with the drag they won't do anything much but hand out a few remarks and ride on," Andy said, in the tone of one who knows exactly what he means to do. "This is my claim-jumper. Chances are I've got three more to handle—or will have. Tell the boys to just rag the fellow a little and ride on, like we did. Get the cattle up here and set Happy and Slim day-herding, and the rest of us'll get busy."

"You wouldn't tell for a dollar, would yuh?" Pink asked him with his dimples showing.

"I've got to think it out first," Andy evaded. "I feel all the symptoms of an idea. Let me alone a while."

"Say, yuh going to tell him he's been found out and yuh know his past," began Slim, "like yuh done to

Dunk? I'll be, by golly—"

"Go on off and lay down!" Andy retorted pettishly. "I never worked the same one off on you twice, did I? It ain't hard to put his nibs on the run—that's dead easy. Trouble is, I went and hobbled myself. I promised a lady I'd be mild."

"Mamma!" muttered Weary, his sunny eyes taking in the shack-dotted horizon. "Mild!—and all these jumpers on our hands!"

"Oh, well—there's more'n one way to kill a cat," Andy reminded them cheerfully. "You go on back and post the boys, Pink, not to get too riled."

He galloped off and left them to say and think what they pleased. From being the official Ananias of the outfit, king of all joke-makers, whose lightest word was suspected of hiding some deep meaning, he had come to the point where they depended upon him to see a way out of every difficulty. They would depend upon him now; of that he was sure—therefore they would wait for his plan.

Strange as it may seem, the Happy Family had not seriously considered the possibility of having their claims "jumped." They meant to stay upon their claims at least seven months in the year, which the law required. They meant to have every blade of grass eaten by their own cattle, which would be counted as improving their claims. They had prepared for every contingency save the one that had arisen. They had not expected that their claims would be jumped and contests filed so early in the game, as long as they maintained their residence.

However, Andy was not dismayed at the turn of

events. It was stimulating to the imagination to be brought face to face with an emergency such as this, and to feel that one must handle it with strength and diplomacy and a mildness of procedure that would find favor in the eyes of a girl.

He looked across the waving grass to where the four-roomed shack was built upon the four corners of four "eighties" so that four women might live together and yet be said to live upon their own claims. That was drawing the line pretty fine, of course; finer than the Happy Family would have dared to draw it. But no one would raise any objection, on account of their being women and timid about living alone. Andy smiled sympathetically because the four conjunctive corners of the four claims happened to lie upon a bald pinnacle bare of grass or water. The shack stood bleakly revealed to the four winds—but also it overlooked the benchland and the half-barren land to the west, which comprised Antelope Coulee and Dry Coulee and several other coulees capable of supporting nothing but coyotes and prairie dogs.

A mile that way Andy rode, and stopped upon the side of a gulch which was an arm of Antelope Coulee. He looked down into the gulch, searched with his eyes for the stake that marked the southeast corner of the eighty lying off in this direction from the shack, and finally saw it fifty yards away on a bald patch of adobe.

He resisted the temptation to ride over and call upon Miss Allen, which was eight o'clock or thereabouts—and rode back to the others very well satisfied with himself and his plan.

He found the whole Happy Family gathered upon the level land just over his west line, extolling resentment while they waited his coming. Grinning, he told them his plan, and set them grinning also. He gave them certain work to be done, and watched them scatter to do his bidding. Then he turned and rode away.

The claim-jumper, watching the benchland through a pair of field glasses, saw a herd of cows and calves feeding contentedly upon the young grass a mile away. Two men on horseback loitered upon the outer fringe of the herd. From a distant hilltop came the staccato sound of hammers where another shack was going up. Of the other horsemen who had come up the bluff with the cattle, he saw not a sign. So the man yawned and went in to his breakfast.

Many times that day he stood at the corner of his shack with the glasses sweeping the benchland. Toward noon the cattle drifted into a coulee where there was water. In a couple of hours they drifted leisurely back upon high ground and scattered to their feeding, still watched and tended by the two horsemen. One was fat and red-faced and spent at least half of his time lying prone upon some slope in the shade of his horse. The other was thin and awkward, and slouched in the saddle or sat upon the ground with his knees drawn up and his arms clasped loosely around them, himself the picture of boredom.

There was nothing whatever to indicate that events were breeding in that peaceful scene, and that adventure was creeping close upon the watcher.

That night he was awakened by a pounding on the side of the shack where was his window. By the time he had reached the middle of the floor similar pounding was at the door. He tried to open the door and couldn't. He went to the window and could see nothing, although the night had not been dark when he went to bed. He shouted, and there was no reply. His name, by the way, was H. J. Owens, though his name does not matter except for convenience in mentioning him. Owens, then, lighted a lamp, and almost instantly was forced to reach out quickly and save it from toppling, because one corner of the shack was lifting . . .

Outside, the Happy Family worked in silence. Before they had left One Man Coulee they had known exactly what they were to do, and how to do it. They knew who was to nail the hastily constructed shutter over the window. They knew who was to fasten the door so that it could not be opened from within. They knew also who were to use the crowbars, who were to roll the skids under the shack.

There were twelve of them—because Bert Rogers had insisted upon helping. In not many more minutes than there were men, they were in their saddles, ready to start. The shack lurched forward after the straining horses. Once it was fairly started it moved easily upon crude runners made of cottonwood logs eight inches or so in diameter and long enough for cross pieces bolted in front and rear. The horses pulled it easily with the ropes tied to the saddle-horns, just as they had many times pulled the roundup wagons across mirey creeks or up steep slopes.

Within, Owens called to them and cursed them. When they had just gained an even pace, he emptied his revolver through the four sides of the shack. But he did

111

not know where they were, exactly, so that he was compelled to shoot at random. And since the five shots seemed to have no effect whatever upon the steady progress of the shack, he decided to wait until he could see where to aim. There was no use, he reflected, in wasting good ammunition when there was a strong probability that he would need it later.

After a half hour or more of continuous travel, the shack tilted on a steep descent. H. J. Owens blew out his lamp and swore when a box came sliding against his shins in the dark. The descent continued until it was stopped with a jolt that made him bite his tongue painfully. He heard a laugh cut short and a muttered command, and that was all. The shack heaved, toppled, righted itself and went on down, and down; jerked sidewise to the left, went forward and then swung the other way. When finally it came to a permanent stand it was sitting with an almost level floor.

Then the four corners heaved upward, two at a time, and settled with a final squeal of twisted boards and nails. There was a sound of confused trampling, and after that the lessening sounds of departure. Mr. Owens tried the door again, and found it still fast. He relighted the lamp, carried it to the window and looked upon rough boards outside the glass. He meditated anxiously and decided to remain quiet until daylight.

The Happy Family worked hard, that night. Before daylight they were in their beds and snoring—except the two who guarded the cattle. Each was in his own cabin. His horse was in his corral, smooth-coated and dry. There was nothing to tell of the night's happen-

ings,—nothing except the satisfied grins on their faces
when they woke and remembered.

CHAPTER XII

SHACKS, LIVE STOCK AND PILGRIMS
PROMPTLY AND PAINFULLY REMOVED

"I'm looking rather seedy now, while holding down my
    claim,
And my grub it isn't always served the best,
And the mice play shyly round me as I lay me down to
    rest
In my little old sod shanty on my claim.
Oh, the hinges are of leather and the windows have no
    glass,
And the roof it lets the howling blizzards in,
And I hear the hungry kiote as he sneaks up through the
    grass—

"Say! have they got down the hill yet, Pink?" Pink
took his cigarette from his fingers, leaned and peered
cautiously through the grimy window. "Unh-huh.
They're coming up the flat."

Whereupon Andy Green, ostentatiously washing his
breakfast dishes, skipped two or three verses and lifted
his voice in song to fit the occasion.

"How I wish that some kind-hearted girl would pity on
    me take,
And relieve me of the mess that I am in!

Oh the angel, how I'd bless her if her home with me
     she'd make,
In my little old sod shanty—

"Got here yet?" And he craned his neck to look. "Aw,
they've pulled up, out there, listening!"

"My clothes are plastered o'er with dough, I'm looking
     like a fright,
And everything is scattered round the room—"

"Why don't yuh stop that caterwauling?" Pink
demanded fretfully. "They'll swear you're drunk!"

There was sense in that. Andy finished the line about
remaining happy lovers in his little old sod shanty, and
went to the door with the dishpan. He threw out the
water and squeezed the dishrag in one hand before he
appeared to discover that Miss Allen and Florence Grace
Hallman were riding up to his door. As a matter of fact,
he had seen them come over the top of the bluff, and had
long ago guessed who they were.

He met them with a smile of surprised innocence, and
invited them inside. They refused to come, and even
Miss Allen showed a certain coolness toward him. Andy
felt hurt at that, but he did not manifest the fact. Instead
he informed them that it was a fine morning. And were
they out taking a look around?

They were. They were looking up the men who had
perpetrated the outrage last night upon four settlers.

"Outrage?" Andy tilted the dishpan against the cabin
wall and went forward, pulling down his sleeves. "What

outrage is that, Miss Hallman? Anybody killed?"

Miss Hallman watched him with her narrowed glance. She saw the quick glance he gave Miss Allen, and her lids narrowed still more. So that was it! But she did not swerve from her purpose.

"You know that no one was killed. But you damaged enough property to place you on the wrong side of the law, Mr. Green. Not one of those shacks can be gotten out of the gulch except in pieces!"

Andy smiled inside his soul, but his face was bewildered. "Me? Damaging property? Miss Hallman, you don't know me yet!" Which was perfectly true. "What shacks are you talking about? In what gulch? All the shacks I've seen so far have been stuck up on bald pinnacles where the blizzards'll hit 'em coming and going next winter."

"Don't try to play innocent, Mr. Green." Florence Grace Hallman drew her brows together. "We all know perfectly well who dragged those shacks off the claims last night."

"Don't you mean that you think you know? I'm afraid you've kinda taken it for granted I'd be mixed up in any deviltry you happened to hear about. I've got in bad with you—I know that—but just the same, I hate to be accused of everything that takes place in the country. All this is sure interesting news to me. Whereabouts was they taken from? Miss Allen, you'll tell me the straight of this, won't you? And I'll get my hoss and you'll show me what gulch she's talking about, won't you?"

Miss Allen puckered her lips into a pout which meant indecision, and glanced at Florence Grace Hallman. And

Miss Hallman frowned at being referred to as *she.*

"Miss Allen prefers to choose her own company," she said with distinct rudeness. "Don't try to wheedle her. And you needn't get your horse to ride anywhere with us, Mr. Green. I just wanted to warn you that nothing like what happened last night will be tolerated. We know all about you Flying U men—you Happy Family." She said it as if she were calling them something perfectly disgraceful. "You may be just as tough and bad as you please—you can't frighten anyone into leaving the country. You ought to be shot for what you did last night."

"Well, if settling up the country means that men are going to be shot for going to bed at dark and sleeping till sun-up, all I've got to say is that things ain't like they used to be. We were all plumb peaceful here till your colony came, Miss Hallman. Why, the sheriff never got out this way often enough to know the trails! If your bunch of town mutts can't behave themselves and leave each other alone, I don't know what's to be done about it. *We* ain't hired to keep the peace."

"No, you've been hired to steal all the land you can. We understand that perfectly."

Andy shook his head in meek denial, and with a sudden impulse turned toward the cabin. "Oh, Pink!" he called, and brought that boyish-faced young man to the door, his eyes as pure as the eyes of a child.

Pink lifted his hat with just the proper degree of confusion to impress the girls with his bashfulness. His eyes were the same pansy-purple as when the Flying U first made tumultuous acquaintance with him. His apparent innocence had completely fooled the Happy Family, you will remember. They had called him Mamma's Little Lamb and had composed poetry for his benefit. The few years had not changed him. His hair was still yellow and curly. The dimples still dodged into his cheeks unexpectedly; he was still much like a stick of dynamite wrapped in white tissue and tied with a ribbon.

Andy introduced him, and Pink bowed and had all the appearance of blushing. "What did you want?" he asked in his soft, girlish voice. But from the corner of his eye Pink saw that a little smile of remembrance had come to soften Miss Hallman's angry features, and that the other girl was smiling also. Pink hated that attitude of pleasant patronage which women were so apt to take toward him, but for the present it suited his purpose to encourage it.

"Pink, what time was it when we went to bed last night?" Andy asked him in the tone of one who wished to eliminate all doubt of his virtue.

"Why—it was pretty early. We didn't light the lamp at all, you remember. You went to bed before I did—we couldn't see the c-ards—" He stopped confusedly, and again he gave the two women the impression that he blushed. "We weren't playing for money," he hurriedly explained. "Just for pastime. It's—pretty lonesome sometimes."

"Somebody did something to somebody last night," Andy informed Pink with a resentful impatience. "Miss Hallman thinks we're guilty parties. It's something about some shacks—damaging property, she called it. Just what was it you said was done, Miss Hallman?" He turned his honest, gray eyes toward her.

Miss Hallman bit her lip. She had been sure of the guilt of Andy Green, and of the others who were his friends. Now, in spite of all reason she was not so sure. And there had been nothing more tangible than two pairs of innocent-looking eyes and the irreproachable manners of two men to change her conviction.

"Well, I naturally took it for granted that you did it," she weakened. "The shacks were moved off eighties that you have filed upon, Mr. Green. Mr. Owens told me this morning that you men came by his place and threatened him yesterday, and ordered him to move. No one else would have any object in molesting him or the others." Her voice hardened again as her mind dwelt upon the circumstances. "It must have been you!" she finished sharply.

Whereupon Pink gave her a distressed look that made Miss Hallman flush. "I'm just about distracted, this morning," she apologized. "I took it upon myself to see these settlers through—and everybody makes it just as hard as possible for me. Why should all you fellows treat us the way you do?"

"Why, we aren't doing a thing!" Pink protested diffidently. "We thought we'd take up some claims and go to ranching for ourselves, when we got f-discharged from the Flying U. We've bought some cattle and we're going to try and get ahead, like other folks."

"Are those your cattle up on the hill? Some men shipped in four carloads of young stock, yesterday, to Dry Lake. They drove them out here intending to turn them on the range, and a couple of men—"

"Four men," Miss Allen corrected.

"Some men refused to let them cross that big coulee back there. They drove the cattle back toward Dry Lake, and told Mr. Simmons and Mr. Chase that they shouldn't come on this bench back here at all. That was another thing I wanted to see you men about."

"Maybe they were going to mix their stock up with ours," Pink ventured mildly.

"Your men shot, and shot, and shot—the atmosphere up there is shot so full of holes that the wind just whistles through!" Miss Allen informed them gravely, with her eyebrows all puckered together and a furtive little twinkle in her eyes. "And they yelled so that we could hear them from the house! They made those poor cows go trotting back across the coulee. My new book on farming says you positively must not hurry cattle. It— oh, it does something to the butter-fat—joggles it all up or something—I'll lend you the book. Why, it was terribly unscientific, the way those men drove those cow-critters!"

"I'll come over and get the book," Andy promised her, with a look in his eyes that displeased Miss Hallman very much. "We're ashamed of our ignorance. We'd like to have you learn us what's in the book."

"I will. And every week—just think of that!—I'm to get a real farm paper."

"I'd like to borrow the paper too," Andy declared.

"Oh, and—what's going to be done about all those bullet-holes? They—they might create a draught—"

"We'll ride around that way and plug 'em up," Andy assured her solemnly. "Whenever you've got time to show me about where they're at."

"It will be a pleasure. I can tell where they are, but they're too high for me to reach. Wherever the wind whistles there's a hole in the atmosphere. And there are places where the air just quivers, so you can see it. That is the shock those bold, bad men gave it with the words they used. They—used—words, Mr. Green! If we could scheme some way to pull out all those wrinkles—I do love a nice, clean, smooth atmosphere where I live. It's so wrinkly—"

"I'll attend to all that, right away."

Miss Hallman decided that she had nothing further to say to Mr. Green. She wheeled her horse rather abruptly and rode off with a curt goodbye. Miss Allen, being new at the business of handling a horse, took more time in pulling her mount around. While her back was turned to Florence Grace and her face was turned toward Pink and Andy, she gave them a twinkling glance that had one lowered eyelid to it, twisted her lips, and spoke sharply to her horse. Florence Grace looked back impatiently— perhaps suspiciously also—and saw Miss Allen coming on with docile haste.

So that ended the interview which Miss Hallman had meant to be so impressive. A lot of nonsense that left a laugh behind and the idea that Miss Allen at least did not disapprove of harassing claim-jumpers. Andy Green was two hundred per cent. more cheerful after that, and his determination more fixed. For all that he stared after them thoughtfully.

"She winked at us—if I've got eyes in my head. What do you reckon she meant, Pink?" he asked when the two riders had climbed over the ridge. "And what she said about the bold, bad men shooting holes that have to be plugged up—and about liking a nice, smooth atmosphere? Do you suppose she meant that it's liable to take bold, bad men to clean the atmosphere?"

"What difference does it make what she meant? There's jumpers left—two on Bud's place—and he's oary-eyed over it, and was going to read 'em the riot act proper, when I left to come over here. And a couple of men drove onto that south eighty of Mig's, with a load of lumber, just as I come by. Looks to me like we've got our hands full, Andy."

"Long as they don't get anything on us I ain't in the state of mind where I give a darn. That little brown-eyed Susan'll keep us posted if they start anything new—what did she mean by that wink, do you reckon?"

"Ah, don't get softening of the emotions," Pink advised. "That's the worst thing we've got to steer clear of, Andy! All them women in the game is going to make it hard to stand 'em off. Irish is foolish over this one you're getting stuck on—you'll be fighting each other, if you don't look out. That Florence Grace lady ain't slow—she's going to use the women to keep us guessing."

Andy sighed. "We can block that play, of course," he said. "Come on, Pink. Let's go round up the boys and see what's been taking place with them cattle. Shipped in four carloads already, have they?" He began pulling on his chaps rather hurriedly. "Worst of it is, you can't stampede a bunch of darned tame cows, either," he complained.

They found Irish and the Native Son on day-herd with

the cattle scattered well along the western line of the claims. Big Medicine, Weary, Cal Emmett and Jack Bates were just returning from driving the settlers' stock well across Antelope Coulee which had been decided upon as a hypothetical boundary line until such time as a fence could be built.

They talked with the day-herders, and they talked with the other four. Chip came up from the ranch with the Kid riding proudly beside him on Silver, and told them that the Honorable Mr. Blake was at the Flying U and had sent word that he would be pleased to take the legal end of the fight. Which was in itself a vast encouragement. The Honorable Blake had said that they were well within their rights thus far, and advised them to permit service of the contest notices, and to go calmly on fulfilling the law. Which was all very well as far as it went, providing they were permitted to go on calmly.

"What about them cattle they're trying to git across our land?" Slim wanted to know. "We got a right to keep 'em off, ain't we?"

Chip said that he thought they had, but to make sure, he would ask the Honorable Blake. Trespassing, he said, might be avoided—

Right there Andy was seized with an idea. He took Chip to one side. Afterwards they departed in haste, with Pink and Weary galloping close at their heels. In a couple of hours they returned to the boundary where the cattle still fed, and behind them drove Pink and Weary in the one wagon which the Family possessed.

"It oughta help some," grinned Andy, when the Native Son came over to see what it was they were erecting on

122

the prairie. "It's a fair warning, and shows 'em where to head in at."

The Native Son read the sign, which was three feet long and stood nailed to two posts ready for planting solidly in the earth. He showed his even, white teeth in a smile of approval. "Back it up, and it ought to do some good," he said.

They dug holes and set the posts, and drove on to where they meant to plant another sign exactly like the first. That day they planted twelve sign-boards along their west line. They might not do any good, but they were a fair warning, and as such were worth the trouble.

That afternoon Andy was riding back along the line when he saw a rider pull up at the first sign and read it carefully. He galloped to the spot and found that his suspicions were correct; it was Miss Allen.

"Well," she said when he came near, "I suppose that means me. Does it?" She pointed to the sign:

WARNING ! !
NO TRESPASSING EAST OF HERE
All Shacks, Live-Stock and Pilgrims Promptly
AND
Painfully Removed From These Premises

"I'm over the line," she notified him, pulling her horse backward a few feet. "You're getting awfully particular, seems to me. Oh, did you know that a lot of men are going to play it's New Year's Eve and hold watch meetings to-night?"

"Never heard a word about it," he declared.

"That's not strange—seeing it's a surprise party. Still—I'm sure you are expected to—attend."

"And where is all this to take place?" Andy looked at her intently, smiling a little.

"Oh, over there—and there—and there." She pointed to three new shacks—the official dwellings of certain contestants. "Stag parties, they are, I believe. But I doubt if they'll have any very exciting time; most of these new settlers are too busy getting the ground ready for crops, to go to parties. Some people are pretty disgusted, I can tell you, Mr. Green. Some people even wonder why it is that folks are interested mainly in their own affairs, and decline to attend watch meetings and—receptions. So I'm afraid very few, except your nearest neighbors, will be present, after all. Might I ask when you expect to—to *move* again, Mr. Green?"

Smiling still, Andy shook his head. "I expect to be busy this spring," he told her evasively. "Aren't any of you ladies invited to those parties?"

"Not a one. But let me tell you something, Mr. Green. Some folks think that perhaps we lady-settlers ought to organize a club for the well being of our—our intellects. Some folks are trying to get up parties just for women—see the point? They think it would be better for the—atmosphere."

"Oh." Andy studied the possibilities of such a move. If Florence Grace should set the women after them, he could see how the Happy Family would be hampered at every turn. "Well, I must be going. Say, did you know this country is full of wild animals, Miss Allen? They prowl around nights. And there's a gang of wild men that hang out up there in those mountains. They're outlaws. They kill off every sheriff's party that tries to round them up, and they kidnap children and ladies. If you should hear any disturbance, any time, don't be scared. Just stay inside after dark and keep your door locked. And if you should organize that ladies' club, you better hold your meetings in the afternoon."

When he had ridden on and left her, Andy was somewhat ashamed of such puerile falsehoods. But then, she had started the allegorical method of imparting advice, he remembered. So presently he went whistling to round up the boys and tell them what he had learned.

CHAPTER XIII

IRISH WORKS FOR THE CAUSE

Big Medicine with Weary and Chip to bear him company, rode up to the shack nearest his own, which had been hastily built by a raw-boned Dane. Big Medicine did not waste time in making threats of what he meant to do. He called the Dane to the door and told him that he was on another man's land, and asked him if he meant to move.

"Sure I don't intend to move!" retorted the Dane. "I'm going to hold 'er down solid."

"Yuh hear what he says, boys." Big Medicine turned to his companions. "Weary, yuh better go tell the bunch I need 'em."

Weary immediately departed. He was not gone so very long, and when he returned the Happy Family was with him, even to Patsy who drove the wagon with all the ease of a veteran of many roundups. The Dane tried bluster, but that did not seem to work. Nothing seemed to work, except the Happy Family.

There in broad daylight, with no more words than were needful, they moved the Dane, and his shack. When they began to raise the building he was so unwise as to flourish a gun, and thereby made it perfectly right and lawful that Big Medicine should take the gun away from him and march him ahead of his own forty-five.

They took the shack directly past one of the trespassing signs, and Big Medicine stopped accommodatingly while the Dane was permitted to read the sign three times aloud. They went on, skidding the little building over the uneven prairie. They took it down into Antelope Coulee and left it there, right side up and with not even a pane of glass broken in the window.

"There, darn yuh, live there awhile!" Andy gritted to the Dane, when the timbers were withdrawn from beneath the cabin. "You can't say we damaged your property—this time. Come back, and there's no telling what we're liable to do."

Since Big Medicine kept his gun, the Dane could do nothing but swear while he watched them ride up the hill and out of sight.

They made straight for the next interloper. There they had an audience, for Florence Grace rode up just as they were getting under way. The Happy Family spoke very nicely to Florence Grace, and when she spoke very sharply to them they became absorbed in their work.

Several settlers came before that shack was moved,

but they only stood around and talked among themselves, and were careful not to get in the way or to hinder, and to lower their voices so that the Happy Family need not hear unless they chose to listen.

So they slid that shack into the coulee, righted it carefully and left it there—where it would be exceedingly difficult to get it out, by the way; since it is much easier to drag a building down hill than up.

They loaded the timbers into the wagon and moved methodically on to the next shack, their audience increased to a couple of dozen perturbed settlers. The owner of this particular shack, feeling the strength of numbers behind him, was disposed to argue the point.

"Oh, you'll sweat for this!" he shouted impotently, when the Happy Family was placing the timbers.

"Ah, get outa the way!" said Andy, coming toward him with a crowbar. "We're sweating now, if that makes you feel any better."

The man got out of the way, and went and stood with the group of onlookers, and talked vaguely of having the law on them—whatever he meant by that.

By the time they had placed the third shack in the bottom of the coulee, the sun was setting. They dragged the timbers up the steep bluff, loaded them on to the wagon and threw the crowbars and rolling timbers in, and turned to look curiously at their audience. Andy, still tacitly their leader, rode a few steps forward.

"That'll be all today," he announced politely. "Except that load of lumber back here on the bench where it don't belong—we aim to haul that over the line. Seeing you're taking considerable interest in our affairs, I'll just say that we filed on our claims according to law, and we're living on 'em according to law. Till somebody proves in court that we're not, there don't any shack, or any stock, stay on our side the line any longer than it takes to get them off."

He lifted his hat to the women—and there were several now—and went away to join his fellows, who had ridden on slowly till he might overtake them. He found Happy Jack grumbling and predicting evil, but he merely laughed at the prophecies.

"As I told you before, there's more than one way to kill a cat," he asserted. "Nobody can say we wasn't mild; and nobody can say we hadn't a right to get those chicken-coops off our land. If you ask me, Florence Grace will have to go some now if she gets the best of the deal. We haven't been served with any contest notices yet, and so we ain't obliged to take their say-so. Who's going to stand guard tonight? We've got to stand our regular shifts, if we want to keep ahead of the game. I'd like to make sure they don't slip any stock across before daylight."

"Say, it's lucky we've got a bunch of boneheads like them to handle," Pink observed thankfully. "Would a bunch of natives have stood around like that with their hands in their pockets and let us get away with the moving job? Not so you could notice!"

"What we'd better do," cut in the Native Son without any misleading drawl, "is try and rustle enough money to build that fence."

"That's right," assented Cal. "Maybe the Old Man—"

"We don't go to the Old Man for so much as a bacon

rind!" cried the Native Son. "We ought to be able to build that fence without help from anybody. I'll stand guard till midnight."

A little more talk and some bickering with Slim and Happy Jack served to knock together a fair working organization. Weary and Andy Green were chosen joint leaders, because Weary could be depended upon to furnish the mental ballast for Andy's imagination. Patsy was told that he would have to cook for the outfit, since he was too fat to ride. Moving houses, they declared, was work.

"Say, we'll have quite a collection of shacks down in Antelope Coulee if we keep on," Jack Bates reminded them. "Wonder where they'll get water?"

"Where's the rest of them going to get water?" Cal Emmett challenged the crowd. "There's that spring the four women up here pick water from—but that goes dry in August. And there's the creek—that goes dry too. On the dead, I feel sorry for the women—and so does Irish," he added drily.

Irish made an uncivil retort and swung away from the group. "I'm going to ride into town, boys," he announced. "I'll be back in the morning and go on day-herd."

"Maybe you will and maybe you won't," Weary amended somewhat impatiently. "This is certainly a poor time for Irish to break out," he added, watching his double go galloping toward the town road.

"I betche he comes back full and tries to clean out all them nesters," Happy Jack predicted. For once no one tried to combat his pessimism—for that was exactly what every one of them believed would happen.

"He's stayed sober a long while," sighed Weary, who never could quite shake off a sense of responsibility for the moral defections of his kinsman. "Maybe I better ride herd on him." Still, he did not go, and Irish presently merged into the dusky distance.

As is often the case with a family's black sheep, his intentions were the best, even though they might have been considered unorthodox. While the Happy Family took it for granted that he was gone because an old thirst awoke within him, Irish was thinking only of the welfare of the outfit. He did not tell them, because he was the sort who does not prattle of his intentions, one way or the other. If he did what he meant to do there would be time enough to explain; if he failed there was nothing to be said.

Irish had thought a good deal about the building of that fence, and about the problem of paying for enough wire and posts to run the fence straight through from Meeker's south line to the north line of the Flying U. He had figured the price of posts and the price of wire and had come somewhere near the approximate cost of the undertaking. He was not at all sure that the Happy Family had faced the actual figures on that proposition.

Irish was hot-headed and impulsive to a degree. He was given to occasional tumultuous sprees, during which he was to be handled with extreme care. He looked almost exactly like Weary, and yet he was almost his opposite in disposition. Weary was optimistic, peace-loving, steady as the sun above him. You could walk all over Weary—figuratively speaking—before he would show resentment. You could not step very close to Irish without running the risk of consequences. That he should, under all that, have a streak of hard-headed business sense, did not occur to them.

They rode on, discussing the situation and how best to meet it; the contingencies of the future, and how best to circumvent the antagonism of Florence Grace Hallman and the colony for which she stood sponsor. They did not dream that Irish was giving his whole mind to solving the problem of raising money to build that fence.

Some of you at least are going to object to his method. Some of you—those of you who live west of the big river—are going to understand his point of view, and you will recognize his method as being perfectly logical to a man of his temperament and manner of life. It is for you that I am going to relate his experiences. Sheltered readers, readers who have never faced life in the raw, should skip the rest of this chapter for the good of their morals. The rest is for you men who have kicked up alkali dust and afterwards washed out the memory in town; who have gone broke between starlight and sun; who know the ways of punchers the West over.

Irish had been easing down a corner of the last shack, with his back turned toward three men who stood looking on with the detached interest which proved they did not own this particular shack. One was H. J. Owens—I don't think you have met the others. Irish had not. He had overheard this scrap of conversation while he worked:

"Going to town tonight?"

"Guess so—I sure ain't going to hang out on this

prairie any more than I have to. You going?"

"Ye-es—I think I will. I hear there's been some pretty swift games going, the last night or two. A fellow in that last bunch Florence rounded up made quite a clean up last night."

"That so. Let's go on in. This claim-holding gets my goat anyway. I don't see where—"

That was all Irish heard, but that was enough. Had he turned in time to catch the wink that one speaker gave the other, and the sardonic grin that answered the lowered eyelid, he would have had the scrap of conversation properly focussed in his mind, and would not have swallowed the bait as greedily as he did. But we all make mistakes. Irish made the mistake of underestimating the cunning of his enemies.

So here he was, kicking up the dust on the town trail just as those three intended that he should do. But that he rode alone instead of in the midst of his fellows was not what the three had intended; and that he rode with the interest of his friends foremost in his mind was also an unforeseen element in the scheme.

Irish did not see H. J. Owens anywhere in town—nor did he see either of the two men who had stood behind him. But there was a poker game running in Rusty Brown's back room, and Irish immediately sat in without further investigation. Bert Rogers was standing behind one of the players, and gave Irish a nod and a wink which may have had many meanings. Irish interpreted it as encouragement to sail in.

There was money enough in sight to build that fence when he sat down. Irish rolled and lighted a cigarette while he waited for that particular jackpot to be taken, and covertly sized up the players.

Every one of them was strange to him. But then, the town was full of strangers since Florence Grace and her Syndicate began to reap a harvest off the open country, so Irish merely studied the faces casually, as a matter of habit. They were nesters, of course—real or prospective. They seemed to have plenty of money—and it was eminently fitting that the Happy Family's fence should be built with nester money.

Irish had in his pockets exactly eighteen dollars and fifty cents. He bought eighteen dollars' worth of chips and began to play. Privately he preferred stud poker to draw, but he was not going to propose a change.

Four hands he played and lost four dollars. He drank a glass of beer then, then settled down to business, feeling that he had but just begun. After the fifth hand he looked up and caught again the eye of Bert Rogers. Bert pulled his eyebrows together in a warning look, and Irish thought better of staying that hand. He did not look at Bert after that, but he did watch the other players more closely.

After awhile Bert wandered away, his interest dulling when he saw that Irish was holding his own and a little better. Irish played on, conservative to such a degree that in two hours he had not won more than fifteen dollars. The Happy Family would have been surprised to see him lay down kings and refuse to draw to them—which he did once, with a gesture of disgust that flipped them face up so that all could see. He turned them over immediately, but the three had seen that this tall stranger would not draw to kings but must have something better before he would stay.

So they played until the crowd thinned; until Irish, by betting safely had sixty dollars' worth of chips piled in front of him.

Some men, playing for a definite purpose, would have quit at that. Irish did not quit, however. He wanted a certain sum from these nesters. He had come to town expecting to win a certain sum from them. He intended to play until he got it or went broke. He was not using any trickery—and he had stopped one man in the middle of a deal, with a certain look in his eye remarking that he'd rather have the top card than the bottom one, so that he was satisfied they were not trying to cheat.

There came a deal when Irish looked at his cards, sent a slanting look at the others and laid down his five cards with a long breath. He raised the ante four blue ones and rolled and lit a cigarette while the three had drawn what cards they thought they needed. The man at Irish's left had drawn only one card. Now he hesitated and then bet with some assurance. Irish smoked imperturbably while the other two came in, and then he raised the bet three stacks of blues. His neighbor raised him one stack, and the next man hesitated and then laid down his cards. The third man meditated for a minute and raised the bet ten dollars. Irish blew forth a leisurely smoke wreath and with a sweep of his hand sent in all his chips.

There was a silent minute, wherein Irish drummed absently upon the table with his fingers that were free. His neighbor frowned and threw down his hand. The third man did the same. Irish made another sweep of his hand and raked the table clean of chips.

"That'll do for tonight," he remarked drily. "I don't like to be a hog."

Had that ended the incident, sensitive readers might still read and think well of Irish. But, one of the players was not quite sober, and he was a poor loser and a pugnacious individual anyway. His underlip pushed out, and when Irish turned away to cash in his chips, this pugnacious one took a look at the cards Irish had held.

It certainly was as rotten a hand as a man could hold. Suits all mixed, and not a face card or a pair in the lot. The pugnacious player had held a king-high straight, and he had stayed until Irish sent in all his chips. He gave a bellow and jumped up and hit Irish a glancing blow back of the ear.

Let us not go into details. You know Irish—or you should know him by this time. A man who will get away with a bluff like that should be left alone or brained in the beginning of the fight—especially when he can look down on the hair of a six-foot man, and has muscles hardened by outdoor living. When the dust settled, two chairs were broken and some glasses swept off the bar by heaving bodies, and two of the three players had forgotten their troubles. The third was trying to find the knob on the back door, and could not because of the buzzing in his head. Irish had welts and two broken knuckles and a clear conscience, and he was so mad he almost wound up by thrashing Rusty, who had stayed behind the bar. Rusty complained because of the damage to his property, and Irish, being the only one present in a condition to listen, took the complaint as a personal insult.

He counted his money to make sure he had it all, evened the edges of the package of bank notes and thrust the package into his pocket. If Rusty had kept his face closed about those few glasses and those chairs, he would have left a "bill" on the bar to pay for them, even though he did need every cent of that money. He told Rusty this, and he accused him of standing in with the nesters and turning down the men who had helped him make money, all these years.

"Why, darn your soul, I've spent money enough over this bar to buy out the whole damn' joint, and you know it!" he cried indignantly. "If you think you've got to collect damages, take it outa these blinkety-blink pilgrims you think so much of. They'll never bring you the money we've brought you, you—"

"They won't because you've likely killed 'em both," Rusty retorted angrily. "You want to remember you can't come into town and rip things up the back the way you used to, and nobody say a word. You better drift, before that feller that went out comes back with an officer. You can't—"

"Officer be damned!" retorted Irish, unawed.

He went out while Rusty was deciding to order him out, and started for the stable. Halfway there he ducked into the shadow of the blacksmith shop and watched two men go up the street to Rusty's place, walking quickly. He went on then, got his horse without waiting to cinch the saddle, led him behind the blacksmith shop and tied him there to the wreck of a freight wagon.

Then he went across lots to where Fred Wilson, manager of the general store, slept in a two-room shack belonging to the hotel. The door was locked so he rapped cautiously upon the window until Fred awoke and wanted to know who in thunder was there.

Irish told his name, and presently went inside. "I'm pulling outa town, Fred," he explained, "and I don't know when I'll be in again. So I want you to take an order for some posts, bob wire and steeples."

"Why didn't you come to the store?" Fred demanded, peevish at being wakened at three o'clock in the morning. "I saw you in town when I closed up."

"I was busy. Crawl back into bed and cover up, while I give you the order. I'll want a receipt for the money, too—I'm paying in advance, so you won't have any excuse for holding up the order. Got anything to write on?"

Fred found part of an order pad and a pencil, and crept shivering into his bed. The offer to pay in advance had silenced his grumbling, as Irish expected it would. So Irish gave the order—thirteen hundred cedar posts, I remember—I don't know just how much wire, but all he would need.

"Holy macintosh! Is this for *you?*" Fred wanted to know as he wrote it down.

"Some of it. We're fencing our claims. If I don't come after the stuff myself, let any of the boys have it that shows up. And get it here as quick as you can—what you ain't got on hand—"

Fred was scratching his jaw meditatively with the pencil, and staring at the order. "I can just about fill that order outa stock on hand," he told Irish. "When all this land rush started I laid in a big supply of posts and wire. How you making it, out there?"

"Fine," said Irish, feeling his broken knuckles. "How much is all that going to cost? You oughta make a rate on it, seeing it's a cash sale, and big."

"I will." Fred tore out a sheet and did some mysterious figuring, afterwards crumpling the paper into a little wad and flipping it behind the bed. "This has got to be on the quiet, Irish. I can't sell wire and posts to these eastern marks at this rate, you know. This is just for you boys— and the profit for us is trimmed right down to a whisper." He named the sum total with the air of one who confers a great favor.

Irish grinned and reached into his pocket. "You musta knocked your profit down to fifty per cent.," he fleered. "But it's a go with me." He peeled off the whole roll, just about. He had two twenties left in his hand when he stopped. He was very methodical that night. He took a receipt for the money before he left, and he looked at it with glistening eyes before he folded it with the money. "Don't sell any posts and wire till our order's filled, Fred," he warned. "We'll begin hauling right away, and we'll want it all."

He let himself out into the cool starlight, walked in the shadows to where he had left his horse, mounted and rode whistling away down the lane which ended where the hills began.

CHAPTER XIV

JUST ONE THING AFTER ANOTHER

A gray clarity of the air told that daylight was near. The skyline retreated, the hills came out of the duskiness like a photograph in the developer tray. Irish dipped down the steep slope into Antelope Coulee, cursing the sprinkle of new shacks that stood stark in the dawn on every ridge and hilltop. He loped along the winding trail through the coulee's bottom and climbed the hill beyond. At the top he glanced across the more level upland to the east and his eyes lightened. Far away stood a shack— Patsy's, that was. Beyond that another, and yet another. Most of the boys had built in the coulees where was water. They did not care so much about the view—over which Miss Allen had grown enthusiastic.

He pulled up in a certain place near the brow of the hill, and looked down into the narrower gulch where huddled the shacks they had moved. He grinned at the sight. His hand went involuntarily to his pocket and the grin widened. He hurried on that he might the sooner tell the boys of their good luck; all the material for that line fence bought and paid for.

First he thought that he would locate the cattle and tell his news to the boys on guard. He therefore left the trail and rode upon a ridge from which he could overlook the whole benchland. The sky was reddening now, save where banked clouds turned purple.

He looked away to where the Bear Paws humped,

blue-black against the sky. He looked past Wolf Butte, where the land was blackened with outcroppings of rock. His eyes came back leisurely to the claim country. A faint surprise widened his lids, and he turned and sent a glance sweeping to the right, toward Flying U Coulee. He frowned, and studied the benchland carefully.

This was daybreak, when the cattle should be getting out for their breakfast-feed. They should be scattered along the level just before him. And there were no cattle anywhere in sight. Neither were there any riders in sight. Irish gave a puzzled grunt and turned in his saddle, looking back toward Dry Lake. But as far as he could see there were no cattle that way, either. Last night when he rode to town the cattle of the colonists had been feeding across Antelope Coulee where he had helped the boys drive them.

He did not waste many minutes studying the empty prairie from the vantage point of that ridge. He sent his horse down the southern slope to the level, and began looking for tracks. He was not long in finding a broad trail in the grass where cattle had lately crossed the coulee from the west. He knew what that meant, and he swore when he saw how the trail pointed straight to the east—to the broken country beyond One Man Coulee. What had the boys been thinking of, to let that nester stock get past them in the night?

Irish had not had much sleep during the past forty-eight hours, and he was ravenously hungry. He followed the trail of the cattle until he saw that they certainly had gotten across the Happy Family claims and into the rough country beyond; then he turned and rode

140

over to Patsy's shack.

There he learned that Dry Lake had not hugged to itself all the events of the night. Patsy, smoking a pipefull of Durham while he waited for the teakettle to boil, was wild with resentment. In the night, while he slept, something had heaved his cabin up at one corner. In a minute another corner heaved upward a foot or more. Patsy had yelled while he felt around in the darkness for his clothes, and had got no answer, save other heavings from below.

Patsy was not the man to submit tamely to such indignities. He had groped and found his old 45-70 rifle, that made a noise like a young cannon. While the shack lurched this way and that, Patsy pointed the gun toward the greatest disturbance and fired. He did not think he hit anybody, but he apologized to Irish for missing and blamed the darkness for the misfortune. Py cosh, he sure tried—witness the bullet holes which he had bored through the four sides of the shack; he besought Irish to count them: which Irish did gravely. And what happened then?

Then? Why, then the Happy Family had come; or at least all those who had been awake and riding the prairie had come pounding up out of the dark, their blood singing the song of battle. They had grappled with certain of the enemy—Patsy broke open the door and saw tangles of struggling forms in the faint starlight. The Happy Family were not the type of men who must settle every argument with a gun, remember. Not while their hands might be used to fight with. Patsy thought that they licked the nesters without much trouble. He knew that the settlers ran, and that the Happy Family chased them clear across the line and then came back and let the shack down where it belonged upon the rock underpinning.

Irish went to the door and looked out. The wind had risen in the last half hour, so that his hat went sailing against the rear wall, but he did not notice that. He was wondering why the settlers had made this night move against Patsy. Was it an attempt to irritate the boys to some real act of violence—something that would put them in fear of the law? Or was it simply a stratagem to call off the night-guard so that they might slip their cattle across into the breaks? They must have counted on some disturbance which would reach the ears of the boys on guard. With that end in view, he could see why Patsy's shack had been chosen for the attack. Patsy's shack was the closest to where they had been holding the cattle. It was absurdly simple, and evidently the ruse had worked to perfection.

"Where are the boys at now?" he asked abruptly, turning to Patsy who had risen and knocked the ashes from his pipe and was slicing bacon.

"Gone after the cattle. Dey stampede alreatty mit all der noise," Patsy growled, with his back to Irish.

So it was just as Irish had suspected. He faced the west and the gathering bank of "thunder heads" that rode swift on the wind, and he hesitated. Should he go after the boys and help them round up the stock, or should he stay where he was and watch the claims? There was that fence—he must see to that, too. He turned and asked Patsy if all the boys were gone. But Patsy did not know.

Irish stood in the doorway until breakfast was ready, whereupon he sat down and ate hurriedly. A gust of wind made the flimsy cabin shake, and Patsy went to close the door against its sudden fury.

"Some riders iss coming now," he said, and held the door half closed against the wind. "It ain't none off der boys," he added. "Pilgrims, I guess—from der ridin'.."

Irish grunted and reached for the coffee pot, giving scarce a thought to Patsy's announcement. While he poured his third cup of coffee he made a sudden decision. He would get that fence off his mind, anyway.

"Say, Patsy, I've rustled wire and posts—all we'll need. I guess I'll just turn this receipt over to you and let you get busy. You take the team and drive in today and get the stuff headed out here *pronto*. The nesters are shipping in more stock—I heard in town that they're bringing in all they can rustle, thinkin' the stock will pay big money while the claims are getting ready to produce. I heard a couple of marks telling each other just how it was going to work out so as to put 'em all on Easy Street. Free grass—that's what they harped on; feed don't cost anything. All yuh do is turn 'em loose and wait till shippin' season, and then collect.

"The sooner that fence is up the better. We can't put in the whole summer hazing their cattle around. I've bought the stuff and paid for it. And here's forty dollars you can use to hire it hauled out here. Us fellows have got to keep cases on the cattle, so you 'tend to this fence." He laid the money on Fred's receipt upon the table and set Patsy's plate over them to hold them safe against the wind that rattled the shack. He had forgotten all about the three approaching riders, until Patsy turned upon him sharply.

"Vot schrapes you been into now?" he demanded querulously. "Py cosh you done somet'ings. It's der constable comin' alreatty. I bet you be pinched."

"I bet I don't," Irish retorted, and made for the one window, which looked toward the hills. "Feed 'em some breakfast, Patsy. And you drive in and tend to that fencing right away, like I told you."

He threw one long leg over the window sill, bent his lean body to pass through the square opening, and drew the other leg outside. He startled his horse, which had walked around there out of the wind, but he caught the bridle-reins and led him a few steps farther where he would be out of the direct view from the window. Then he stopped and listened.

He heard the three ride up to the other side of the shack and shout to Patsy. He heard Patsy open the door. He heard the constable ask Patsy if he knew anything about Irish, and where he could be found; and he heard Patsy declare that he had enough to do without keeping track of that boneheaded cowpuncher who was good for nothing but to get into schrapes.

After that he heard Patsy ask the constable if they had had any breakfast before leaving town. He heard certain saddle-sounds which told of their dismounting in response to the tacit invitation. And then, pulling his hat down upon his head, Irish led his horse into a hollow behind the shack, and so out of sight and hearing of those three who sought him.

He did not believe that he was wanted for anything

144

very serious; they meant to arrest him, probably, for laying out those two gamblers with a chair and a bottle of whisky respectively. A trumped-up charge, very likely, chiefly calculated to make him some trouble and to eliminate him from the struggle for a time. Irish did not worry at all over their reason for wanting him, but he did not intend to let them come close enough to state their errand, because he did not want to become guilty of resisting an officer—which would be much worse than fighting nesters with fists and chairs.

In the hollow he mounted and rode down the depression and debouched upon the grassy coulee where lay a part of his own claim. He was not sure of the intentions of that constable, but he took it for granted that he would ride on to Irish's cabin in search of him; also that he would look for him further, which would in a measure hamper the movements and therefore the usefulness of Irish. For that reason he was resolved to take no chance that could be avoided.

The sun slid behind the scurrying forerunners of the storm. From where he was Irish could not see the full extent of the storm-clouds, and while he had been on high land he had been too absorbed in other matters to pay much attention. Even now he did no more than glance up casually at the inky mass above him, and decided that he would do well to ride on to his cabin and get his slicker.

By the time he reached his shack the storm was beating up against the wind which had turned unexpectedly to the northeast. Mutterings of thunder grew to sharper booming. It was the first real thunderstorm of the season, but it was going to be a hard one, if looks meant anything. Irish went in and got his slicker and put it on, and then hesitated over riding on in search of the cattle and the men in pursuit of them.

Still, the constable might take a notion to ride over this way in spite of the storm. And if he came there would be delay, even if there were nothing worse. So Irish, being one to fight but never to stand idle, mounted again and turned his long-suffering horse down the coulee as the storm swept up.

First a few large drops of rain pattered upon the earth and left blobs of wet where they fell. Then the clouds opened recklessly the headgates and let the rain down in one solid rush of water that sluiced the hillsides and drove muddy torrents down channels that had been dry since the snow left.

Irish bent his head so that his hat shielded somewhat his face, and rode doggedly on. It was not the first time that he had been out in a driving thunderstorm, and it would not be his last. But it was not the more comfortable because it was an oft-repeated experience. And when the first fury had passed and still it rained steadily, his optimism suffered appreciably.

His luck in town no longer cheered him. He began to feel the loss of sleep and the bone-weariness of his fight and the long ride afterwards.

He went into One Man Coulee and followed it to the arm that would lead to the open land beyond, where the "breaks" of the Badlands reached out to meet the prairie. He came across the track of the herd, and followed it to the plain. Once out in the open, however, the herd had seemed to split into several small bunches, each going in a different direction. Which puzzled Irish a little at first. Later, he thought he understood.

The cattle, it would seem, had been driven purposefully into the edge of the breaks and there made to scatter out through the winding gulches and canyons that led deeper into the Badlands. It was the trick of rangemen—he could not believe that the strange settlers, ignorant of the country and the conditions, would know enough to do this. He hesitated before several possible routes, the rain pouring down upon him. If there had been hoof-prints to show which way the boys had gone, the rain had washed them so they looked dim and old.

He chose what seemed to him the gorge which the boys would be most likely to follow—especially at night and if they were in open pursuit of those who had driven the cattle off the benchland; and that the cattle had been driven beyond this point was plain enough, for otherwise he would have overtaken stragglers long before this.

It was nearing noon when he came out finally upon a little, open flat and found there Big Medicine and Pink holding a bunch of perhaps a hundred cattle which they had gleaned from the surrounding gulches. The two were wet to the skin, and they were chilled and hungry and as amiable as a she-bear sent up a tree by yelping dogs.

Big Medicine it was who spied him first through the haze of falling water, and galloped toward him.

"Say!" he bellowed when he was yet a hundred yards away. "Got any grub with yuh?"

"No!" Irish called back.

"Y'ain't?" Big Medicine's voice was charged with incredulous reproach. "What'n hell yuh doin' here without *grub?* Is Patsy comin' with the wagon?"

"No. I sent Patsy on in to town after—"

"Town? And us out here—" Big Medicine choked over his wrongs.

Irish waited until he could get in a word and then started to explain. But Pink rode up with his hatbrim flapping soggily against one dripping cheek, looking pinched and draggled and wholly miserable.

"Say! Got anything to eat?" he shouted.

"No!" snapped Irish.

"Well, why ain't yuh? Where's Patsy?" Pink came closer and eyed the newcomer truculently.

"How'n hell do I know?" Irish snapped.

"Well, why don't yuh know? What do yuh think you're out here for? To tell us you think it's going to rain? It's a wonder you come alive enough to ride out this way at all! I don't reckon you've even got anything to drink!" Pink paused a second, saw no move toward producing anything wet and cheering, and swore disgustedly. "Of course not! You needed it all yourself! So help me Josephine, if I was as low-down ornery as some I could name I'd tie myself to a mule's tail and let him kick me to death! Ain't got any grub! Ain't got—"

Irish interrupted him then with a sentence that stung. Irish, remember, approved of himself and his actions. True, he had forgotten to bring anything to eat with him, but there was excuse for that in the haste with which he had left his own breakfast. Besides how could he be expected to know that the cattle had been driven away

148

down here? Did they think he was a mind-reader?

Pink, with biting sarcasm, retorted that they did not. That it took a mind to read a mind. He added that, from the looks of Irish, he must have started home drunk, anyway, and his horse had wandered this far of his own accord. Then three or four cows started up a gulch to the right of them and Pink rode off to turn them back. So they did not actually come to blows, those two, though they were near it.

Big Medicine lingered to bawl unforgivable things at Irish, and Irish shouted back recklessly that they had all acted like a bunch of sheepherders, or the cattle would never have been driven off the bench at all. He declared that anybody with the brains of a sick sagehen would have stopped the thing right in the start.

Big Medicine said things in reply, and Pink, returning to the scene with his anger grown hotter from feeding upon his discomfort, made a few comments pertinent to the subject of Irish's shortcomings.

You may scarcely believe it, unless you have really lived, and have learned how easily small irritations grow to the proportions of real trouble, and how swiftly—but this is a fact: Irish and Big Medicine became so enraged that they dismounted simultaneously and Irish jerked off his slicker while Big Medicine was running up to smash him for some needless insult.

They fought, there in the rain and the mud. They fought just as relentlessly as though they had long been enemies. They pounded and smashed until Pink tore them apart and swore at them for crazy men and implored them to have some sense. They let the cattle that had been gathered with so much trouble drift away into the gulches and draws where they must be routed out of the brush again.

When the first violence of their rage had like the storm settled to a cold steadiness of animosity, the two remounted painfully and turned backs upon each other. Big Medicine and Pink drew close together as against a common foe, and Irish cursed them both and rode away—whither he did not know nor care.

CHAPTER XV

THE KID HAS IDEAS OF HIS OWN

The Old Man sat out in his big chair on the porch, staring dully at the trail which led up the bluff by way of the Hog's Back to the benchland beyond. Facing him in an old, cane rocking chair, the Honorable Blake smoked with that air of leisurely enjoyment which belongs to the man who can afford to burn good tobacco and who has the sense to burn it consciously, realizing in every whiff its rich fragrance. The Honorable Blake flicked a half-inch of ash from his cigar upon a porch support and glanced at the Old Man's face.

"No, it wouldn't do," he observed with the accent of a second consideration of a subject that coincides exactly with the first. "You could save the boys time, I've no doubt—time and trouble so far as getting the cattle back where they belong is concerned. I can see how they must be hampered for lack of saddle-horses, for instance. But—it wouldn't do, Whitmore. If they come to you and ask for horses, don't let them have them. They'll manage somehow—trust them for that. They'll manage—"

"But doggone it, Blake, it's for—"

"Sh-sh—" Blake held up a warning hand. "These young fellows have taken claims in—er—good faith." His bright blue eyes sparkled with a sudden feeling. "I—admire them intensely for what they have started out to do. But—they have certain things which they must do, and do alone. If you would not thwart them in accomplishing what they have set out to do, you must go carefully; which means that you must not run to their aid with your camp-wagons and your saddle-horses, so they can gather the cattle again and drive them back where they belong. You would not be helping them."

"But doggone it, Blake, them boys have lived right here at the Flying U—why, this has been their home, yuh might say. Why, doggone it, what they done here when I got hurt in Chicago and they was left to run themselves, why, that alone puts me under obligations to help 'em out in this scrape. Ain't I a neighbor? Ain't neighbors got a right to jump in and help each other? There ain't no law again—"

"Not against neighbors—no." Blake uncrossed his perfectly trousered legs. "But this syndicate—or these contestants—will try to prove that you are not a neighbor only, but a—backer of the boys in a land-grabbing scheme. To avoid—"

"Well, doggone your hide, Blake, I've told you fifty times I ain't!" The Old Man sat forward in his chair and shook his fist at his guest. "Them boys cooked that up themselves, and went and filed on that land before ever

I knowed a thing about it. How can yuh set there and say I backed 'em? And that blonde Jezebel—riding down here bold as brass and turnin' up her nose at Dell, and callin' me a conspirator to my face!"

"I sticked a pin in her saddle blanket, Uncle Gee-gee. I'll bet she wished she'd stayed away from here when her horse bucked her off." The Kid looked up from trying to tie a piece of paper to the end of a brindle kitten's switching tail, and smiled his adorable smile—that had a gap in the middle.

"Hey? You leave that cat alone or he'll scratch yuh. Blake, if you can't see—"

"He! He's a her and her name's Adeline. Where's the boys, Uncle Gee-gee?"

"Hey? Oh, away down in the breaks after their cattle that got away. You keep still and never mind where they've gone." His mind swung back to the Happy Family, combing the breaks for their stock with an average of one saddle-horse apiece and a camp outfit of the most primitive sort. The Old Man had eased too many roundups through that rough country not to realize the difficulties of the Happy Family.

"They need horses," he groaned to Blake, "and they need help. If you knowed the country and the work as well as I do you'd know they've got to have horses and help. And there's their claims—fellers squatting down on every eighty—four different nesters for every dog-goned one of the bunch to handle! And you tell me I can't put men to work on that fence they want built. You tell me I can't lend 'em so much as a horse!"

Blake nodded. "I tell you that and, I emphasize it," he

assured the other. "If you want to help those boys hold their land, you must not move a finger."

"He's wiggling all of 'em!" accused the Kid sternly, and pointed to the Old Man drumming irritatedly upon his chair arms. "He don't want to help the boys, but I do. I'll lend 'em my string."

"You've been told before not to butt in to grownup talk," his uncle reproved him irascibly. "Now you cut it out. And take that string off'n that cat!" he added harshly. "Dell! Come and look after this kid! Doggone it, a man can't talk five minutes—"

The Kid giggled irrepressibly. "That's one on you, old man. You saw Doctor Dell go away a long time ago. Think she can hear yuh when she's away up on the bench?"

"You go on off and play!" commanded the Old Man. "I dunno what yuh want to pester a feller to death for— and say! Take that string off'n that cat!"

"Aw gwan! It ain't hurting the cat. She likes it." He lifted the kitten and squeezed her till she yowled. "See? She said yes, she likes it."

The Old Man returned to the trials of the Happy Family, and the Kid sat and listened, with the brindle kitten snuggled uncomfortably, head downward in his arms. The Kid had heard a good deal, lately, about the trials of his beloved "bunch." About the "nesters" who brought cattle in to eat up the grass that belonged to the cattle of the bunch. The Kid understood that perfectly— since he had been raised in the atmosphere of range talk. He had heard about the men building shacks on the claims of the Happy Family. He knew all about the

153

attack on Patsy's cabin and how the Happy Family had been fooled, and the cattle driven off and scattered. The breaks—he was a bit hazy upon the subject of breaks. He had heard about them all his life. The stock got amongst them and had to be hunted out. He thought that it must be a place where all the brakes grow that are used on wagons and buggies. These were of wood, therefore they must grow somewhere. They grew where the Happy Family went sometimes, when they were gone for days and days after stock. They were down there now—it was *down* in the breaks; always—and they couldn't round up their cattle because they hadn't horses enough. They needed help, so they could hurry back and slide those other shacks off their claims and into Antelope Coulee. On the whole, the Kid had a very fair conception of the state of affairs. Claimants and contestants—those words went over his head. But he knew perfectly well that the nesters were the men that didn't like the Happy Family, and lived in shacks on the way to town, and plowed big patches of prairie and had children that went barefooted in the furrows and couldn't ride horses to save their lives.

After a while, when the Honorable Blake became the chief speaker and tapped the Old Man frequently on a knee with his finger, and used long words that carried no meaning, and said contestant and claimant and evidence so often that he became tiresome, the Kid slid off the porch and went away, his small face sober with deep meditations.

He would need some grub—maybe the bunch was hungry without any camp-wagons. The Kid had stood around in the way, many's the time, and watched certain members of the Happy Family stuff emergency rations into flour sacks, and afterwards tie the sack to their saddles and ride off.

He hunted up a flour sack that had not had all the string pulled out of it so it was no longer a sack but a dish-towel, and held it behind his back while he went cautiously to the kitchen door. The Countess was nowhere in sight—but it was just as well to make sure. The Kid went in, took a basin off the table, held it high and deliberately dropped it on the floor. It made a loud bang, but it did not elicit any shrill protest from the Countess; therefore the Countess was nowhere around. The Kid went in boldly and filled his flour sack so full it dragged on the floor when he started off.

At the door he went down the steps ahead of the sack, and bent his small back from the third step and pulled the sack upon his shoulders. It wobbled a good deal, and the Kid came near falling sidewise off the last step before he could balance his burden. But he managed it, having a good deal of persistence in his makeup; and he went, by a round-about way, to the stable with the grub-sack bending him double. Still it was not so very heavy; it was made bulky by about two dozen fresh-made doughnuts and a loaf of bread and a jar of honey and a glass of wild-currant jelly and a pound or so of raw, dried prunes.

Getting that sack tied fast to the saddle after the saddle was on Silver's back was no easy task for a boy who is six. Still, being Chip's Kid and the Little Doctor's he did it—with the help of the oats box and Silver's patient disposition.

There were other things which the bunch always tied on their saddles; a blanket for instance, and a rope. The Kid made a trip to the bunk-house and pulled a gray blanket off Ole's bed, and spent a quarter of an hour rolling it. The oats box, with Silver standing beside it, came in handy again. He found a discarded rope and after much labor coiled it crudely and tied it beside the saddle-fork.

The Kid went to the door, stood beside it and leaned away over so that he could peek out and not be seen. Voices came from the house—the voice of the Old Man, to be exact—high-pitched and combative. The Kid looked up the bluff, and the trail lay empty in the after-noon sun. Still, he did not like to take that trail. Doctor Dell might come riding down there almost any minute. The Kid did not want to meet Doctor Dell just right then.

He went back, took Silver by the bridle-reins and led him out of the barn and around the corner where he could not be seen from the White House. He thought he had better go down the creek, and out through the wire gate and on down the creek that way. He was sure that the "breaks" were somewhere beyond the end of the coulee, though he could not have explained why he was sure of it. Perhaps the boys, in speaking of the breaks, had tilted heads in that direction.

The Kid went quickly down along the creek through the little pasture, leading Silver by the reins. He was hor-ribly afraid that his mother might ride over the top of the hill and see him and call him back. If she did that, he would have to go, of course. Deliberate, open disobedi-ence had never yet occurred to the Kid as a moral possibility. If your mother or your Daddy Chip told you to come back, you had to come; therefore he did not want to be told to come. Doctor Dell had told him that he could go on roundup some day—the Kid had decided that this was the day, but that it would be foolish to mention the decision to anyone. The Kid thought he was getting pretty big, since he could stand on something and put the saddle on Silver his own self, and cinch it and everything; plenty big enough to get out and help the bunch when they needed help.

He did not look so very big as he went trudging down alongside the creek, stumbling now and then in the coarse grass that hid the scattered rocks. He could not keep his head twisted around to look under Silver's neck and watch the hill trail, and at the same time see where he was putting his feet. And if he got on Silver now he would be seen and recognized at the first glance which Doctor Dell would give to the coulee when she rode over the brow of the hill. Walking beside Silver's shoulder, on the side farthest from the bluff, he might not be seen at all.

The Kid was anxious that he should not be seen. The bunch needed him. Uncle Gee-gee said they needed help. The Kid thought they would expect him to come and help with his "string." He helped Daddy Chip drive the horses up from the little pasture, these days; just yesterday he had brought the whole bunch up, all by his own self, and had driven them into the big corral alone.

When a turn in the narrow creek-bottom hid him completely from the ranch buildings and the hill trail, the Kid led Silver alongside a low bank, and climbed into the saddle. Then he made Silver lope all the way to the gate.

He had some trouble with that gate. It was a barbed wire gate, such as bigger men than the Kid sometimes swear over. It went down all right, but when he came to put it up again, that was another matter. He simply had to put it up before he could go on. You always had to shut gates if you found them shut—that was a law of the range. And there was another reason—he did not want them to know he had passed that way, if they took a notion to call him back. So he worked and he tugged and he grew so red in the face it looked as if he were choking. But he got the gate up and the wire loop over the stake—though he had to hunt up an old piece of a post to stand on.

He even remembered to scrape out the tell-tale prints of his small feet in the bare earth there, and the prints of Silver's feet where he went through.

After a while he left that winding creek-bottom and climbed a long ridge. Then he went down hill and pretty soon he climbed another hill that made old Silver stop and rest before he went on to the top. The Kid stood on the top for a few minutes and stared wistfully out over the tumbled mass of hills. He could not see any of the bunch; but then, he could not see any brakes growing anywhere, either. The bunch was down in the brakes— he had heard that often enough to get it fixed firmly in his mind. Well, when he came to where the brakes grew—and he would know them, all right, when he saw them!—he would find the bunch. He thought they'd be s'prised to see him ride up! The bunch didn't know that he could drive stock all his own self, and that he was a real, old cowpuncher now.

The brakes must be farther over. Maybe he would have to go over on the other side of that biggest hill before he came to the place where they grew. He rode unafraid down a steep, rocky slope where Silver picked his way very, very carefully.

The Kid let him choose his path—Daddy Chip had taught him to leave the reins loose and let Silver cross ditches and rough places where he wanted to cross. So Silver brought him safely down that hill where even the Happy Family would have hesitated to ride unless the need was urgent.

He could not go right up over the next hill—there was a rock ledge that was higher than his head when he sat on Silver. He went down a narrow gulch—oh, an awfully narrow gulch! Sometimes he was afraid Silver was too fat to squeeze through; but Silver always did squeeze through somehow. And still there were no brakes growing anywhere. Just choke-cherry trees, and service-berries, and now and then a little flat filled with cottonwoods and willows.

So the Kid went on and on, over hills or around hills or down along the side of hills. But he did not find the Happy Family, and he did not find the brakes. He found cattle that had the Flying U brand—they had a comfortable, homey look. One bunch he drove down a wide coulee, hazing them out of the brush and yelling "*Hy-ah!*" at them, just the way the Happy Family yelled. He thought maybe these were the cattle the Happy Family were looking for; so he drove them ahead of him and didn't let one break back on him, and he was the happiest

Kid in all Montana with those range cattle, that had the Flying U brand, galloping awkwardly ahead of him down that big coulee.

CHAPTER XVI

"A RELL OLD COWPUNCHER"

The hills began to look bigger, and kind of chilly and blue in the deep places. The Kid was beginning to get hungry, and he had long ago begun to get tired. But he was undismayed, even when he heard a coyote yap-yap-yapping up a brushy canyon. It might be that he would have to camp out all night. The Kid had loved those cowboy yarns where the teller had been caught out somewhere and had been compelled to make a "dry camp." His favorite story of that type was the story of how Happy Jack had lost his clothes and had to go naked through the breaks. And there were other times; when Pink had got lost, down in the breaks, and had found a cabin just—in—*time,* with Irish sick inside and a blizzard just blowing outside, and all they had to eat was one weenty, teenty snow-bird, till the yearling heifer came and Pink killed it and they had beef-steak. And there were other times, that others of the boys could tell about, and that the Kid thought about now with pounding pulse. It was not all childish fear of the deepening shadows that made his eyes big and round while he rode slowly on, farther and farther into the breaks.

He still drove the cattle before him; rather, he followed where the cattle led. He felt very big and very proud—

but he did wish he could find the Happy Family! Somebody ought to stand guard, and he was getting sleepy already.

Silver stopped to drink at a little creek of clear, cold water. There was grass, and over there was a little hollow under a rock ledge. The Kid thought maybe he had better camp here till morning. He reined Silver against a bank and slid off, and stood looking around him at the strange hills with the huge, black boulders that looked like houses unless you knew, and the white cliffs that looked—queer—unless you knew they were just cliffs.

For the first time since he started, the Kid wished guiltily that his dad was here, or—he did wish the bunch would happen along! He wondered if they weren't camped, maybe, around that point. Maybe they would hear him if he hollered as loud as he could. Which he did, two or three times; and quit because the hills hollered back at him and they wouldn't stop for the longest time—it was just like people yelling at him from behind those rocks.

The Kid knew, of course, who they were; they were Echo-boys, and they wouldn't hurt, and they wouldn't let you see them. They just ran away and hollered from some other place. The Kid was not afraid—but there seemed to be an awful lot of Echo-boys down in these hills. They were quiet after a minute or so, and he did not call again.

The Kid was six, and he was big for his age; but he looked very little, there alone in that deep coulee that was really more like a canyon—very little and lonesome and as if he needed his Doctor Dell to take him on her lap and rock him. It was just about the time of day when Doctor Dell always rocked him and told him stories. The Kid hated to be suspected of baby ways, but he loved those times, when his legs were tired and his eyes wanted to go shut, and Doctor Dell laid her cheek on his hair and called him her baby man.

The Kid's lips quivered a little. Doctor Dell would be s'prised when he didn't show up for supper, he guessed. He turned to Silver and to his man ways, because he did not like to think about Doctor Dell just right now.

"Well, old feller, I guess you want your saddle off, huh?" he quavered, and slapped the horse upon the shoulder. He lifted the stirrup—it was a little stock saddle, with everything just like a big saddle except the size—and began to undo the latigo, whistling self-consciously and finding that his lips kept trying to tremble just the way they did when he cried. He had no intention of crying.

"Gee! I always wanted to camp out and watch the stars," he told Silver stoutly. "Honest to gran'ma, I think this is just—simply—*great!* I bet them nester kids would be scared. Hunh!"

That helped a lot. The Kid could whistle better after that. He pulled off the saddle, laid it down on its side so that the skirts would not bend out of shape, and untied the rope from beside the fork. "I'll have to anchor you to a tree, old-timer," he told the horse briskly. "I'd sure hate to be set afoot in this man's country!" And a minute later—"Oh, funder! I never brought you any sugar!"

Would you believe it, that small child of the Flying U picketed his horse where the grass was best, and the knots he tied were the knots his dad would have tied in his place. He unrolled his blanket and carried it to the sheltered little nook under the ledge, and dragged the bag of doughnuts and the jelly and honey and bread after it. He had heard about thievish animals that will carry off bacon and flour and such. He knew that he ought to hang his grub in a tree, but he could not reach up as far as the fox who might try to help himself, so that was out of the question.

The Kid ate a doughnut while he studied the matter out for himself. "If a coyote or a skink came pestering around *me,* I'd frow rocks at him," he said. So when he had finished the doughnut he collected a pile of rocks. He ate another doughnut, went over and laid himself down on his stomach the way the boys did, and drank from the little creek.

So the Kid, trying very hard to act just like his Daddy Chip and the boys, flopped the blanket vigorously this way and that in an effort to get it straightened, flopped himself on his knees and folded the blanket round and round him until he looked like a large, gray cocoon, and cuddled himself under the ledge with his head on the bag of doughnuts and his wide eyes fixed upon the first pale stars and his mind clinging sturdily to his mission and to this first real, man-sized adventure that had come into his small life.

"I'm a rell ole cowpuncher, all right," he told himself bravely; but he had to blink his eyelashes pretty fast when he said it. A "rell ole cowpuncher" wouldn't cry! He was afraid Doctor Dell would be *awfully* s'prised, though . . .

An unexpected sob broke loose, and another. He wasn't afraid—but . . . Silver, cropping steadily at the grass which must be his only supper, turned and came slowly toward the Kid in his search for sweeter grass-tufts. The Kid choked off the third sob and sat up ashamed. He tugged at the bag and made believe to Silver that his sole trouble was with his pillow.

"By cripes, that jelly glass digs right into my ear," he complained aloud, to help along the deception. "You go back, old-timer—I'm all right. We're makin' a dry-camp, just like—Happy Jack. I'm a rell—ole—" The Kid went to sleep before he finished saying it. There is nothing like the open air to make one sleep from dusk till dawn. The rell ole cowpuncher forgot his little white bed in the corner of the big bedroom. He forgot that Doctor Dell would be awfully s'prised, and that Daddy Chip would maybe be cross. The rell ole cowpuncher lay with his yellow curls pillowed on the bag of doughnuts, and slept soundly; and his lips were curved in the half smile that came often to his sleeping face and made him look ever so much like his Daddy Chip.

CHAPTER XVII

"LOST CHILD!"

"Djuh find 'im?" The Old Man had limped down to the big gate and stood there bareheaded under the stars, waiting, hoping—fearing to hear the answer.

"Hasn't he showed up yet?" Chip and the Little Doctor rode out of the gloom and stopped before the gate. Chip did not wait for an answer. One question answered the other and there was no need for more. "I brought Dell home," he said. "She's about all in—and he's just as likely to come back himself as we are to run across him. Silver'll bring him home, all right. You go up to the house and lie down, Dell. I—the Kid's all right."

His voice held all the tenderness of the lover, and all the protectiveness of the husband and all the agony of a father—but Chip managed to keep it firm and even for all that. He lifted the Little Doctor bodily from the saddle, held her very close in his arms for a minute, kissed her twice and pushed her gently through the gate.

"You better stay right here," he said authoritatively. "You can't do any good riding—and you don't want to be gone when he comes." He reached over the gate, got hold of her arm and pulled her towards him. "Buck up, old girl," he whispered, and kissed her lingeringly. "Now's the time to show the stuff you're made off. You needn't worry one minute about that kid. Yuh couldn't lose him if you tried. Go up and go to bed."

"Go to bed!" echoed the Little Doctor. "J. G., are you sure he didn't say anything about going anywhere?"

"No. He was settin' there on the porch tormentin' the cat." The Old Man swallowed a lump. "I told him to quit. He set there a while after that—I was talkin' to Blake. I dunno where he went to."

"'S that you, Dell? Did yuh find 'im?" The Countess came flapping down the path in a faded, red kimono. "What under the shinin' sun's went with him, do yuh s'pose? Yuh never know what a day's got up its sleeve— 'n I always said it. Man plans and God displans—the poor little tad'll be scairt plumb to death, out all alone in the dark—"

"Oh, for heaven's sake shut up!" cried the tortured Little Doctor, and fled past her up the path. "Poor little tad, all alone in the dark,"—the words followed her and were like sword thrusts through the mother heart of her. Then Chip overtook her, knowing too well the hurt which the Countess had given with her blundering anxiety. Just at the porch he caught up with her, and she clung to him, sobbing wildly.

"You don't want to mind what that old hen says," he told her brusquely. "The Kid's all right. Some of the boys have run across him by this time, most likely, and are bringing him in. He'll be good and hungry, and the scare will do him good." He forced himself to speak as though the Kid had merely fallen off the corral fence. "You've got to make up your mind to these things," he argued, "if you tackle raising a boy, Dell. Why, I'll bet I ran off and scared my folks into fits fifty times when I was a kid."

"But—he's—just a baby!" sobbed the Little Doctor with her face pressed hard against Chip's strong, comforting shoulder.

"He's a little devil!" amended Chip fiercely. "He ought to be walloped for scaring you like this. He's just as capable of looking after himself as most kids twice his size. He'll get hungry and head for home—and if he don't know the way, Silver does."

"But he may have fallen and—"

"Come, now! If you insist on thinking up horrors to scare yourself with, I don't know as anybody can stop you. Dell! Brace up and quit worrying. I tell you—he's—all right!"

That did well enough—seeing the Little Doctor did not get a look at Chip's face, which was white and drawn. He kissed her hastily and told her he must go, and that he'd hurry back as soon as he could. So he went half running down the path and passed the Countess and the Old Man without a word; piled onto his horse and went off up the hill road again.

They could not get it out of their minds that the Kid must have ridden up on the bluff to meet his mother, had been too early to meet her—for the Little Doctor had come home rather later than she expected to do—and had wandered off to visit the boys, perhaps, or to meet his Daddy Chip who was over there somewhere on the bench trying to figure out a system of ditches that might logically be expected to water the desert claims of the Happy Family—if they could get the water.

They firmly believed that the kid had gone up on the hill, and so they hunted for him up there. The Honorable Blake had gone to Dry Lake and taken the train for Great Falls, before ever the Kid had been really missed. The Old Man had not seen the Kid ride up the hill—but he had been sitting with his chair turned away from the road, and he was worried about other things and so might easily have missed seeing him. The Countess had been taking a nap, and she was not expected to know anything about his departure. And she had not looked into the doughnut jar—indeed, she was so upset by supper time that, had she looked she would not have missed the doughnuts. For the same reason Ole did not miss his blanket. Ole had not been near his bed; he was out riding and searching.

No one dreamed that the Kid had started out with a camp-outfit—if one might call it that—and with the intention of joining the Happy Family in the breaks. How could they realize that a child who still liked to be told bedtime stories and to be rocked to sleep, should harbor such man-size thoughts and ambitions?

That night the whole Happy Family, just returned from the Badlands and warned by Chip at dusk that the Kid was missing, hunted the coulees that bordered the bench-land. A few of the nesters who had horses and could ride them hunted also. The men who worked at the Flying U hunted, and Chip hunted frantically.

At sunrise they straggled in to the ranch, caught up fresh horses, swallowed a cup of coffee and what food they could choke down and started out again. At nine o'clock a party came out from Dry Lake, learned that the Kid was not yet found, and went out under a captain to comb systematically through the hills.

Before night all the able-bodied men in the country were searching. It is astonishing how quickly a small army will volunteer in such an emergency.

The Little Doctor—oh, let us not talk about the Little Doctor. Such agonies as she suffered go too deep for words.

The next day after that, Chip saddled a horse and let her ride beside him. Chip was afraid to leave her at the ranch—afraid that she would go mad. So he let her ride—they rode together. They did not go far from the ranch. There was always the fear that someone might bring him in while they were gone. That fear drove them back, every hour or two.

Up in another county there is a creek called Lost Child Creek. A child was lost—or was it two children?—and men hunted and hunted and it was months before anything was found. Then a cowboy riding that way found—just bones. Chip knew about that creek which is called Lost Child. He had been there and he had heard the story, and he had seen the father and had shuddered—and that was long before he had known the feeling a father has for his child. What he was afraid of now was that the Little Doctor would hear about that creek, and how it had gotten its name.

What he dreaded most for himself was to think of that creek. He kept the Little Doctor beside him and away from that Job's comforter, the Countess, and tried to keep her hope alive while the hours dragged their leaden feet over the hearts of them all.

A camp was hastily organized in One Man Coulee, and another out beyond Denson's place, and men went there to the camps for a little food and a little rest, when they could hold out no longer. Chip and the Little Doctor rode from camp to camp, intercepted every party of searchers they glimpsed on the horizon, and came back to the ranch, hollow-eyed and silent for the most part. They would rest an hour, perhaps. Then they would ride out again.

The Happy Family seemed never to think of eating, never to want sleep. Two days—three days—four days—the days became a nightmare. Irish, with a warrant out for his arrest, rode with the constable, perhaps—

if the search chanced to lead them together. Or with Big Medicine, whom he had left in hot anger. H. J. Owens and those other claim-jumpers hunted with the Happy Family and apparently gave not a thought to claims.

Miss Allen started out on the second day and hunted through all the coulees and gulches in the neighborhood of her claim. She had no time to make whimsical speeches to Andy Green, nor he to listen. When they met, each asked the other for news, and separated without a thought for each other. The Kid—they must find him.

The third day, Miss Allen put up a lunch, told her three claim partners that she should not come back until night unless that poor child was found, and set out with the twinkle all gone from her humorous brown eyes and her mouth very determined.

She met Pink and the Native Son and was struck with the change which two days of killing anxiety had made in them. True, they had not slept for forty-eight hours. True, they had not eaten except in snatches. But it was not that alone which made their faces look haggard and old and haunted. They, too, were thinking of Lost Child Creek and how it had gotten its name.

Miss Allen gleaned a little information from them regarding the general whereabouts of the various searching parties. And then, having learned that the foothills of the mountains were being searched minutely because the Kid might have taken a notion to visit Meeker's; and that the country around Wolf Butte was being searched, because he had once told Big Medicine that when he got bigger and his dad would let him, he was going over there and kill wolves to make Doctor Dell some rugs; and that the country toward the river was being searched because the Kid always wanted to see where the Happy Family drove the sheep to, that time when Happy Jack got shot under the arm; that all the places the Kid had seemed most interested in were being searched minutely—having learned all that, Miss Allen struck off by herself, straight down into the Bad-lands where nobody seemed to have done much searching.

The reason for that was, that the Happy Family had come out of the breaks on the day that the Kid was lost. They had not ridden together, but in twos and threes because they drove out several small bunches of cattle that they had gleaned, to a common center in One Man Coulee. They had traveled by the most feasible routes through that rough country, and they had seen no sign of the Kid or any other rider.

It never occurred to anyone that the Kid might go down Flying U Creek and so into the breaks and the Badlands. Flying U Creek was fenced, and the wire gate was in its place—Chip had looked down along there, the first night, and had found the gate up just as it always was kept. Why should he suspect that the Kid had man-aged to open that gate and to close it after him? A little fellow like that?

So the searching parties, having no clue to that one incident which would at least have sent them in the right direction, kept to the outlying fringe of gulches which led into the broken edge of the benchland, and to the country west and north and south of those gulches. At that, there was enough broken country to keep them busy for several days.

Miss Allen did not want to go tagging along with some party. She did not feel as if she could do any good that way. She wanted to find that poor little fellow and take him to his mother. She had met his mother, just the day before, and had ridden with her for several miles. The look in the Little Doctor's eyes haunted Miss Allen until she felt sometimes as if she must scream curses to the heavens for so torturing a mother.

She left the more open valley and rode down a long, twisting canyon that was lined with cliffs so that it was impossible to climb out with a horse. She was sure she could not get lost or turned around, in a place like that, and it seemed to her as hopeful a place to search as any. When you came to that, they all had to ride at random and trust to luck, for there was not the faintest clue to guide them. So Miss Allen considered that she could do no better than search all the patches of brush in the canyon, and keep on going.

The canyon ended abruptly in a little flat, which she crossed. She had not seen the tracks of any horse going down, but when she was almost across the flat she discovered tracks of cattle, and now and then the print of a shod hoof. Miss Allen began to pride herself on her astuteness in reading these signs. They meant that some of the Happy Family had driven cattle this way; which meant that they would have seen little Claude Bennett— that was the Kid's real name, which no one except perfect strangers ever used—they would have seen the Kid or his tracks, if he had ridden down here.

Miss Allen, then, must look farther than this. She hesitated before three or four feasible outlets to the little flat, and chose the one farthest to the right. That carried her farther south, and deeper into a maze of gulches and gorges and small, hidden valleys. She did not stop, but she began to see that it was going to be pure chance if one ever did find anybody in this horrible jumble. She believed that poor little tot *had* come down in here, after all; she could not see why, but then you seldom did know why children took a notion to do certain unbelievable things. Miss Allen had taught the primary grade in a city school, and she knew a little about small boys and girls and the big ideas they sometimes harbored.

She rode and rode, trying to put herself mentally in the Kid's place. Trying to pick up the thread of logical thought—children were logical sometimes.

"I wonder," she thought suddenly, "if he started out with the idea of hunting cattle! I wouldn't be a bit surprised if he did—living on a cattle ranch, and probably knowing that the men were down here somewhere." Miss Allen, you see, came pretty close to the truth with her guess.

Still, that did not help her find the Kid. She saw a high, bald peak standing up at the mouth of the gorge down which she was at that time picking her way, and she made up her mind to climb that peak and see if she might not find him by looking from that point of vantage. So she rode to the foot of the pinnacle, tied her horse to a bush and began to climb.

Peaks like that are very deceptive in their height. Miss Allen was slim and her lungs were perfect, and she climbed steadily. For all that it took her a long while to reach the top. When she reached the black rock that looked, from the bottom, like the highest point of the hill, she found that she had not gone much more than two-thirds of the way up, and that the real peak sloped back so that it could not be seen from below at all.

Miss Allen was a persistent young woman. She kept climbing until she did finally reach the highest point, and could look down into gorges and flats and tiny basins and upon peaks and ridges and patches of timber and patches of grass all jumbled up together—. Miss Allen gasped from something more than the climb, and sat down upon a rock, stricken with a sudden, overpowering weakness.

"God in heaven!" she whispered, appalled. "What a place to get lost in!"

She sat there a while and stared dejectedly down upon that wild orgy of the earth's upheaval which is the Badlands. It was worse than a mountain country, because in the mountains there is a certain semblance of some system in the canyons and high ridges and peaks. Here everything—peaks, gorges, tiny valleys and all—seemed to be just dumped down together.

"Oh!" she cried aloud, jumping up and gesticulating wildly. "Baby! Little Claude! Here! Look up this way!" She saw him, down below, on the opposite side from where she had left her horse.

The Kid was riding slowly up a gorge. Silver was picking his way over the rocks—they looked tiny, down there! And they were not going toward home. They were headed directly away from home.

174

The cheeks of Miss Allen were wet while she shouted and called and waved her hands. He was alive, anyway. Oh, if his mother could only be told that he was alive!

Miss Allen called again, and the Kid heard her. She was sure that he heard her, because he stopped and she thought he looked up at her. Yes, she was sure he heard her, and that finally he saw her; because he took off his hat and waved it over his head—just like a man, the poor baby!

Miss Allen considered going straight down to him, and then walking around to where her horse was tied. She was afraid to leave him while she went for the horse and rode around to where he was. She was afraid she might miss him somehow—the Badlands had stamped that fear deep into her soul.

"Wait!" she shouted, her hands cupped around her trembling lips. "Wait, baby! I'm coming for you." She hoped that the Kid heard what she said, but she could not be sure, for she did not hear him reply. But he did not go on at once, and she thought he would wait.

Miss Allen started running down the steep slope. The Kid, away down below, stared up at her. She went down a third of the way, and stopped just in time to save herself from going over a sheer wall of rock—stopped because a rock which she dislodged with her foot rolled down the slope a few feet, gave a leap into space and disappeared.

A step at a time Miss Allen crept down where the rock had bounced off into nothingness, and gave one look and crouched close to the earth. A hundred feet, it must be, straight down. After the first shock she looked to the right and the left and saw that she must go back, and down upon the other side.

Away down there at the bottom, the Kid sat still on his horse and stared up at her. And Miss Allen, calling to him that she would come, started back up to the peak.

CHAPTER XVIII

THE LONG WAY ROUND

Miss Allen turned to call encouragingly to the Kid, and she saw that he was going on slowly, his head turned to watch her. She told him to wait where he was, and she would come around the mountain and get him and take him home. "Do you hear me, baby?" she asked imploringly after she had told him just what she meant to do. "Answer me, baby!"

"I ain't a baby!" his voice came faintly shrill after a minute. "I'm a rell ole cowpuncher!"

Miss Allen thought that was what he said, but at the time she did not quite understand, except his denial of being a baby; that was clear enough. She turned to the climb, feeling that she must hurry if she expected to get him and take him home before dark. It was well after noon—she had forgotten to eat her lunch, but her watch said it was nearly one o'clock already. She had no idea how far she had ridden, but she thought it must be twelve miles at least.

She had no idea, either, how far she had run down the butte to the cliff—until she began to climb back. Every rod or so she stopped to rest and to look below, and to call to the Kid who seemed such a tiny mite of humanity among those huge peaks and fearsome gorges.

From the top of the peak she could see the hazy outline of the Bear Paws, and she knew just about where the Flying U Coulee lay. She turned and looked wishfully down at the Kid, a tinier speck now than before—for she had climbed quite a distance. She waved her hand to him, and her warm brown eyes held a maternal tenderness. He waved his hat—just like a man; he must be brave! she thought. She turned reluctantly and went hurrying down the other side, her blood racing with joy of having found him, and of knowing that he was safe.

It seemed to take a long time to climb down that peak; much longer than she thought it would take. She looked at her watch nervously—two o'clock, almost! She must hurry, or they would be in the dark getting home. That did not worry her very much, however, for there would be searching parties—she would be sure to strike one somewhere in the hills before dark.

She came finally down to the level—except that it was not level at all, but a trough-shaped gulch that looked unfamiliar. Still, it was the same one she had used as a starting point when she began to climb—of *course* it was the same one. How in the world could a person get turned around going straight up the side of a hill and straight down again in the very same place? This was the gorge where her horse was tied, only it might be that she was a little below the exact spot; that could happen, of course. So Miss Allen went up the gorge until it petered out against the face of the mountain—one might as well call it a mountain and be done with it, for it certainly was more than a mere hill.

It was some time before Miss Allen would admit to herself that she had missed the gorge, where she had left her horse, and that she did not know where the gorge was. She had gone down the mouth of the gulch before she made any admissions, and she had seen not one solitary thing that she could remember having ever seen before. Not even the peak she had climbed looked familiar from where she was.

After an hour or two she decided to climb the peak again, get her bearings from the top and come down more carefully. She was wild with apprehension—though I must say it was not for her own plight but on account of the Kid. So she climbed. And then everything looked so different that she believed she had climbed another hill entirely. So she went down again, and turned into a gorge which seemed to lead in the direction where she had seen the little lost boy. She followed that quite a long way—and that one petered out like the first.

Miss Allen found the gorges filling up with shadows, and she looked up and saw the sky crimson and gold, and she knew then without any doubts that she was lost. Miss Allen was a brave young woman, or she would not have been down in that country in the first place; but just the same she sat down with her back against a clay bank and cried because of the eeriness and the silence, and because she was hungry—but mostly because she could not find that brave little boy who had waved his hat when she left him.

In a few minutes she pulled herself together and went on; there was nothing to be gained by sitting in one place and worrying. She walked until it was too dark to see, and then, because she had come upon a little, level canyon bottom she stopped there where a high bank sheltered her from the wind that was too cool for comfort. She called, a few times, until she was sure that the child was not within hearing. After that she repeated poetry to keep her mind off the loneliness and the pity of that poor baby alone like herself. She would not think of him if she could help it.

When she began to shiver so that her teeth chattered, she would walk up and down before the bank until she felt warm again; then she would sit with her back against the clay and close her eyes and try to sleep. It was not a pleasant way in which to pass a whole night, but Miss Allen endured it as best she could. When the sun tinged the hilltops she got up stiffly and dragged herself out of the canyon where she could get the direction straight in her mind, and then set off resolutely to find the Kid. She no longer had much thought of finding her horse, though she missed him terribly, and wished she had the lunch that was tied to the saddle.

This, remember, was the fourth day since the Kid rode down through the little pasture. Men had given up hope of finding him alive. They searched now for his body. And then the three women who lived with Miss Allen began to inquire about the girl, and so the warning went out that Miss Allen was lost; and they began looking for her also.

Miss Allen, along towards noon of that fourth day, found a small stream of water that was fit to drink. Beside the stream she found the footprints of a child, and they looked quite fresh—as if they had been made that day. She whipped up her flagging energy and went on.

It was a long while afterwards that she met him coming down a canyon on his horse. It must have been past three o'clock, and Miss Allen could scarcely drag herself along. When she saw him she turned faint, and sat down heavily on the steep-sloping bank.

The Kid rode up and stopped beside her. His face was terribly dirty and streaked with the marks of tears he would never acknowledge afterwards. He seemed to be all right, though, and because of his ignorance of the danger he had been in he did not seem to have suffered half as much as had Miss Allen.

"Howdy do," he greeted her. "Are you the lady up on the hill? Do you know where the bunch is? I'm—lookin' for the bunch."

Miss Allen found strength enough to stand up and put her arms around him as he sat very straight in his little stock saddle; she hugged him tight.

"You poor baby!" she cried, and her eyes were blurred with tears. "You poor little lost baby!"

"I ain't a baby!" The Kid pulled himself free. "I'm six years old goin' on thirty. I'm a rell ole cowpuncher. I can slap a saddle on my string and ride like a son-a-gun. And I can put the bridle on him my own self and everything. I—I was lookin' for the bunch. I had to make a dry-camp and my doughnuts is all smashed up and the jelly glass broke but I never cried when a skink came. I shooed him away and I never cried once. I'm a rell ole cowpuncher, ain't I?"

Miss Allen stepped back and the twinkle came into her

eyes. She knew children. Not for the world would she offend this man-child.

"Well, I should say you are a real old cowpuncher!" she exclaimed. "Now I'm afraid of skinks. And last night when I was lost and hungry and it got dark, I—cried!"

"Hunh!" The Kid studied her with a condescending pity. "Oh, well—you're dust a woman. Us fellers have to take care of women. Daddy Chip takes care of Doctor Dell—I guess she'd cry if she couldn't find the bunch and had to make dry-camp and skinks come around—but I never."

"Of course you never!" Miss Allen agreed emphatically, trying not to look conscious of any tear-marks on the Kid's sunburned cheeks. "Women are regular cry babies, aren't they? I suppose," she added guilefully. "I'd cry again if you rode off to find the bunch and left me down here all alone. I've lost my horse, and I've lost my lunch, and I've lost myself, and I'm awfully afraid of skunks—skinks."

"Oh, I'll take care of you," the Kid comforted. "I'll give you a doughnut if you're hungry. I've got some left, but you'll have to pick out the glass where the jelly broke on it." He reined closer to the bank and slid off and began untying the sadly depleted bag from behind the cantle. Miss Allen offered to do it for him, and was beautifully snubbed. The Kid may have been just a frightened, lost little boy before he met her—but that was a secret hidden in the silences of the deep canyons. Now he was a real old cowpuncher, and he was going to take care of Miss Allen because men always had to take care of women.

Miss Allen offended him deeply when she called him Claude. She was told bluntly that he was Buck, and that he belonged to the Flying U outfit, and was riding down here to help the bunch gather some cattle. "But I can't find the brakes," he admitted grudgingly.

"Don't you think you ought to go home to your mother?" Miss Allen asked him while he was struggling with the knot he had tied in the bag.

"I've got to find the bunch. The bunch needs me," said the Kid. "I—I guess Doctor Dell is s'prised—"

"Who's Doctor Dell? Your mother? Your mother has just about cried herself sick, she's so lonesome without you."

The Kid looked at her wide-eyed. "Aw, gwan!" he retorted after a minute, imitating Happy Jack's disbelief of any unpleasant news. "I guess you're jest loadin' me. Daddy Chip is takin' care of her. He wouldn't let her be lonesome."

The Kid got the sack open and reached an arm in to the shoulder. He groped there for a minute and drew out a battered doughnut smeared with wild currant jelly, and gave it to Miss Allen with an air of princely generosity. Miss Allen took the doughnut and did not spoil the Kid's pleasure by hugging him as she would have liked to do. Instead she said: "Thank you, Buck of the Flying U." Then something choked Miss Allen and she turned her back upon him.

"I've got one, two, free, fourteen left," said the Kid, counting them gravely. "If I had 'membered to bring matches," he added regretfully, "I could have a fire and toast rabbit legs. I guess you got some glass, didn't you?

I got some and it cutted my tongue so the bleed came—but I never cried," he made haste to deny stoutly. "I'm a rell ole cowpuncher now. I dust cussed." He looked at her gravely. "You can't cuss where women can hear," he told Miss Allen reassuringly. "Bud says—"

"Let me see the doughnuts," said Miss Allen abruptly. "I think you ought to let me keep the lunch. That's the woman's part. Men can't bother with lunch—"

"It ain't lunch, it's grub," corrected the Kid. But he let her have the bag, and Miss Allen looked inside. There were some dried prunes that looked like lumps of dirty dough, and six dilapidated doughnuts in a mess of jelly, and a small jar of honey.

"I couldn't get the cover off," the Kid explained, "'thout I busted it, and then it would all spill like the jelly. Gee! I wish I had a beef-steak under my belt!"

Miss Allen leaned over with her elbows on the bank and laughed. Miss Allen was closer to hysterics than she had ever been in her life. The Kid looked at her in astonishment and turned to Silver, standing with drooping head beside the bank. Miss Allen pulled herself together and asked him what he was going to do.

"I'm going to locate your horse," he said, "and then I'm going to take you home." He looked at her disapprovingly. "I don't like you so very much," he added. "It ain't p'lite to laugh at a feller all the time."

"I won't laugh any more. I think we had better go home right away," said Miss Allen contritely. "You see, Buck, the bunch came home. They—they aren't hunting cattle now. They want to find you and tell you. And your father and mother need you awfully bad, Buck. They've

183

been looking all over for you, everywhere, and wishing you'd come home."

Buck looked wistfully up and down the canyon. His face at that moment was not the face of a real old cow-puncher, but the sweet, dirty, mother-hungry face of a child. "It's a far ways," he said plaintively. "It's a million miles, I guess. I wanted to go home, but I couldn't des' 'zactly 'member—and I thought I could find the bunch, and they'd know the trail better. Do you know the trail?"

Miss Allen evaded that question and the Kid's wide, wistful eyes. "I think if we start out, Buck, we can find it. We must go toward the sun, now. That will be towards home. Shall I put you on your horse?"

The Kid gave her a withering glance and squirmed up into the saddle with the help of both horn and cantle and by the grace of good luck. Miss Allen gasped while she watched him.

The Kid looked down at her triumphantly. He frowned a little and flushed guiltily when he remembered something. " 'Scuse me," he said. "I guess you better ride my horse. I guess I better walk. It ain't p'lite for ladies to walk and men ride."

"No, no!" Miss Allen reached up with both hands and held the Kid from dismounting. "I'll walk, Buck. I wouldn't dare ride that horse of yours. I'd be afraid he might buck me off." She pinched her eyebrows together and pursed up her lips in a most convincing manner.

"Hunh!" Scorn of her cowardice was in his tone. "Well, a course *I* ain't scared to ride him."

So with Miss Allen walking close to the Kid's stirrup and trying her best to be cheerful and to remember that she must not treat him like a little, lost boy but like a real old cowpuncher, they started up the canyon toward the sun which hung low above a pine-covered hill.

CHAPTER XIX

HER NAME WAS ROSEMARY

Andy Green came in from a twenty-hour ride through the Wolf Butte country and learned that another disaster had followed on the heels of the first; that Miss Allen had been missing for thirty-six hours. While he bolted what food was handiest in the camp where old Patsy cooked for the searchers, and the horse wrangler brought up the saddle-bunch just as though it was a roundup that held here its headquarters, he heard all that Slim and Cal Emmett could tell him about the disappearance of Miss Allen.

One fact stood in the foreground, and that was that Pink and the Native Son had been the last to speak with her, so far as anyone knew. That was it—so far as anyone knew. Andy's lips tightened. There were many strangers riding through the country, and where there are many strangers there is also a certain element of danger. That Miss Allen was lost was not the greatest fear that drove Andy Green forth without sleep and with food enough to last him a day or two.

First he meant to hunt up Pink and Miguel—which was easy enough, since they rode into camp exhausted and disheartened while he was saddling a fresh horse. From them he learned the direction which Miss Allen had taken when she left them, and he rode that way and never stopped until he had gone down off the benchland and had left the fringe of coulees and canyons behind. Pink and the Native Son had just come from down in here, and they had seen no sign of either her or the Kid. Andy intended to begin where they had left off, and comb the breaks as carefully as it is possible for one man to do. He was beginning to think that the Badlands held the secret of the Kid's disappearance, even though they had seen nothing of him when they came out four days ago. Had he seen Chip he would have urged him to send all the searchers into the Badlands and keep them there until the Kid was found. But he did not see Chip and had no time to hunt him up. And having managed to keep clear of all parties, he meant to go alone and see if he could find a clue, at least.

It was down in the long canyon which Miss Allen had followed, that Andy found hoof-prints which he recognized. The horse Miss Allen had ridden whenever he saw her—one which she had bought somewhere north of town—had one front foot which turned in toward the other. "Pigeon-toed," he would have called it. The track it left in soft soil was unmistakable. Andy's face brightened when he saw it and knew that he was on her trail. The rest of the way down the canyon he rode alertly, for though he knew she might be miles from there by now, to find the route she had taken into the Badlands was something gained.

The flat, which Andy knew very well—having driven the bunch of cattle whose footprints had so elated Miss Allen—he crossed uneasily. There were so many outlets to this rich little valley. He tried several of them, which took time; and always when he came to soft earth and saw no track of the hoof that turned in toward the other, he would go back and ride into another gulch. And when you are told that these were many, and that much of the ground was rocky, you will not be surprised that when Andy finally took up her trail in the canyon farthest to the right, it was well towards noon. He followed her easily enough until he came to the next valley, which he examined over and over before he found where she had left it to push deeper into the Badlands. And it was the same experience repeated when he came out of that gulch into another open space.

He came into a network of gorges and stopped to water his horse and let him feed for an hour or so. A man's horse meant a good deal to him, down here on such a mission, and even his anxiety could not betray him into letting his mount become too fagged.

After a while he mounted and rode on without having any clue to follow; one must trust to chance, to a certain extent, in a place like this. He had not seen any sign of the Kid, either, and the gorges were filling with shadows that told how low the sun was sliding down the sky. At that time he was not more than a mile or so from the canyon up which Miss Allen was toiling afoot toward the sun; but Andy had no means of knowing that. He went on with drooping head and eyes that stared achingly here and there. That was the worst of his discomfort—his eyes. Lack of sleep and the strain of looking, looking against wind and sun, had made them red-rimmed and bloodshot.

In spite of himself Andy's eyes closed now. He had not slept for two nights, and he had been riding all that time. Before he realized it he was asleep in the saddle, and his horse was carrying him into a gulch that had no outlet—there were so many such!—but came up against a hill and stopped there. The shadows deepened, and the sky above was red and gold.

Andy woke with a jerk, his horse having stopped because he could go no further. But it was not that which woke him. He listened. He would have sworn that he had heard the shrill whinny of a horse not far away. He turned and examined the gulch, but it was narrow and grassy and had no possible place of concealment, and save himself and his own horse it was empty. And it was not his own horse that whinnied—he was sure of that. Also, he was sure that he had not dreamed it. A horse had called insistently. Andy knew horses too well not to know that there was anxiety and rebellion in that call.

He turned and started back down the gulch, and then stopped suddenly. He heard it again—shrill, prolonged, a call from somewhere; where he could not determine because of the piled masses of earth and rock that flung the sound riotously here and there and confused him as to direction.

Then his own horse turned his head and looked toward the left, and answered the call. From far off the strange horse made shrill reply. Andy got down and began climbing the left-hand ridge on the run. Not many horses ranged down in here—and he did not believe, anyway, that this was any range horse. It did not sound like Silver, but it might be the pigeon-toed horse of Miss Allen. And if it was, then Miss Allen would be there. He took a deep breath and went up the last steep pitch in a spurt of speed that surprised himself.

At the top he stood panting and searched the canyon below him. Just across the canyon was the high peak which Miss Allen had climbed afoot. But down below him he saw her horse circling about in a trampled place under a young cottonwood.

You would never accuse Andy Green of being weak, or of having unsteady nerves, I hope. But it is the truth that he felt his knees give way while he looked; and it was a minute or two before he had any voice with which to call to her. Then he shouted, and the great hill opposite flung back the echoes maddeningly.

He started running down the ridge, and brought up in the canyon's bottom near the horse. It was growing shadowy now to the top of the lower ridges. The horse whinnied and circled restively when Andy came near. Andy needed no more than a glance to tell him that the horse had stood tied there for twenty-four hours, at the very least. That meant . . .

Andy turned pale. He shouted, and the canyon mocked him with echoes. He looked for her tracks. At the base of the peak he saw the print of her riding boots; farther along, up the slope he saw the track again. Miss Allen, then, must have climbed the peak, and he knew why she had done so. But why had she not come down again?

There was only one way to find out, and he took the method in the face of his weariness. He climbed the peak also, with now and then a footprint to guide him. He was not one of those geniuses at trailing who could tell, by a mere footprint, what had been in Miss Allen's mind when she had passed that way; but for all that it seemed logical that she had gone up there to see if she could not glimpse the Kid—or possibly the way home.

At the top he did not loiter. He saw, before he reached the height, where Miss Allen had come down again—and he saw where she had, to avoid a clump of boulders and a broken ledge, gone too far to one side. He followed that way. She had descended at an angle, after that, which took her away from the canyon.

In Montana there is more of daylight after the sun has gone than there is in some other places. Andy, by hurrying, managed to trail Miss Allen to the bottom of the peak before it grew really dusky. He knew that she had been completely lost when she reached the bottom, and had probably wandered about at random since then. At any rate, there were no tracks anywhere save her own, so that he felt less anxiety over her safety than when he had started out looking for her.

Andy knew those breaks pretty well. He went over a rocky ridge which Miss Allen had not tried to cross because to her it seemed exactly in the opposite direction from where she had started, and so he came to her horse again. He untied the poor beast and searched for a possible trail over the ridge to where his own horse waited; and by the time he had found one and had forced the horse to climb to the top and then descend into the gulch, the darkness lay heavy upon the hills.

He picketed Miss Allen's horse with his rope and fashioned a hobble for his own mount. Then he ate a little of the food he carried and sat down to rest and smoke and consider how best he could find Miss Allen or the Kid—or both. He believed Miss Allen to be somewhere not far away—since she was afoot, and had left her lunch tied to the saddle.

After a little he climbed back up the ridge to where he had noticed a patch of brush, and there he started a fire. Not a very large one, but large enough to be seen for a long distance. Then he sat down beside it and waited and listened and tended the fire. It was all that he could do for the present, and it seemed pitifully little. If she saw the fire, he believed that she would come; if she did not see it, there was no hope of his finding her in the dark.

Heavy-eyed, tired in every fibre of his being, Andy dragged up a dead buck-bush and laid the butt of it across his blaze. There he lay down near it—and went to sleep as quickly as if he had been chloroformed.

It may have been an hour after that—it may have been more. He sat up suddenly and listened. Through the stupor of his sleep he had heard Miss Allen call. At least, he believed he had heard her call, though he knew he might easily have dreamed it. He knew he had been asleep, because the fire had eaten part of the way to the branches of the bush and had died down to smoking embers. He kicked the branch upon the coals and a blaze shot up into the night. He stood up and walked a little distance away from the fire so that he could see better, and stood staring down into the canyon.

From below he heard a faint call—he was sure of it. The wonder to him was that he had heard it at all in his sleep. His anxiety must have been strong enough even then to send the signal to his brain and rouse him. He shouted, and again he heard a faint call. It seemed to be far down the canyon. He started running that way.

The next time he shouted, she answered him more clearly. And farther along he distinctly recognized her voice. You may be sure he ran, after that!

After all, it was not so very far, to a man who is running recklessly down hill. Before he realized how close he was he saw her standing before him in the starlight. Andy did not stop. He kept right on running until he could catch her in his arms; and when he had her there he held her close and then he kissed her. That was not proper, of course—but a man does sometimes do improper things under the stress of big emotions; Andy had been haunted by the fear that she was dead.

Well, Miss Allen was just as improper as he was, for that matter. She did say "Oh!" in a breathless kind of way, and then she must have known who he was. There surely could be no other excuse for the way she clung to him and without the faintest resistance let him kiss her.

"Oh, I've found him!" she whispered after the first terribly unconventional greetings were over. "I've found him, Mr. Green. I couldn't come up to the fire, because he's asleep and I couldn't carry him, and I wouldn't wake him unless I had to. He's just down here—I was afraid to go very far, for fear of losing him again. Oh, Mr. Green! I—"

"My name is Andy," he told her. "What's your name?"

"Mine? It's—well, it's Rosemary. Never mind now. I should think you'd be just wild to see that poor little fellow—he's a brick, though."

"I've been wild," said Andy, "over a good many

things—you, for one. Where's the Kid?"

They went together, hand in hand to where the Kid lay wrapped in the gray blanket in the shelter of a bank. Andy struck a match and held it so that he could see the Kid's face—and Miss Allen, looking at the man whose wooing had been so abrupt, saw his lashes glisten as he stared down while the match-blaze lasted.

"Poor little tad—he's sure a great Kid," he said huskily when the match went out. He stood up and put his arm around Miss Allen just as though that was his habit. "And it was you that found him!" he murmured with his face against hers. "And I've found you both, thank God."

CHAPTER XX

THE RELL OLE COWPUNCHER GOES HOME

I don't suppose anything can equal the aplomb of a child that has always had his own way and has developed normally. The Kid, for instance, had been wandering in the wild places—this was the morning of the sixth day. The whole of Northern Montana waited for news of him. The ranch had been turned into a rendezvous for searchers. Men rode as long as they could sit in the saddle. And yet, the Kid himself opened his eyes to the sun and his mind was untroubled save where his immediate needs were concerned. He was up thinking of breakfast, and he spied Andy Green humped on his knees over a heap of camp-fire coals, toasting rabbit-hams—the joy of it!—on a forked stick. Opposite him

Miss Allen crouched and held another rabbit-leg on a forked stick. The Kid sat up as if a spring had been suddenly released, and threw off the gray blanket.

"Say, I want to do that too!" he cried. "Get me a stick, Andy, so I can do it. I never did and I want to!"

Andy grabbed him as he came up and kissed him—and the Kid wondered at the tremble of Andy's arms. He wondered also at the unusual caress; but it was very nice to have Andy's arms around him and of a sudden the baby of him came to the surface.

"I want my Daddy Chip!" he whimpered, and laid his head down on Andy's shoulder. "And I want my Doctor Dell and my—cat! I forgot to take the string off her tail and maybe it ain't comf'table any more!"

"We're going to hit the trail, old-timer, just as soon as we get outside of a little grub." Andy's voice was so tender that Miss Allen gulped back a sob of sympathy. "You take this stick and finish roasting the meat, and then see what you think of rabbit-hams. I hear you've been a real old cowpuncher, Buck. The way you took care of Miss Allen proves you're the goods, all right. Not quite so close, or you'll burn it, Buck. I'll get another stick and roast the back."

The Kid, squatting on his heels by the fire, watched gravely the rabbit-leg on the two prongs of the willow stick he held. He glanced across at Miss Allen and smiled his Little Doctor smile.

"He's my pal," he announced. "I bet if I stayed we could round up all them cattle our own selves. And I bet he can find your horse, too. He—he's 'customed to this country. I'd a found your horse today, all right—but I guess Andy could find him quicker. Us punchers'll take care of you all right." The rabbit-leg sagged to the coals and began to scorch, and the Kid lifted it startled and was grateful when Miss Allen did not seem to have seen the accident.

"I'd a killed a rabbit for you," he explained, "only I didn't have no gun or no matches so I couldn't. When I'm ten my Daddy Chip is going to give me a gun. And then if you get lost I can take care of you like Andy can. I'll be ten next week, I guess." He turned as Andy came back slicing off the branches of a willow the size of his thumb.

"Say, old-timer, where's the rest of the bunch?" he inquired. "Did you git your cattle rounded up?"

"Not yet." Andy sharpened the prongs of his stick and carefully impaled the back of the rabbit.

"Well, I'll help you out. But I guess I better go home first—I guess Doctor Dell might need me, maybe."

"I know she does, Buck." Andy's voice had a peculiar, shaky sound that the Kid did not understand. "She needs you right bad. We'll hit the high places right away quick."

Since Andy had gone at daybreak and brought the horses over into this canyon, his statement was a literal one. They ate hurriedly and started—and Miss Allen insisted that they were going in exactly the wrong direction, and blushed and was silent when Andy, turning his face full toward her, made a kissing motion with his lips.

"You quit that!" the Kid commanded him sharply. "She's my girl. I guess I found her first 'fore you did, and you ain't goin' to kiss her."

After that there was no lovemaking but the most decorous conversation between those two.

Flying U Coulee lay deserted under the warm sunlight of early forenoon. Deserted, and silent with the silence that tells where Death has stopped with his sickle. Even the Kid seemed to feel a strangeness in the atmosphere—a stillness that made his face sober while he looked around the little pasture and up at the hill trail. In all the way home they had not met anyone—but that may have been because Andy chose the way up Flying U Creek as being shorter and therefore more desirable.

At the lower line fence of the little pasture Andy refused to believe the Kid's assertion of having opened and shut the gate, until the Kid got down and proved that he could open it—the shutting process being too slow for Andy's raw nerves. He lifted the Kid into the saddle and shut the gate himself, and led the way up the creek at a fast trot.

"I guess Doctor Dell will be glad to see me," the Kid observed wistfully. "I've been gone most a year, I guess."

Neither Andy nor Miss Allen made any reply to this. Their eyes were searching the hilltop for riders. But there was no one in sight anywhere.

"Hadn't you better shout?" suggested Miss Allen. "Or would it be better to go quietly—"

Andy did not reply; nor did he shout. Andy, at that moment, was fighting a dryness in his throat. He could not have called out if he had wanted to. They rode to the stable and stopped. Andy lifted the Kid down and set him on his two feet by the stable door while he turned to Miss Allen. For once in his life he was at a loss. He did not know how best to bring the Kid to the Little Doctor; how best to lighten the shock of seeing safe and well the man-child she had thought was dead. Perhaps he should have ridden on to the house with him. Perhaps he should have fired the signal when first he came into the coulee. Perhaps . . .

The Kid himself swept aside Andy's uncertainties. Adeline, the cat, came out of the stable and looked at them contemplatively. Adeline still had the string tied to her tail, and a wisp of paper tied to the string. The Kid pounced and caught her by the middle.

"I guess I can tie knots so they stay, by cripes!" he shouted vaingloriously. "I guess Happy Jack can't tie strings any better 'n me, can he? Nice kitty—c'm back here, you son-a-gun!"

Adeline had not worried over the absence of the Kid, but his hilarious arrival seemed to worry her considerably. She went bounding up the path to the house, and after her went the Kid, yelling epithets which were a bit shocking for one of his age.

So he came to the porch just when Chip and the Little Doctor reached it, white-faced and trembling. Adeline paused to squeeze under the steps, and the Kid, catching her by the tail, dragged her back yowling. While his astounded parents watched him unbelievingly, the Kid gripped Adeline firmly and started up the steps.

"I ketched the son-a-gun!" he cried jubilantly. "Say, I seen a skink, Daddy Chip, and I frowed a rock and knocked his block off 'cause he was going to swipe my grub. Was you s'prised, Doctor Dell?"

Doctor Dell did not say. Doctor Dell was kneeling on the porch floor with the Kid held closer in her arms than ever he held the cat, and she was crying and laughing and kissing him all at once—though nobody except a mother can perform that feat.

CHAPTER XXI

THE FIGHT GOES ON

It is amazing how quickly life swings back to the normal after even so harrowing an experience as had come to the Flying U. Tragedy had hovered there a while and had turned away with a smile, and the smile was reflected upon the faces and in the eyes of everyone upon whose souls had fallen her shadow. The Kid was safe, and he was well, and he had not suffered from the experience; on the contrary he spent most of his waking hours in recounting his adventures to an admiring audience. He was a real old cowpuncher. He had gone into the wilderness and he had proven the stuff that was in him. He had slept out under the stars rolled in a blanket—and do you think for one minute that he would ever submit to lace-trimmed nighties again? If you do, ask the Little Doctor what the Kid said on the first night after his return, when she essayed to robe him in spotless white and rock him, held tight in her starved arms. Or you might ask his Daddy Chip, who hovered pretty close to them both, his eyes betraying how his soul gave thanks. Or—never mind, I'll tell you myself.

The Little Doctor brought the nightie, and reached out her two arms to take the Kid off Chip's knees where he was perched contentedly relating his adventures with sundry hair-raising additions born of his imagination. The Kid was telling Daddy Chip about the skunk he saw, and he hated to be interrupted. He looked at his Doctor Dell and at the familiar, white garment with lace at the neck and wristbands, and he waved his hand with a gesture of dismissal.

"Aw, take that damn' thing away!" he told her in the tone of the real old cowpuncher. "When I get ready to hit the bed-ground, a blanket is all I'll need."

Lest you should think him less lovable than he really was, I must add that, when Chip set him down hastily so that he himself could rush off somewhere and laugh in secret, the Kid spread his arms with a little chuckle and rushed straight at his Doctor Dell and gave her a real bear hug.

"I want to be rocked," he told her—and was her own baby man again, except that he absolutely refused to reconsider the nightgown. "And I want you to tell me a story—about when Silver breaked his leg. I don't know what I'd done 'thout Silver. And tell about the bunch makin' a man outa straw to scare you, and the horses runned away. I was such a far ways, Doctor Dell, and I couldn't get back to hear them stories and I've most forgot about 'em."

The Little Doctor rocked him and told him of the old days, and she never again brought him his lace-trimmed nightie at bedtime. The Little Doctor was learning some things about her man-child, and one of them was this:

When he rode away into the Badlands and was lost, other things were lost, and lost permanently; he was no longer her baby, for all he liked to be rocked. He had come back to her changed, so that she studied him amazedly while she worshipped. He had entered boldly into the life which men live, and he would never come back entirely to the old order of things. He would never be her baby; there would be a difference, even while she held him in her arms and rocked him to sleep.

She knew that it was so, when the Kid insisted, next day, upon going home with the bunch; with Andy, rather, who was just now the Kid's particular hero. He had to help the bunch he said; they needed him, and Andy needed him and Miss Allen needed him.

"Aw, you needn't be scared, Doctor Dell," he told her shrewdly. "I ain't going to find them brakes any more. I'll stick with the bunch, cross my heart. And I'll come back tonight if you're scared 'thout me. Honest to gran'ma, I've got to go and help the bunch lick the stuffin' outa them nesters, Doctor Dell."

The Little Doctor hugged him tight—and let him go. Chip would be with them, and he would bring the Kid home safely, and—the limitations of dooryard play no longer sufficed; her fledgling had found what his wings were for, and the nest was too little now.

"We'll take care of him," Andy promised her understandingly. "If Chip don't come up, this afternoon, I'll bring him home myself. Don't worry a minute about *him*."

"I'd tell a man she needn't!" added the Kid.

"I suppose he's a lot safer with you boys than he is here

at the ranch—unless one of us stood over him all the time, or we tied him up," she told Andy gamely. "I feel like a hen trying to raise a duck! Go on, Buck—but give mother a kiss first."

The Kid kissed her violently and with a haste that betrayed where his thoughts were, in spite of the fact that never before had his mother called him Buck. To her it was a supreme surrender of his babyhood—to him it was merely his due. The Little Doctor sighed and watched him ride away beside Andy. "Children are such self-centered little beasts!" she told J. G. ruefully. "I almost wish he were a girl."

"Ay? If he was a girl he wouldn't git lost, maybe, but some feller'd take him away from yuh just the same. The Kid's all right. He's just the kind you expect him to be and want him to be. You're tickled to death because he's like he is. Doggone it, Dell, that Kid's got the real stuff in him! He's a dead ringer fer his dad—that ought to do yuh."

"It does," the Little Doctor declared. "But it does seem as if he might be contented here with me for a little while—after such a horrible time—"

"It wasn't horrible to him, yuh want to recollect. Doggone it, I wish that Blake would come back. You write to him, Dell, and tell him how things is stacking up. He oughta be here on the ground. No tellin' what them nesters'll build up next."

So the Old Man slipped back into the old channels of worry and thought, just as life itself slips back after a stressful period. The Little Doctor sighed again and sat down to write the letter and to discuss with the Old Man what she should say.

There was a good deal to say. For one thing, more contests had been filed and more shacks built upon claims belonging to the Happy Family. She must tell Blake that. Also, Blake must help make some arrangement whereby the Happy Family could hire an outfit to gather their stock and the alien stock which they meant to drive back out of the Badlands. And there was Irish, who had quietly taken to the hills again as soon as the Kid returned. Blake was needed to look into that particular bit of trouble and try and discover just how serious it was. The man whom Irish had floored with a chair was apparently hovering close to death—and there were those who emphasized the adverb and asserted that the hurt was only apparent, but could prove nothing.

"And you tell 'im," directed the Old Man querulously, "that I'll stand good for his time while he's lookin' after things for the boys. And tell 'im if he's so doggoned scared I'll buy into the game, he needn't to show up here at the ranch at all; tell him to stay in Dry Lake if he wants to—serve him right to stop at that hotel for a while. But tell him for the Lord's sake git a move on. The way it looks to me, things is piling up on them boys till they can't hardly see over the top, and something's got to be done. Tell 'im—here! Give me a sheet of paper and a pencil and I'll tell him a few things myself! Chances are you'd smooth 'em out too much, gitting 'em on paper. And the things I've got to say to Blake don't want any smoothing."

The things he wrote painfully with his rheumatic hand were not smoothed for politeness' sake, and it made the

Old Man feel better to get them off his mind. He sent one of his new men to town for the express purpose of mailing that letter, and he felt a glow of satisfaction at actually speaking his mind upon the subject.

Perhaps it was just as well he did not know that Blake was in Dry Lake when the letter reached his office in Helena, and that it was forwarded to the place whence it had started. Blake was already "getting a move on," and he needed no such spur as the Old Man's letter. But the letter did the Old Man a lot of good, so that it served its purpose.

Blake had no intention of handling the case from the Flying U porch, for instance. He had laid his plans quite independently of the Flying U outfit. He had no intention of letting Irish be arrested upon a trumped up charge, and he managed to send word of warning to that hot-headed young man not to put himself in the way of any groping arm of the law; it was so much simpler than arrest and preliminary trial and bail, and all that. He had sent word to Weary to come and see him, before ever he received the Old Man's letter, and he had placed at Weary's disposal what funds would be needed for the immediate plans of the Happy Family. He had attended in person to the hauling of the fence material to their boundary line on the day he arrived and discovered by sheer accident that the stuff was still in the warehouse of the general store.

After he did all that, the Honorable Blake received the Old Man's letter, read it through slowly and afterwards stroked down his Vandyke beard and laughed quietly to himself. The letter itself was both peremptory and profane, and commanded the Honorable Blake to do exactly what he had already done, and what he intended to do when the time came for the doing.

CHAPTER XXII

LAWFUL IMPROVEMENTS

Florence Grace Hallman must not be counted a woman without principle or kindness of heart. She was a pretty nice young woman, unless one roused her antagonism. Had Andy Green, for instance, accepted in good faith her offer of a position with the Syndicate, he would have found her generous and humorous and loyal and kind. He would probably have fallen in love with her before the summer was over, and he would never have discovered in her nature that ability for spiteful scheming which came to the surface and made the whole Happy Family look upon her as an enemy.

Florence Grace Hallman was intensely human, as well as intensely loyal to her firm. She had liked Andy Green better than anyone—herself included—realized. It was not altogether her vanity that was hurt when she discovered how he had worked against her. She felt chagrined and humiliated and as though nothing save the complete subjugation of Andy Green and the complete thwarting of his plans could ease her own hurt.

Deep in her heart she hoped that he would eventually want her to forgive him his treachery. She would give him a good, hard fight—she would force him to respect her as a foe; after that—Andy Green was human, certainly. She trusted her feminine intuition to say just what should transpire after the fight; trusted to her feminine charm also to bring her whatever she might desire.

That was the personal side of the situation. There was also the professional side, which urged her to do battle for the interests of her firm. And since both the personal and professional aspects of the case pointed to the same general goal, it may be assumed that Florence Grace was prepared to make a stiff fight.

Then Andy Green proceeded to fall in love with that sharp-tongued Rosemary Allen; and Rosemary Allen had no better taste than to let herself be lost and finally found by Andy, and had the nerve to show plainly that she not only approved of his love but returned it. After that, Florence Grace was in a condition to stop at nothing—short of murder—that would defeat the Happy Family in their latest project.

While all the Bear Paws country was stirred up over the lost child, Florence Grace Hallman said it was too bad, and had they found him yet? and went right along planting contestants upon the claims of the Happy Family. She encouraged the building of claim-shacks and urged firmness in holding possession of them. She visited the man whom Irish had knocked down with a bottle of whisky, and she had a long talk with him and with the doctor who attended him. She saw to it that the contest notices were served promptly upon the Happy Family. Oh, she was very busy indeed, during the week that was spent in hunting the Kid. When he was found, and the rumor of an engagement between Rosemary Allen and that treacherous Andy Green reached her, she was busier still; but since she had changed her methods and was careful to mask her real purpose behind an air of passive resentment, her industry became less apparent.

The Happy Family did not pay much attention to Florence Grace Hallman and her studied opposition. They were pretty busy attending to their own affairs; Andy Green was not only busy but very much in love, so that he almost forgot the existence of Florence Grace except on the rare occasions when he met her riding over the prairie trails.

First of all they rounded up the stock that had been scattered and they did not stop when they crossed Antelope Coulee with the settlers' cattle. They bedded them there until after dark. Then they drove them on to the valley of Dry Lake, crossed that valley on the main traveled road and pushed the herd up on Lonesome Prairie and out as far upon the benchland as they had time to drive them.

They did not make much effort toward keeping it a secret. Indeed Weary told three or four of the most indignant settlers, next day, where they would find their cattle. But he added that the feed was pretty good back there, and advised them to leave the stock out there for the present.

"It isn't going to do you fellers any good to rear up on your hind legs and make a holler," he said calmly. "We haven't hurt your cattle. We don't want to have trouble with anybody. But we're pretty sure to have a fine, large row with our neighbors if they don't keep on their own side of the fence."

That fence was growing to be more than a mere figure of speech. The Happy Family did not love the digging of post-holes and the stretching of barbed wire; yet they put in long hours at the fence-building.

They had to take the work in shifts on account of having their own cattle to watch day and night. Sometimes it happened that a man tamped posts or helped stretch wire all day, and then stood guard two or three hours on the herd at night.

New shipments of cattle, too, kept coming to Dry Lake. Invariably these would be driven out towards Antelope Coulee and would have to be driven back again with what patience the Happy Family could muster. No one helped them among the settlers. There was every attitude among the claim-dwellers, from open opposition to latent antagonism. None were quite neutral—and yet the Happy Family did not bother any save those who had filed contests to their claims, or who took active part in the cattle driving.

The Happy Family were not half as brutal as they might have been. In spite of their no-trespassing signs they permitted settlers to drive across their claims with wagons and water-barrels, to haul water from One Man Creek when the springs and the creek in Antelope Coulee went dry.

They did not attempt to move the shacks of the later contestants off their claims. Though they hated the sight of them, they grudged the time the moving would take. Besides that the Honorable Blake had told them that moving the shacks would accomplish no real, permanent good. Within thirty days they must appear before the register and receiver and file answer to the contest, and he assured them that forbearance upon their part would serve to strengthen their case with the Commissioner.

It goes to prove how deeply in earnest they were, that they immediately began to practice the virtues of mildness and forbearance. They could, he told them, postpone the filing of their answers until close to the end of the thirty days; which would serve also to delay the date of actual trial of the contests, and give the Happy Family more time for their work.

Their plans had enlarged somewhat. They talked now of fencing the whole tract on all four sides, and of building a dam across the mouth of a certain coulee in the foothills which drained several miles of rough country, thereby converting the coulee into a reservoir that would furnish water for their desert claims. It would take work, of course; but the Happy Family were beginning to see prosperity on the trail ahead and nothing in the shape of hard work could stop them from coming to hang-grips with fortune.

Chip helped them all he could, but he had the Flying U to look after, and that without the good team-work of the Happy Family which had kept things moving along so smoothly. The team-work now was being used in a different game; a losing game, one would say at first glance.

So far the summer had been favorable to dry-farming. The more enterprising of the settlers had some grain and planted potatoes upon freshly broken soil, and these were growing apace. They did not know about those scorching August winds, that might shrivel crops in a day. They became enthusiastic over dry-farming, and their resentment toward the Happy Family increased as their enthusiasm waxed strong. The Happy Family complained to one another that you couldn't pry a nester loose from his claim with a crowbar.

In this manner did civilization march out and take possession of the high prairies that lay close to the Flying U. They had a Sunday School organized, with the meetings held in a double shack near the trail to Dry Lake. The Happy Family, riding that way, sometimes heard voices mingled in the shrill singing of some hymn where, a year before, they had listened to the hunting song of the coyote.

Eighty acres to the man—with that climate and that soil they never could make it pay; with that soil especially, since it was mostly barren. The Happy Family knew it, and could find it in their hearts to pity the men who were putting in dollars and time and hard work there.

They fenced their west line in record time. There was only one gate in the whole length of it, and that was on the trail to Dry Lake. Not content with trusting to the warning of four strands of barbed wire, they took turns in watching it—"riding fence," in range parlance—and in watching the settlers' cattle.

To H. J. Owens and his fellow contestants they paid not the slightest attention, because the Honorable Blake had urged them to ignore any and all claimants. To Florence Grace Hallman they gave no heed, believing that she had done her worst, and that her worst was after all pretty weak, since the contests she had caused to be filed could not possibly be approved by the government so long as the Happy Family continued to abide by every law and condition in their present thorough-going manner.

You should have seen how mild-mannered and how industrious the Happy Family were, during those three weeks which followed the excitement of the Kid's adventuring into the wild. You would have been astonished, and you would have made the mistake of thinking that they had changed permanently and might be expected to settle down with wives and raise families and hay and cattle and potatoes.

The Happy Family were almost convinced that they were actually leaving excitement behind them for good and all. They might hold back the encroaching tide of immigration from the rough land along the river—that sounded like something exciting, to be sure. But they must hold back the tide with legal proceedings and by pastoral pursuits, and that promised little in the way of brisk, decisive action and strong nerves and all those qualities which set the Happy Family somewhat apart from their fellows.

CHAPTER XXIII

THE WATER QUESTION AND SOME GOSSIP

Miss Rosemary Allen rode down into One Man Coulee and boldly up to the cabin of Andy Green, and shouted for him to come forth. Andy made a pass at his hair with a brush and came out eagerly. There was no hesitation in his manner. He went straight up to her and reached up to pull her from the saddle, that he might hold her in his arms and kiss her. But Miss Rosemary Allen stopped him with a push that was not altogether playful, and scowled at him viciously.

"I am in a most furious mood today," she said. "I want to scratch somebody's eyes out! Don't come close, or I might pull your hair or something, James." She called him James because that was not his name, and because she had learned a good deal about his past misdeeds and liked to take a sly whack at his tendency to forget the truth, by calling him Truthful James.

"All right; that suits me fine. It's worth a lot to have you close enough to pull hair. Where have you been all this long while?" Being a bold young man and very much in love, he kissed her in spite of her professed viciousness.

"Oh, I've been to town—it hasn't been more than three days since we met and had that terrible quarrel, James. What was it about?" She frowned down at him thoughtfully. "I'm still furious about it—whatever it is. Do you know, Mr. Man, that I am an outlaw amongst the neighbors, and that our happy little household, up there on the hill, is a house divided against itself? I've put up a green burlap curtain on my southwest corner, and bought me a smelly oil stove and I pos-i-tively refuse to look at my neighbors or speak to them. I'm going to get some lumber and board up that side of my house.

"Those three cats—they get together on the other side of my curtain and say the meanest things!"

Andy Green had the temerity to laugh. "That sounds

good to me," he told her unsympathetically. "Now maybe you'll come down and keep house for me and let that pinnacle go to thunder. That whole eighty acres of yours wouldn't support a family of jackrabbits a month. What—"

"And let those old hens say they drove me off? That Kate Price is the limit. The things she said to me you wouldn't believe. And it all started over my going with little Buck a few times to ride along your fence when you boys were busy. I consider that I had a perfect right to ride where I pleased. Of course they're furious anyway, because I don't side against you boys and—and all that. When—when they found out about—you and me, James, they said some pretty sarcastic things, but I didn't pay any attention to that. Poor old freaks, I expected them to be jealous, because nobody ever pays any attention to *them*.

"Well, I didn't mind the things they said then; I took that for granted. But a week or so ago Florence Hallman came, and she did stir things up in great style! Since then the girls have hardly spoken to me except to say something insulting. And Florence Grace called me a traitor; that was before little Buck and I took to 'riding fence' for you boys. You imagine what they've been saying since then!"

"Well, what do you care? You don't have to stay with them, and you know it. I'm just waiting—"

"Well, but I'm no quitter, James. I'm going to hold down that claim now if I have to wear a six-shooter!" Her eyes twinkled at that idea. "Besides, I can stir them up now and then and get them to say things that are useful. For instance, Florence Hallman told Kate Price about that last trainload of cattle coming, and that they were going to cut your fence and drive them through in the night—and I stirred dear little Katie up so she couldn't keep still about that. And therefore—" She reached out and gave Andy Green's ear a small tweak. "—somebody found out about it, and a lot of somebodys happened around that way and just quietly managed to give folks a hint that there was fine grass somewhere else. That saved a lot of horseflesh and words and work, didn't it?"

"It sure did." Andy smiled up at her worshipfully. "Just the same—"

"But listen here! Katie-girl has lost her temper since then, and let out a little more that is useful knowledge to somebody. There's one great weak point in the character of Florence Hallman. She's just simply *got* to have somebody to tell things to, and she doesn't always show the best judgment in her choice of a confessional—"

"I've noticed that before," Andy Green admitted, and smiled reminiscently. "She sure does talk too much—for a lady that has so much up her sleeve."

"Yes—and she's been making a chum of Kate Price since she discovered what an untrustworthy creature I am. I did a little favor for Irish Mallory, James. I over-heard Florence Grace talking to Kate about that man who is supposed to be at death's door. So I made a trip to Great Falls, if you please, and I scouted around and located the gentleman—well, anyway, I gave that nice, sleek little lawyer of yours a few facts that will let Irish come back to his claim—"

"Irish has been coming back to his claim pretty regular as it is," Andy informed her quietly. "Did you think he was hiding out, all this time? Why"—he laughed at her "—you talked to him yourself, one day, and thought he was Weary. Remember when you came over with the mail? That was Irish helping me string wire. He's been wearing Weary's hat and clothes and cultivating a twinkle in his eyes—that's all."

"Why, I—well, anyway, that man they've been making a fuss over is just as well as you are, James. They only wanted to get Irish in jail and make a little trouble— pretty cheap warfare at that, if you want my opinion."

"Oh, well—what's the odds? While they're wasting time and energy that way, we're going right along doing what we've laid out to do. Say, do you know, I'm kinda getting stuck on this ranch proposition. If I just had a housekeeper—"

Miss Rosemary Allen seldom let him get beyond that point, and she interrupted him now by wrinkling her nose at him in a manner that made Andy Green forget altogether that he had begun a sentence upon a subject forbidden. Later she went back to her worries; she was a very persistent young woman.

"I hope you boys are going to attend to the contest business right away," she said, with a pucker between her eyes and not much twinkle in them. "There's something about that which I don't quite understand. I heard Florence Hallman and Kate talking yesterday about it going by default. Are you sure it's wise to put off filing your answers so long? When are you supposed to appear, James?"

214

"Me? On or before the twenty-oneth day of July, my dear girl. They lumped us up and served us all on the same day—I reckon to save shoe-leather; therefore, inasmuch as said adverse parties of the first part have got over a week left—"

"You'd better not take a chance, waiting till the last day in the afternoon," she warned him vaguely. "Maybe they think you've forgotten the date or something—but whatever they think, I believe they're counting on your not answering in time. I think Florence Hallman knows they haven't any real proof against you. She's perfectly wild over the way you boys have stuck here and worked. And from what I can gather, she hasn't been able to scrape up the weentiest bit of evidence that the Flying U is backing you—and of course that is the only ground they could contest your claims on. So if it comes to trial, you'll all win; you're bound to. I told Kate Price so— and those other old hens, yesterday, and that's what we had the row over."

"My money's on you, girl," Andy told her, grinning. "How are the wounded?"

"The wounded? Oh, they've clubbed together this morning and are washing hankies and collars and things, and talking about me. And they have snouged every speck of water from the barrel—I paid my share for the hauling, too—and the man won't come again till day after tomorrow with more. Fifty cents a barrel, straight, he's charging now, James. And you boys with a great, big, long creekful of it that you can get right in and swim in! I've come over to borrow two water-bags of it, if you please, James. Florence Hallman ought to be made to live on one of these dry claims she's fooled us into taking. I really don't know, James, what's going to become of some of these poor farmers. You knew, didn't you, that Mr. Murphy spent nearly two hundred dollars boring a well—and now it's so strong of alkali they daren't use a drop of it? Mr. Murphy is living right up to his name and nationality, since then. He's away back there beyond the Sands place, you know. He has to haul water about six miles. Believe me, James, Florence Hallman had better keep away from Murphy! I met him as I was coming out from town, and he called her a Jezebel!"

"That's mild!" Andy commented drily. "Get down, why don't you? I want you to take a look at the inside of my shack and see how bad I need a housekeeper—since you won't take my word for it. I hope every drop of water leaks outa these bags before you get home. I've a good mind not to let you have any, anyway. Maybe you could be starved and tortured into coming down here where you belong."

"Maybe I couldn't. I'll get me a barrel of my own, and hire Simpson to fill it four times a week, if you please! And I'll put a lid with a padlock on it, so Katie dear can't rob me in the night—and I'll use a whole quart at a time to wash dishes, and two quarts when I take a bath! I shall," she asserted with much emphasis, "live in luxury, James!"

Andy laughed and waved his hand toward One Man Creek. "That's all right—but how would you like to have that running past your house, so you could wake up in the night and hear it go gurgle-gurgle? Wouldn't that be all right?"

Rosemary Allen clasped her two gloved hands together and drew a long breath. "I should want to run out and stop it," she declared. "To think of water actually running around loose in this world! And think of us up on that dry prairie, paying fifty cents a barrel for it—and a lot slopped out of the barrel on the road!" She glanced down into Andy's love-lighted eyes, and her own softened. She placed her hand on his shoulder and shook her head at him with a tender remonstrance.

"I know, boy—but it isn't in me to give up anything I set out to do, any more than it is in you. You wouldn't like me half so well if I could just drop that claim and think no more about it. I've got enough money to commute, when the time comes, and I'll feel a lot better if I go through with it now I've started. And—James!" She smiled at him wistfully. "Even if it is only eighty acres, it will make good pasture, and—it will help some, won't it?"

After that you could not expect Andy Green to do any more badgering or to discourage the girl. He did like her better for having grit and a mental backbone—and he found a way of telling her so and of making the assurance convincing enough.

He filled her canvas water-bags and went with her to carry them, and he cheered her much with his air-castles. Afterwards he took the team and rustled a water-barrel and hauled her a barrel of water, and gave Kate Price a stony-eyed stare when she was caught watching him superciliously; and in divers ways managed to make Rosemary Allen feel that she was fighting a good fight and that the odds were all in her favor and in the favor of the Happy Family—and of Andy Green in particular. She felt that the spite of her three very near neighbors was really a matter to laugh over, and the spleen of Florence Hallman a joke.

But for all that she gave Andy Green one last warning when he climbed up to the spring seat of the wagon and unwound the lines from the brake-handle, ready to drive back to his own work. She went close to the front wheel, so that eavesdroppers could not hear, and held her front hair from blowing across her earnest, wind-tanned face while she looked up at him.

"Now remember, boy, do go and file your answer to those contests—all of you!" she urged. "I don't know why—but I've a feeling some kind of a scheme is being hatched to make you trouble on that one point. And if you see Buck, tell him I'll ride fence with him tomorrow again. If you realized how much I like that old cowpuncher, you'd be horribly jealous, James."

"I'm jealous right now, without realizing a thing except that I've got to go off and leave you here with a bunch of lemons," he retorted—and he spoke loud enough so that any eavesdroppers might hear.

CHAPTER XXIV

THE KID IS USED FOR A PAWN IN THE GAME

Did you ever stop to think of the tremendous moral lesson in the Bible tale of David and Goliath? And how great human issues are often decided one way or the other by little things? Not all crises are passed in the clashing of swords and the boom of cannon. It was a pebble the size of your thumb-end, remember, that slew the giant.

In the struggle which the Happy Family was making to preserve the shrunken range of the Flying U, and to hold back the sweeping tide of immigration, one might logically look for some overwhelming element to turn the tide one way or the other. With the Homeseekers' Syndicate backing the natural animosity of the settlers, who had filed upon semi-arid land because the Happy Family had taken all of the tract that was tillable, a big clash might be considered inevitable.

And yet the struggle was resolving itself into the question of whether the contest filings should be approved by the land office, or the filings of the Happy Family be allowed to stand as having been made in good faith. Florence Hallman therefore, having taken upon herself the leadership in the contest fight, must do one of two things if she would have victory to salve the hurt to her self-esteem and to vindicate the firm's policy in the eyes of the settlers.

She must produce evidence of the collusion of the Flying U outfit with the Happy Family, in the taking of the claims. Or she must connive to prevent the filing of answers to the contest notices within the time-limit fixed by law, so that the cases would go by default. That, of course, was the simplest—since she had not been able to gather any evidence of collusion that would stand in court.

There was another element in the land struggle—that

was the soil and climate that would fight inexorably against the settlers; but with them we have little to do, since the Happy Family had nothing to do with them save in a purely negative way.

A four-wire fence and a systematic patrol along the line was having its effect upon the stock question. If the settlers drove their cattle south until they passed the farthest corner of Flying U fence, they came plump against Bert Rogers' barbed boundary line. West of that was his father's place—and that stretched to the railroad right-of-way, fenced on either side with a stock-proof barrier and hugging the Missouri all the way to the Marias— where were other settlers. If they went north until they passed the fence of the Happy Family, there were the Meeker holdings to bar the way to the very foot of Old Centennial, and as far up its sides as cattle would go.

The Happy Family had planned wisely when they took their claims in a long chain that stretched across the benchland north of the Flying U. Florence Grace knew this perfectly well—but what could she prove? The Happy Family had bought cattle of their own, and were grazing them lawfully upon their own claims. A lawyer had assured her that there was no evidence to be gained there. They never went near J. G. Whitmore, nor did they make use of his wagons, his teams or his tools or his money; instead they hired what they needed, openly and from Bert Rogers. They had bought their cattle from the Flying U, and that was the extent of their business relations—on the surface. And since collusion had been the ground given for the contests, it will be easily seen what slight hope Florence Grace and her clients must have of winning any contest suit. Still, there was that alternative—the Happy Family had been so eager to build that fence and gather their cattle and put them back on the claims, and so anxious lest in their absence the settlers should slip cattle across the deadline and into the breaks, that they had postponed their trip to Great Falls as long as possible. The Honorable Blake had tacitly advised them to do so; and the Happy Family never gave a thought to their being hindered when they did get ready to attend to it.

But—a pebble killed Goliath.

H. J. Owens, whose eyes were the wrong shade of blue, sat upon a rocky hilltop which overlooked the trail from Flying U Coulee and a greater portion of the shack-dotted benchland as well, and swept the far horizons with his field glasses. Just down the eastern slope, where the jutting sandstone cast a shadow, his horse stood tied to a dejected wild-currant bush. He laid the glasses across his knees while he refilled his pipe, and tilted his hatbrim to shield his pale blue eyes from the sun that was sliding past midday.

H. J. Owens looked at his watch, nevertheless, as though the position of the sun meant nothing to him. He scowled a little, stretched a leg straight out before him to ease it of cramp, and afterwards moved farther along in the shade. The wind swept past with a faint whistle, and laid the ripening grasses flat where it passed. A cloud shadow moved slowly along the slope beneath him, and he watched the darkening of the earth where it touched, and the sharp contrast of the sun-yellowed sea of grass all around it. H. J. Owens looked bored and sleepy; yet he did not leave the hilltop—nor did he go to sleep.

Instead, he lifted the glasses, turned them toward Flying U Coulee a half mile to the south of him, and stared long at the trail. After a few minutes he made a gesture to lower the glasses, and then abruptly fixed them steadily upon one spot, where the trail wound up over the crest of the bluff. He looked for a minute, and laid the glasses down upon a rock.

H. J. Owens fumbled in the pocket of his coat, which he had folded and laid beside him on the yellow gravel of the hill. He found something he wanted, stood up, and with his back against a boulder he faced to the southwest. He was careful about the direction. He glanced up at the sun, squinting his eyes at the glare; he looked at what he held in his hand.

A glitter of sun on glass showed briefly. H. J. Owens laid his palm over it, waited while he could count ten, and took his palm away. Replaced it, waited, and revealed the glass again with the sun glare upon it full. He held it so for a full minute, and slid the glass back into his pocket.

He glanced down toward Flying U Coulee again—toward where the trail stretched like a brown ribbon through the grass. He seemed to be in something of a hurry now—if impatient movement meant anything—yet he did not leave the place at once. He kept looking off there toward the southwest—off beyond Antelope Coulee and the sparsely dotted shacks of the settlers.

A smudge of smoke rose thinly there; behind a hill. Unless one had been watching the place, one would scarcely have noticed it, but H. J. Owens saw it at once and smiled his twisted smile and went running down the hill to where his horse was tied. He mounted and rode down to the level, skirted the knoll and came out on the trail, down which he rode at an easy lope until he met the Kid.

The Kid was going to see Rosemary Allen and take a ride with her along the new fence; but he pulled up with the air of condescension which was his usual attitude toward "nesters," and in response to the twisted smile of H. J. Owens he grinned amiably.

"Want to go on a bear-hunt with me, Buck?" began H. J. Owens with just the right tone of comradeship to win the undivided attention of the Kid.

"I was goin' to ride fence with Miss Allen," the Kid declined regretfully. "There ain't any bears. Not very close, there ain't. I guess you musta swallowed something Andy told you." He looked at H. J. Owens tolerantly.

"No sir. I never talked to Andy about this." Had he been perfectly truthful he would have added that he had not talked with Andy about anything whatever, but he let it go. "This is a bear den I found myself. There's two little baby cubs, Buck, and I was wondering if you wouldn't like to go along and get one for a pet. You could learn it to dance and play soldier, and all kinds of stunts."

The Kid's eyes shone, but he was wary. This man was a nester, so it would be just as well to be careful. "Where 'bouts is it?" he therefore demanded in a tone of doubt that would have done credit to Happy Jack.

"Oh, down over there in the hills. It's a secret, though,

till we get them out. Some fellows are after them for themselves Buck. They want to—skin them."

"The mean devils!" condemned the Kid promptly. "I'd take a fall outa them if I ketched 'em skinning any baby bear cubs while *I* was around."

H. J. Owens glanced behind him with an uneasiness not altogether assumed.

"Let's go down into this next gully to talk it over, Buck," he suggested with an air of secretiveness that fired the Kid's imagination. "They started out to follow me, and I don't want 'em to see me talking to you, you know."

The Kid went with him unsuspectingly. In all the six years of his life, no man had ever offered him injury. Fear had not yet become associated with those who spoke him fair. Nesters he did not consider friends because they were not friends with his bunch. Personally he did not know anything about enemies. This man was a nester—but he called him Buck, and he talked very nice and friendly, and he said he knew where there were some little baby bear cubs. The Kid had never before realized how much he wanted a bear cub for a pet. So do our wants grow to meet our opportunities.

H. J. Owens led the way into a shallow draw between two low hills, glancing often behind him and around him until they were shielded by the higher ground. He was careful to keep where the grass was thickest and would hold no hoof-prints to betray them, but the Kid never noticed. He was thinking how nice it would be to have a bear cub for a pet. But it was funny that the Happy Family had never found him one, if there were any in the country.

He turned to put the question direct to H. J. Owens, but that gentleman forestalled him.

"You wait here a minute, Buck, while I ride back on this hill a little ways to see if those fellows are on our trail," he said, and rode off before the Kid could ask him the question.

The Kid waited obediently. He saw H. J. Owens get off his horse and go sneaking up to the brow of the hill, and take some field glasses out of his pocket and look over the prairie with them. The sight tingled the Kid's blood so that he almost forgot about the bear cub. It was almost exactly like fighting Injuns, like Uncle Gee-gee told about when he wasn't cross.

In a few minutes Owens came back to the Kid, and they went on slowly, keeping always in the low, grassy places where there would be no tracks left to tell of their passing that way. Behind them a yellow-brown cloud drifted sullenly with the wind. Now and then a black flake settled past them to the ground. A peculiar, tangy smell was in the air—the smell of burning grass.

H. J. Owens related a long, full-detailed account of how he had been down in the hills along the river, and had seen the old mother bear digging ants out of a sand-hill for her cubs.

"I know—that's jes' 'zactly the way they do!" the Kid interrupted excitedly. "Daddy Chip seen one doing it on the Musselshell one time. He told me 'bout it."

H. J. Owens glanced sidelong at the Kid's flushed face, smiled his twisted smile and went on with his story. He had not bothered them, he said, because he did not have any way of carrying both cubs, and he hated to kill them. He had thought of Buck, and how he would like a pet cub, so he had followed the bear to her den and had come away to get a sack to carry them in, and to tell Buck about it.

The Kid never once doubted that it was so. Whenever any of the Happy Family found anything in the hills that was nice, they always thought of Buck, and they always brought it to him. You would be amazed at the number of rattlesnake rattles, and eagle's claws, and elk teeth, and things like that, which the Kid possessed and kept carefully stowed away in a closet kept sacred to his uses.

" 'Course you'd 'member I wanted a baby bear cub for a pet," he assented gravely and with a certain satisfaction. "Is it a far ways to that mother bear's home?"

"Why?" H. J. Owens turned from staring at the rolling smoke cloud, and looked at the Kid curiously. "Ain't you big enough to ride far?"

" 'Course I'm big enough!" The Kid's pride was touched. "I can ride as far as a horse can travel. I bet I can ride farther and faster 'n you can, you pilgrim!" He eyed the other disdainfully. "Huh! You can't ride. When you trot you go this way!" The Kid kicked Silver into a trot and went bouncing along with his elbows flapping loosely in imitation of H. J. Owens' ungraceful riding.

"I don't want to go a far ways," he explained when the other was again riding alongside, " 'cause Doctor Dell would cry if I didn't come back to supper. She cried when I was out huntin' the bunch. Doctor Dell gets lonesome awful easy." He looked over his shoulder uneasily. "I guess I better go back and tell her I'm goin' to git a baby bear cub for a pet," he said, and reined Silver around to act upon the impulse.

"No—don't do that, Buck." H. J. Owens pulled his horse in front of Silver. "It isn't far—just a little ways. And it would be fun to surprise them at the ranch. Gee! When they saw you ride up with a pet bear cub in your arms—" H. J. Owens shook his head as though he could not find words to express the surprise of the Kid's family.

The Kid smiled his Little Doctor smile. "I'd tell a man!" he assented enthusiastically. "I bet the Countess would holler when she seen it. She scares awful easy. She's scared of a mice, even! Huh! My kitty ketched a mice and she carried it right in her mouth and brought it into the kitchen and let it set down on the floor a minute, and it started to run away—the mice did. And it runned right up to the Countess, and she jes' hollered and yelled! And she got right up and stood on a chair and hollered for Daddy Chip to come and ketch that mice. He didn't do it though. Adeline ketched it herself. And I took it away from her and put it in a box for a pet. I wasn't scared."

"She'll be scared when she sees the bear cub," H. J. Owens declared absent-mindedly. "I know you won't be, though. If we hurry maybe we can watch how he digs ants for his supper. That's lots of fun, Buck."

"Yes—I 'member it's fun to watch baby bear cubs dig ants," the Kid assented earnestly, and followed willingly where H. J. Owens led the way.

That the way was far did not impress itself upon the Kid, beguiled with wonderful stories of how baby bear cubs might be taught to do tricks. He listened and believed, and invented some very wonderful tricks that he meant to teach his baby bear cub. Not until the shadows began to fill the gullies through which they rode did the Kid awake to the fact that night was coming close and that they were still traveling away from home and in a direction which was strange to him. Never in his life had he been tricked by anyone with unfriendly intent. He did not guess that he was being tricked now. He rode away into the wild places in search of a baby bear cub for a pet.

CHAPTER XXV

"LITTLE BLACK SHACK'S ALL BURNT UP!"

It is a penitentiary offense for anyone to set fire to prairie grass or timber; and if you know the havoc which one blazing match may work upon dry grassland when the wind is blowing free, you will not wonder at the penalty for lighting that match with deliberate intent to set the prairie afire.

Within five minutes after H. J. Owens slipped the bit of mirror back into his pocket after flashing a signal that the Kid was riding alone upon the trail, a line of fire several rods long was creeping up out of a grassy hollow to the hilltop beyond, whence it would go racing away to the east and the north, growing bigger and harder to fight with every grass tuft it fed upon.

The Happy Family were working hard that day upon the system of irrigation by which they meant to reclaim and make really valuable their desert claims. They happened to be, at the time when the fire was started, six or seven miles away, wrangling over the best means of getting their main ditch around a certain coulee without building a lot of expensive flume. A surveyor would have been a blessing, at this point in the undertaking; but a surveyor charged good money for his services, and the Happy Family were trying to be very economical with money; with time, and effort, and with words they were not so frugal.

The fire had been burning for an hour and had spread so alarmingly before the gusty breeze that it threatened several claim-shacks before they noticed the telltale, brownish tint to the sunlight and smelled other smoke than the smoke of the word-battle then waging fiercely among them. They dropped stakes, flags and ditch-level and ran to where their horses waited sleepily the pleasure of their masters.

They reached the level of the benchland to see disaster sweeping down upon them like a race-horse. They did not stop then to wonder how the fire had started, or why it had gained such headway. They raced their horses after sacks, and after the wagon and team and water-barrels with which to fight the flames. For it was not the claim-shacks in its path which alone were threatened. The grass that was burning meant a great deal to the stock, and therefore to the welfare of every settler upon that bench.

Florence Grace Hallman had, upon one of her periodical visits among her "clients," warned them of the danger of prairie fires and urged them to plow and burn guards around all their buildings. A few of the settlers had done so, and were comparatively safe in the face of that leaping, red line. But there were some who had delayed—and these must fight now if they would escape.

The Happy Family, to a man, had delayed; rather they had not considered that there was any immediate danger from fire; it was too early in the season for the grass to be tindery dry, as it would become a month or six weeks later. They were wholly unprepared for the catastrophe, so far as any expectation of it went. But for all that they knew exactly what to do and how to go about doing it, and they did not waste a single minute in meeting the emergency.

While the Kid was riding with H. J. Owens into the hills, his friends, the bunch, were riding furiously in the opposite direction. And that was exactly what had been planned beforehand. There was an absolute certainty in the minds of those who planned that it would be so. Florence Grace Hallman, for instance, knew just what would furnish complete occupation for the minds and the hands of the Happy Family and of every other man in that neighborhood, that afternoon. Perhaps a claim-shack or two would go up in smoke, and some grass would burn. But when one has a stubborn disposition and is fighting for prestige and revenge and the success of one's business, a shack or two and a few acres of prairie grass do not count for very much.

For the rest of that afternoon the boys of the Flying U fought side by side with hated nesters and told the inexperienced how best to fight. For the rest of that afternoon no one remembered the Kid, or wondered why H. J. Owens was not there in the grimy line of fire-fighters who slapped doggedly at the leaping flames with sacks kept wet from the barrels of water hauled here and there as they were needed. No one had time to call the roll and see who was missing among the settlers. No one dreamed that this mysterious fire that had crept up out of a coulee and spread a black, smoking blanket over the hills where it passed, was nothing more nor less than a diversion while a greater crime was being committed behind their backs.

In spite of them the fire, beaten out of existence at one point, gained unexpected fury elsewhere and raced on. In spite of them women and children were in actual danger of being burned to death, and rushed weeping from flimsy shelter to find safety in the nearest barren coulee. The sick lady whom the Little Doctor had been tending was carried out on her bed and laid upon the blackened prairie, hysterical from the fright she had received. The shack she had lately occupied smoked while the tarred paper on the roof crisped and curled; and then the whole structure burst into flame and sent blazing bits of paper and boards to spread the fire faster.

Fire guards which the inexperienced settlers thought safe were jumped without any perceptible check upon the flames. The wind was just right for the fanning of the fire. It shifted now and then erratically and sent the yellow line leaping in new directions. Florence Grace Hallman was in Dry Lake that day, and she did not hear until after dark how completely her little diversion had been a success; how more than half of her colony had been left homeless and hungry upon the charred prairie. Florence Grace Hallman would not have relished her supper, I fear, had the news reached her earlier in the evening.

At Antelope Coulee the Happy Family and such of the settlers as they could muster hastily for the fight, made a desperate stand against the common enemy. Flying U Coulee was safe, thanks to the permanent fire guards which the Old Man maintained year after year as a matter of course. But there were the claims of the Happy Family and all the grassland east of there which must be saved.

Men drove their work horses at a gallop after plows, and when they had brought them they lashed the horses into a trot while they plowed crooked furrows in the sun-baked prairie sod, just over the eastern rim of Antelope Coulee. The Happy Family knelt here and there along the fresh-turned sod, and started a line of fire that must beat up against the wind until it met the flames rushing before it. Backfiring is always a more or less ticklish proceeding, and they would not trust the work to strangers.

Every man of them took a certain stretch of furrow to watch, and ran backward and forward with blackened, frayed sacks to beat out the wayward flames that licked treacherously through the smallest break in the line of fresh soil. They knew too well the danger of those little, licking flame tongues; not one was left to live and grow and race leaping away through the grass.

They worked—heaven, how they worked!—and they stopped the fire there on the rim of Antelope Coulee.

Florence Grace Hallman would have been sick with fury, had she seen that dogged line of fighters, and the ragged hem of charred black ashes against the yellow-brown, which showed how well those men whom she hated had fought.

So the fire was stopped well outside the fence which marked the boundary of the Happy Family's claims. All west of there and far to the north the hills and the coulees lay black as far as one could see—which was to the rim of the hills which bordered Dry Lake valley on the east. Here and there a claim-shack stood forlorn amid the blackness. Here and there a heap of embers still smoked and sent forth an occasional spitting of sparks when a gust fanned the heap. Men, women and children stood about blankly or wandered disconsolately here and there, coughing in the acrid clouds of warm grass cinders kicked up by their own lagging feet.

No one missed the Kid. No one dreamed that he was lost again. Chip was with the Happy Family and did not know that the Kid had left the ranch that afternoon. The Little Doctor had taken it for granted that he had gone with his daddy, as he so frequently did; and with his daddy and the whole Happy Family to look after him, she never doubted that he was perfectly safe, even among the fire-fighters. She supposed he would be up on the seat beside Patsy, proudly riding on the wagon that hauled the water-barrels.

The Little Doctor had troubles of her own to occupy her mind. She had ridden hurriedly up the hill and straight to the shack of the sick woman, when first she discovered that the prairie was afire. And she had found the sick woman lying on a makeshift bed on the smoking, black area that was pathetically safe now from fire because there was nothing more to burn.

"Little black shack's all burnt up! Everything's black now. Black hills, black hollows, black future, black world, black hearts—everything matches—everything's black. Sky's black, I'm black—you're black—little black shack won't have to stand all alone any more— little black shack's just black ashes—little black shack's all burnt up!" And then the woman laughed shrilly, with that terrible, meaningless laughter of hysteria.

She was a pretty woman, and young. Her hair was that bright shade of red that goes with a skin like thin, rose-tinted ivory. Her eyes were big and so dark a blue that they sometimes looked black, and her mouth was sweet and had a tired droop to match the mute pathos of her eyes. Her husband was a coarse lout of a man who seldom spoke to her when they were together. The Little Doctor had felt that all the tragedy of womanhood and poverty and loneliness was synthesized in this woman with the unusual hair and skin and eyes and expression. She had been coming every day to see her; the woman was rather seriously ill, and needed better care than she could get out there on the bald prairie, even with the Little Doctor to watch over her. If she died, her face would haunt the Little Doctor always. Even if she did not die she would remain a vivid memory. Just now even the Little Doctor's mother instinct was submerged under her professional instincts and her woman sympathy. She did not stop to wonder whether she was perfectly sure that the Kid was with Chip. She took it for granted and dismissed the Kid from her mind, and worked to save the woman.

Yes, the little diversion of a prairie fire that would call all hands to the westward so that the Kid might be lured away in another direction without the mishap of being seen, proved a startling success. As a diversion it could scarcely be improved upon—unless Florence Grace Hallman had ordered a wholesale massacre or something like that.

CHAPTER XXVI

ROSEMARY ALLEN DOES A SMALL SUM IN ADDITION

Miss Rosemary Allen, having wielded a wet gunny sack until her eyes were red and smarting and her lungs choked with cinders and her arms so tired she could scarcely lift them, was permitted by fate to be almost the first person who discovered that her quarter of the four-room shack built upon the four contiguous corners of four claims, was afire in the very middle of its roof. Miss Rosemary Allen stood still and watched it burn, and was a trifle surprised because she felt so little regret.

Other shacks had caught fire and burned hotly, and she had wept with sympathy for the owners. But she did not weep when her own shack began to crackle and show yellow, licking tongues of flame. Those three old cats— I am using her own term, which was spiteful—would probably give up now and go back where they belonged. She hoped so. And for herself—

"By gracious, I'm glad to see that one go, anyhow!"

Andy Green paused long enough in his headlong gallop to shout to her. "I was going to sneak up and touch it off myself, if it wouldn't start any other way. Now you and me'll get down to cases, girl, and have a settlement. And say!" He had started on but he pulled up again. "The Little Doctor's back here, somewhere. You go home with her when she goes, and stay till I come and get you."

"I like your nerve!" Rosemary retorted.

"Sure—folks generally do. I'll tell her to stop for you. You know she'll be glad enough to have you—and so will the Kid."

"Where *is* Buck?" Rosemary was the first person who asked that question. "I saw him ride up on the bench just before the fire started. I was watching for him, through the glasses—"

"Dunno—haven't seen him. With his mother, I guess." Andy rode on to find Patsy and send him back down the line with the water wagon. He did not think anything more about the Kid, though he thought a good deal about Miss Allen.

Now that her shack was burned, she would be easier to persuade into giving up that practically worthless eighty. That was what filled the mind of Andy Green to the exclusion of everything else except the fire. He was in a hurry to deliver his message to Patsy, so that he could hunt up the Little Doctor and bespeak her hospitality for the girl he meant to marry just as soon as he could persuade her to stand with him before a preacher.

He found the Little Doctor still fighting a dogged battle with death for the life of the woman who laughed wildly because her home was a heap of smoking embers. The Little Doctor told him to send Rosemary Allen on down to the ranch, or take her himself, and to tell the Countess to send up her biggest medicine case immediately. She could not leave, she said, for some time yet. She might have to stay all night—or she would if there was any place to stay. She was half decided, she said, to have someone take the woman into Dry Lake right away, and up to the hospital in Great Falls. She supposed she would have to go along. Would Andy tell J. G. to send up some money? Clothes didn't matter—she would go the way she was; there were plenty of clothes in the stores, she declared. And would Andy rustle a team, right away, so they could start? If they went at all they ought to catch the evening train. The Little Doctor was making her decisions and her plans while she talked, as is the way with those strong natures who can act promptly and surely in the face of an emergency.

By the time she had thought of having a team come right away, she had decided that she would not wait for her medicine case or for money. She could get all the money she needed in Dry Lake; and she had her little emergency case with her. Since she was going to take the woman to a hospital, she said, there was no great need of more than she had with her. She was a thoughtful Little Doctor. At the last minute she detained Andy long enough to urge him to see that Miss Allen helped herself to clothes or anything she needed; and to send a goodbye message to Chip—in case he did not show up before she left—and a kiss to her man-child.

Andy was lucky. He met a man driving a good team

and spring wagon, with a barrel of water in the back. He promptly dismounted and helped the man unload the water-barrel where it was, and sent him bumping swiftly over the burned sod to where the Little Doctor waited. So Fate was kinder to the Little Doctor than were those who would wring anew the mother heart of her that their own petty schemes might succeed. She went away with the sick woman laughing crazily because all the little black shacks were burned and now everything was black so everything matched nicely—nicely, thank you. She was terribly worried over the woman's condition, and she gave herself wholly to her professional zeal and never dreamed that her man-child was at that moment riding deeper and deeper into the Badlands with a tricky devil of a man, looking for a baby bear cub for a pet.

Neither did Chip dream it, nor any of the Happy Family, nor even Miss Rosemary Allen, until they rode down into Flying U Coulee at supper-time and were met squarely by the fact that the Kid was not there. The Old Man threw the bomb that exploded tragedy in the midst of the little group. He heard that "Dell" had gone to take a sick woman to the hospital in Great Falls, and would not be back for a day or so, probably.

"What'd she do with the Kid?" he demanded. "Take him with her?"

Chip stared blankly at him, and turned his eyes finally to Andy's face. Andy had not mentioned the Kid to him.

"He wasn't with her," Andy replied to the look. "She sent him a kiss and word that he was to take care of Miss Allen. He must be somewhere around here."

"Well, he ain't. I was looking for him myself," put in

the Countess sharply. "Somebody shut the cat up in the flour chest and I didn't study much on who it was done it! If I'd a got my hands on 'em—"

"I saw him ride up on the hill trail just before the fire started," volunteered Rosemary Allen. "I had my opera glasses and was looking for him, because I like to meet him and hear him talk. He said yesterday that he was coming to see me today. And he rode up on the hill in sight of my claim. I saw him." She stopped and looked from one to the other with her eyebrows pinched together and her lips pursed.

"Listen," she went on hastily. "Maybe it has nothing to do with Buck—but I saw something else that was very puzzling. I was going to investigate, but the fire broke out immediately and put everything else out of my mind. A man was up on that sharp-pointed knoll off east of the trail where it leaves this coulee, and he had field glasses and was looking for something over this way. I thought he was watching the trail. I just caught him with the glasses by accident as I swung them over the edge of the benchland to get the trail focussed. He was watching something—because I kept turning the glasses on him to see what he was doing.

"Then Buck came into sight, and I started to ride out and meet him. I hate to leave the little mite riding alone anywhere—I'm always afraid something may happen. But before I got on my horse I took another look at this man on the hill. He had a mirror or something bright in his hands. I saw it flash, just exactly as though he was signalling to someone—over that way." She pointed to the west. "He kept looking that way, and then back this way; and he covered up the piece of mirror with his hand and then took it off and let it shine a minute, and put it in his pocket. I know he was making signals.

"I got my horse and started to meet little Buck. He was coming along the trail and rode into a little hollow out of sight. I kept looking and looking toward Dry Lake—because the man looked that way, I guess. And in a few minutes I saw the smoke of the fire—"

"Who was that man?" Andy took a step toward her, his eyes hard and bright in their inflamed lids.

"The man? That Mr. Owens who jumped your south eighty."

"Good Lord, what fools!" He brushed past her without a look or another word, so intent was he upon this fresh disaster. "I'm going after the boys, Chip. You better come along and see if you can pick up the Kid's trail where he left the road. It's too bad Florence Grace Hallman ain't a man! I'd know better what to do if she was."

"Oh, do you think—?" Miss Rosemary looked at him wide-eyed.

"Doggone it, if she's tried any of her schemes with fire and—why, doggone it, being a woman ain't going to help her none!" The Old Man, also, seemed to grasp the meaning of it almost as quickly as had Andy. "Chip, you have Ole hitch up the team. I'm going to town myself, by thunder, and see if she's going to play any of her tricks on this outfit and git away with it! Burnt out half her doggoned colony tryin' to git a whack at you boys! Where's my shoes? Doggone it, what yuh all standin' round with your jaws hangin' down for? We'll see about this fire-settin' and this—where's them shoes?"

The Countess found his shoes, and his hat, and his second-best coat and his driving gloves which he had not worn for more months than anyone cared to reckon. Miss Rosemary Allen did what she could to help, and wondered at the dominant note struck by this bald old man from the moment when he rose stiffly from his big chair and took the initiative so long left to others.

While the team was being made ready the Old Man limped here and there, collecting things he did not need and trying to remember what he must have, and keeping the Countess moving at a flurried trot. Chip and Andy were not yet up the bluff when the Old Man climbed painfully into the covered buggy, took the line and the whip and cut a circle with the wheels on the hard-packed earth as clean and as small as Chip himself could have done, and went whirling through the big gate and across the creek and up the long slope beyond. He shouted to the boys and they rode slowly until he overtook them—though their nerves were all on edge and haste seemed to them the most important thing in the world. But habit is strong—it was their Old Man who called to them to wait.

"You boys want to git out after that Owens," he shouted when he passed them. "If they've got the Kid, killing's too good for 'em!" The brown team went trotting up the grade with back straightened to the pull of the lurching buggy, and nostrils flaring wide with excitement. The Old Man leaned sidewise and called back to the two loping after him in the obscuring dust-cloud he left behind.

"I'll have that woman arrested on suspicion uh setting

241

prairie fires!" he called. "I'll git Blake after her. You git that Owens if you have to haze him to hell and back! Yuh don't want to worry about the Kid, Chip—they ain't goin' to hurt him. All they want is to keep you boys huntin' high and low and combin' the breaks to find 'im. I see their scheme, all right."

CHAPTER XXVII

"IT'S AWFUL EASY TO GET LOST"

The Kid wriggled uncomfortably in the saddle and glanced at the narrow-browed face of H. J. Owens, who was looking this way and then at the enfolding hills and scowling abstractedly. The Kid was only six, but he was fairly good at reading moods and glances, having lived all his life amongst grown-ups.

"It's a pretty far ways to them baby bear cubs," he remarked. "I bet you're lost, old-timer. It's awful easy to get lost. I bet you don't know where that mother-bear lives."

"You shut up!" snarled H. J. Owens. The Kid had hit uncomfortably close to the truth.

"You shut up your own self, your darned pilgrim," the Kid flung back instantly. That was the way he learned to say rude things; they were said to him and he remembered and gave them back in full measure.

"Say, I'll slap you if you call me that again." H. J. Owens, because he did not relish the task he had undertaken, and because he had lost his bearings here in the confusion of hills and hollows and deep gullies, was in a very bad humor.

"You darn pilgrim, you dassent slap me. If you do the bunch'll fix you, all right. I guess they'd just about kill you. Daddy Chip would just knock the stuffin' outa you." He considered something very briefly, and then tilted his small chin so that he looked more than ever like the Little Doctor. "I bet you was just lying all the time," he accused. "I bet there ain't any baby bear cubs."

H. J. Owens laughed disagreeably, but he did not say whether or not the Kid was right in his conjecture. The Kid pinched his lips together and winked very fast for a minute. Never, never in all the six years of his life had anyone played him so shabby a trick. He knew what the laugh meant; it meant that this man had lied to him and led him away down here in the hills where he had promised his Doctor Dell, cross-his-heart, that he would never go again. He eyed the man resentfully.

"What made you lie about them baby bear cubs?" he demanded. "I didn't want to come such a far ways."

"You keep quiet. I've heard about enough from you, young man. A little more of that and you'll get something you ain't looking for."

"I'm a going home!" The Kid pulled Silver half around in the grassy gulch they were following. "And I'm going to tell the bunch what you said. I bet the bunch'll make you hard to ketch, you—you son-a-gun!"

"Here! You come back here, young man!" H. J. Owens reached and caught Silver's bridle. "You don't go home till I let you go; see? You're going right along with me, if anybody should ask you. And you ain't going to talk like that either. Now mind!" He turned his pale blue eyes threateningly upon the Kid. "Not another word out of you if you don't want a good thrashing. You come along and behave yourself or I'll cut your ears off."

The Kid's eyes blazed with anger. He did not flinch while he glared back at the man, and he did not seem to care, just at that moment, whether he lost his ears or kept them. "You let go my horse!" he gritted. "You wait. The bunch'll fix *you,* and fix you right. You wait!"

H. J. Owens hesitated, tempted to lay violent hands upon the small rebel. But he did not. He led Silver a rod or two, found it awkward, since the way was rough and he was not much of a horseman, and in a few minutes let the rein drop from his fingers.

"You come on, Buck, and be a good boy—and maybe we'll find them cubs yet," he conciliated. "You'd die a-laughing at the way they set up and scratch their ears when a big, black ant bites 'em, Buck. I'll show you in a little while. And there's a funny camp down here, too, where we can get some supper."

The Kid made no reply, but he rode along docilely beside H. J. Owens and listened to the new story he told of the bears. That is, he appeared to be listening; in reality he was struggling to solve the biggest problem he had ever known—the problem of danger and of treachery. Poor little tad, he did not even know the names of his troubles. He only knew that this man had told him a lie about those baby bear cubs, and had brought him away down here where he had been lost, and that it was getting dark and he wanted to go home and the man was mean and would not let him go. He did not understand why the man should be so mean—but the man *was* mean to him, and he did not intend to "stand for it." He wanted to go home. And when the Kid really wanted to do a certain thing, he nearly always did it, as you may have observed.

H. J. Owens would not let him go home; therefore the Kid meant to go anyway. Only he would have to sneak off, or run off, or something, and hide where the man could not find him, and then go home to his Doctor Dell and Daddy Chip, and tell them how mean this pilgrim had been to him. And he would fix him all right! The thought cheered the Kid so that he smiled and made the man think he was listening to his darned old bear story that was just a big lie. Think he would listen to any story that pilgrim could tell? Huh!

The gulches were growing dusky now. The Kid was tired, and he was hungry and could hardly keep from crying, he was so miserable. But he was the son of his father—he was Chip's kid; it would take a great deal more misery and unkindness to make him cry before this pilgrim who had been so mean to him. He rode along without saying a word. H. J. Owens did not say anything, either. He kept scanning each jagged peak and each gloomy canyon as they passed, and he seemed uneasy about something. The Kid knew what it was, all right; H. J. Owens was lost.

They came to a wide, flat-bottomed coulee with high-ragged bluffs shutting it in upon every side. The Kid dimly remembered that coulee, because that was where Andy got down to tighten the cinch on Miss Allen's horse, and looked up at her the way Daddy Chip looked at Doctor Dell sometimes, and made a kiss with his lips—and got called down for it, too. The Kid remembered.

He looked at the man, shut his mouth tight and wheeled Silver suddenly to the left. He leaned forward as he had always seen the Happy Family do when they started a race, and struck Silver smartly down the rump with the braided romal on his bridle-reins. H. J. Owens was taken off his guard and did nothing but stare open-mouthed until the Kid was well under way; then he shouted and galloped after him, up the little flat.

He might as well have saved his horse's wind and his own energy. He was no match for little Buck Bennett, who had the whole Flying U outfit to teach him how to ride, and the spirit of his Daddy Chip and the Little Doctor combined to give him grit and initiative. H. J. Owens pounded along to the head of the coulee, where he had seen the Kid galloping dimly in the dusk. He turned up into the canyon that sloped invitingly up from the level, and went on at the top speed of his horse—which was not fast enough to boast about.

When he had left the coulee well behind him, the Kid rode out from behind a clump of bushes that was a mere black shadow against the coulee wall, and turned back whence he had come. The Kid giggled a little over the way he had fooled the pilgrim, and wished that the bunch had been there to see him do it. He kept Silver galloping until he had reached the other end of the level, and then he pulled him down to a walk and let the reins drop loosely upon Silver's neck. That was what Daddy Chip and the boys had told him he must do, next time he got lost and did not know the way home. He must just let

Silver go wherever he wanted to go, and not try to guide him at all. Silver would go straight home; he had the word of the whole bunch for that, and he believed it implicitly.

Silver looked back inquiringly at his small rider, hesitated and then swung back up the coulee. The Kid was afraid that H. J. Owens would come back and see him and cut off his ears if he went that way—but he did not pull Silver back and make him go some other way, for all that. If he left him alone, Silver would take him right straight home. Daddy Chip and the boys said so. And he would tell them how mean that man was. They would fix him, all right!

Halfway up the coulee Silver turned into a narrow gulch that seemed to lead nowhere at all except into the side of a big, black-shadowed bluff. Up on the hillside a coyote began to yap with a shrill staccato of sounds that trailed off into a disconsolate whimper. The Kid looked that way interestedly. He was not afraid of coyotes. They would not hurt anyone; they were more scared than you were—the bunch had told him so. He wished he could get a sight of him, though. He liked to see their ears stick up and their noses stick out in a sharp point, and see them drop their tails and go sliding away out of sight. When he was ten and Daddy Chip gave him a gun, he would shoot coyotes and skin them his own self.

The coyote yapped shrilly again, and the Kid wondered what his Doctor Dell would say when he got home. He was terribly hungry, and he was tired and wanted to go to bed. He wished the bunch would happen along and fix that man. His heart swelled in his chest with rage and disappointment when he thought of those baby bear cubs that were not anywhere at all—because the man was just lying all the time. In spite of himself the Kid cried whimperingly to himself while he rode slowly up the gorge which Silver had chosen to follow because the reins were drooping low alongside his neck and he might go where he pleased.

By and by the moon rose and lightened the hills so that they glowed softly; and the Kid, looking sleepily around him, saw a coyote slinking along the barren slope. He was going to shout at it and see it run, but he thought of the man who was looking for him and glanced fearfully over his shoulder. The moon shone full in his face and showed the tear-streaks and the tired droop to his lips.

The Kid thought he must be going wrong, because at the ranch the moon came up in another place altogether. He knew about the moon. Doctor Dell had explained to him how it kept going round and round the world and you saw it when it came up over the edge. That was how Santa Claus found out if kids were good; he lived in the moon, and it went round and round so he could look down and see if you were bad. The Kid rubbed the tears off his cheeks with his palm, so that Santa Claus could not see that he had been crying. After that he rode bravely, with a consciously straight spine, because Santa Claus was looking at him all the time and he must be a rell ole cowpuncher.

After a long while the way grew less rough, and Silver trotted down the easier slopes. The Kid was pretty tired now. He held on by the horn of his saddle so Silver would not jolt him so much. He was terribly hungry, too, and his eyes kept going shut. But Santa Claus kept looking at him to see if he were a dead game sport, so he did not cry any more. He wished he had some grub in a sack, but he thought he must be nearly home now. He had come a terribly far ways since he ran away from that pilgrim who was going to cut off his ears.

The Kid was so sleepy and so tired that he almost fell out of the saddle once when Silver, who had been loping easily across a fairly level stretch of ground, slowed abruptly to negotiate a washout crossing. He had been thinking about those baby bear cubs digging ants and eating them. He had almost seen them doing it; but he remembered now that he was going home to tell the bunch how the man had lied to him and tried to make him stay down here. The bunch would sure fix him when they heard about that.

He was still thinking vengefully of the punishment which the Happy Family would surely mete out to H. J. Owens when Silver lifted his head, looked off to the right and gave a shrill whinny. Somebody shouted, and immediately a couple of horsemen emerged from the shadow of a hill and galloped toward him.

The Kid gave a cry and then laughed. It was his Daddy Chip and somebody. He thought the other was Andy Green. He was too tired to kick Silver in the ribs and race toward them. He waited until they came up, their horses pounding over the uneven sod urged by the jubilance of their riders.

Chip rode up and lifted the Kid bodily from the saddle and held him so tight in his arms that the Kid kicked half-heartedly with both feet, to free himself. But he had a message for his Daddy Chip, and as soon as he could get his breath he delivered it.

"Daddy Chip, I just want you to kill that damn' pilgrim!" he commanded. "There wasn't any baby bear cubs at all. He was just a-stringin' me. And he was going to cut off my ears. He said it wasn't a far ways to where the baby bear cubs lived with the old mother bear, and it was. I wish you'd lick the stuffin' outa him. I'm awful hungry, Daddy Chip."

"We'll be home pretty quick," Chip said in a queer choked voice. "Who was the man, Buck? Where is he now?"

The Kid lifted his head sleepily from his Daddy Chip's shoulder and pointed vaguely toward the moon. "He's the man that jumped Andy's ranch right on the edge of One Man," he explained. "He's back there ridin' the rimrocks a lookin' for me. I'd a come home before, only he wouldn't let me come. He said he'd cut my ears off. I runned away from him, Daddy Chip. And I cussed him a plenty for lying to me—but you needn't tell Doctor Dell."

"I won't, Buck." Chip lifted him into a more comfortable position and held him so. While the Kid slept he talked with Andy about getting the Happy Family on the trail of H. J. Owens. Then he rode thankfully home with the Kid in his arms and Silver following docilely after.

CHAPTER XXVIII

AS IT TURNED OUT

They found H. J. Owens the next forenoon wandering hopelessly lost in the hills. Since killing him was barred, they tied his arms behind him and turned him toward the Flying U. He was sullen, like an animal that is trapped and will do nothing but lie flattened to the ground and glare red-eyed at its captors. For that matter, the Happy Family themselves were pretty sullen. They had fought fire for hours—and that is killing work; and they had been in the saddle ever since, looking for the Kid and for this man who rode bound in their midst.

Weary and Irish and Pink, who had run across him in a narrow canyon, fired pistol-shot signals to bring the others to the spot. But when the others emerged from various points upon the scene, there was very little said about the capture.

In town, the Old Man had been quite eager to come close to Florence Grace Hallman—but he was not so lucky. Florence Grace had heard the news of the fire a good half hour before the train left for Great Falls. She would have preferred a train going the other way, but she decided not to wait. She watched the sick woman put aboard the one Pullman coach, and then she herself went into the stuffy day-coach. Florence Grace Hallman was not in the habit of riding in day-coaches in the night-time when there was a Pullman sleeper attached to the train. She did not stop at Great Falls; she went on to Butte—

and from there I do not know where she went. Certainly she never came back.

That, of course, simplified matters considerably for Florence Grace—and for the Happy Family as well. For at the preliminary hearing of H. J. Owens for the high crime of kidnapping, that gentleman proceeded to unburden his soul in a way that would have horrified Florence Grace, had she been there to hear. Remember, I told you that his eyes were the wrong shade of blue.

A man of whom you have never heard tried to slip out of the court room during the unburdening process, and was stopped by Andy Green, who had been keeping an eye on him for the simple reason that the fellow had been much in the company of H. J. Owens during the week preceding the fire and the luring away of the Kid. The sheriff led him off somewhere—and so they had the man who had set the prairie afire.

As is the habit of those who confess easily the crimes of others, H. J. Owens professed himself as innocent as he consistently could in the face of the Happy Family and of the Kid's loud-whispered remarks when he saw him there. He knew absolutely nothing about the fire, he said, and had nothing to do with the setting of it. He was two miles away at the time it started.

And then Miss Rosemary Allen took the witness stand and told about the man on the hilltop and the bit of mirror that had flashed sun-signals toward the west. H. J. Owens crimpled down visibly in his chair. Imagine for yourself the trouble he would have in convincing men of his innocence after that.

Just to satisfy your curiosity, at the trial a month later

he failed absolutely to convince the jury that he was anything but what he was—a criminal without the strength to stand by his own friends. He was sentenced to ten years in Deer Lodge, and the judge informed him that he had been dealt with leniently at that, because after all he was only a tool in the hands of the real instigator of the crime. That real instigator, by the way, was never apprehended. The other man—he who had set fire to the prairie—got six years, and cursed the judge and threatened the whole Happy Family with death when the sentence was passed upon him—as so many guilty men do.

To go back to that preliminary trial: The Happy Family, when H. J. Owens was committed safely to the county jail, along with the fire-bug, took the next train to Great Falls with witnesses and the Honorable Blake. They filed their answers to the contests two days before the time-limit had expired. You may call that shaving too close the margin of safety. But the Happy Family did not worry over that—seeing there was a margin of safety. Nor did they worry over the outcome of the matter. With the Homeseekers' Syndicate in extremely bad repute, and with fully half of the colonists homeless and disgusted, why should they worry over their own ultimate success?

They planned great things with their irrigation scheme. . . . I am not going to tell any more about them just now. Some of you will complain, and want to know a good many things that have not been told in detail. But if I should try to satisfy you, there would be no more meetings between you and the Happy Family—since there would be no more to tell.

So I am not even going to tell you whether Andy succeeded in persuading Miss Rosemary Allen to go with him to the parson. Nor whether the Happy Family really did settle down to raise families and alfalfa and beards. Not another thing shall you know about them now.

You may take a look at them as they go trailing contentedly away from the land office, with their hats tilted at various characteristic angles and their well-known voices mingled in more or less joyful converse, and their toes pointed toward Central Avenue and certain liquid refreshments. You need not worry over that bunch, surely. You may safely leave them to meet future problems and emergencies as they have always met them in the past—on their feet, with eyes that do not waver or flinch, shoulder to shoulder, ready alike for grim fate or a frolic.